Moriarty's Men

BOOK TWO

THE TEMPTATION OF FOUR

EVA CHASE

CHAPTER ONE

Jemma

Hidden by the velvety folds of the brocade curtain, I peered out my hotel room window. Shoppers and tourists strolled through the mid-morning sunlight along the road below. One of Zagreb's bright blue trams whirred past. The glossy signs at street level, nearly as many of them in English as in Croatian, stood out against the aged stone that rose two or three stories above them.

The hotel rose taller still, but even from my sixth floor vantage point, I should have been able to recognize the men I was searching for if they'd been in view. I'd gotten to know Sherlock Holmes, John Watson, and Garrett Lestrade rather intimately during the time I'd spent with them in London weeks ago.

"Do you have eyes on them?" Bash asked. My right-hand man had gotten up from the table where we'd been enjoying a room service breakfast, his newspaper discarded. His fingers veered instinctively toward the pistol I knew he was wearing in a concealed holster at his hip.

"Not from here." I drew back from the window. Honestly, I'd have been a little disappointed if the trio of London's top criminal investigators had tracked me all this way only to carelessly reveal themselves that quickly.

They might not even realize I was in this hotel. The porter who'd called to warn me that an "old man" had come in asking about me had said the staff at the front desk had denied any knowledge. But that man had almost certainly been Sherlock in one of his elaborate disguises, and if anyone in the lobby had given a hint that they knew more than they were letting on, he'd have picked up on it.

I hadn't exactly left the three of them in the lurch when I'd vanished from London, but I *had* lured them into committing a heist that would have cost them all their careers if they'd fumbled. And I'd told them plenty of lies along the way. After realizing that, they might not be in the friendliest mood toward me.

I turned to Bash. "There's no way they could charge me with any crime they know of without revealing their own. They don't even know *you* exist. So they don't pose any real threat, as long as they keep out of my other business. I'm thinking we head off potential interruptions by finding out what exactly they want."

Bash raised an eyebrow. Otherwise his tan face was as deadpan as usual. "It looks like giving them their evidence didn't stop them from wanting revenge after all."

I'd gone a little out of my way to ensure the trio didn't end up embarrassed after the heist was over. At the time,

I'd told Bash it was to protect myself. They'd gotten their man, even if he hadn't actually committed the one crime I'd planted evidence of. Stefan Richter had been guilty of plenty of other indiscretions. If Sherlock and company had figured out his innocence in that one murder, they'd decided to let him hang for it anyway.

"Maybe they'd have caught up with us three weeks sooner if they'd been angrier," I said. "And we might have had Richter's people harassing us on top of that. Let's go. You take the front, and I'll take the back—we'll meet up at Franjo's. Watch from the back room?"

"Of course. I'll be there before you walk in, Majesty." Bash gave me a mock salute, swiped his hand over the black stubble of his hair, and headed out the door. With well-honed self-control, I avoided spending more than a second admiring the sculpted muscle of his backside.

I took more time than he had with my own preparations, pulling my thick red waves into a braid and covering my head with a gauzy scarf as if I wanted to hide it. The casual cotton dress I'd put on would work well enough.

When I'd given Bash a couple minutes' head start, I slipped out into the hall and made for the staircase at the back of the building. If the trio suspected I was staying there, they'd be watching that exit.

In the alley, I let the warm spring breeze tug a strand of my hair from beneath the scarf and paused to put on a pair of sunglasses before I emerged. I hadn't heard any definite signs of pursuit, but these three were better than that. My heart thumped at a pace that might have been slightly giddy as I wove through the streets to the pub Bash and I had been frequenting.

Franjo's held an eclectic mix of styles and offerings. I stepped inside to exposed brick walls and a buoyant Europop song. The tables scattered throughout the middle of the room were old wood carved with a checkerboard pattern, but the bar on one side and the booths on the other shone with slick indigo laminate. The smell of pickles, barbeque wings, and fine wine mingled in the air.

I slid onto one of the padded booth benches in view of both the entrance and the black curtain that hung over the doorway to the back room. Franjo Junior, the grizzled son of the original Franjo who'd established the pub decades ago, nodded to me from behind the counter, where he acted as primary bartender as well as owner. Bash and I had gotten ourselves into his very good graces by handling an extortion racket that'd been breathing down his neck.

It always paid to make friends with the locals.

The waitress brought over my usual, a sidecar. It might have been early in the day for alcohol, but there was a little orange in it, and anyway, I deserved a drink. As invigorating as the prospect of tangling with the London trio again was, especially after the dull drudgery of the last six weeks, it was also a hassle.

Where had I slipped up to allow them to track me here? What the hell were they hoping to get out of following me?

I didn't have to wait long for the opportunity to ask those questions directly. I'd just taken my first sip of the sidecar's tangy sweetness when a stooped figure with shaggy gray hair came in. The man took a seat at the bar—not directly across from my booth but close enough that he could easily keep an eye on it—and ordered a local beer.

Sherlock truly was a master of disguise. I wasn't completely sure it was him and not a regular getting started on his daily boozing until he dropped his napkin and reached down to pick it up, giving him the perfect excuse to steal a surreptitious glance my way. His long lithe fingers confirmed my suspicions. I restrained a smile, pretending to be absorbed in my drink. When he'd gotten back on his stool, I ambled over with my glass.

"Hello, Sherlock," I said, sliding onto the stool one over from him. "What a coincidence, bumping into you here."

Sherlock's hand tightened around his beer mug, just slightly. He rubbed his narrow face, his posture straightening to reach his full remarkable height, and suddenly it wasn't so hard to see the man I knew within the disguise. His cool blue eyes studied me with their usual penetrating sharpness. He gave me a crooked smile.

"Hello, Jemma," he said evenly. "I'm guessing it isn't such a coincidence on either of our sides after all."

"I'll give credit where it's due," I said. "I don't think I'd have seen through the disguise if I hadn't been waiting for you."

He made a dismissive sound that seemed to say he wasn't going to be mollified in his failure and took a sip of his beer. His lips twisted with a grimace. Sherlock was more the brandy type.

I leaned back against the bar. "Should we invite John and Garrett in too? Make it a full reunion?"

"I think it's probably best to keep the conversation simple. One-to-one."

"All right. Let's converse then. How did you track me to Zagreb?"

A hint of his earlier smile came back. "If I tell you that, you'll know how to cover your tracks better next time."

He did enjoy being able to hold his superior strategizing over a person. I set aside that question. I'd find out eventually if I needed to. "Fine. I assume you'll at least tell me *why* you tracked me here. This is an awfully long way to come just to have a drink together."

Sherlock turned toward me on his stool as if he could read my reactions better that way, which maybe he could. A whole lot went on in that admittedly brilliant mind of his that I couldn't entirely follow. His thoughts and deductions moved in patterns different from my own. Which was part of what had made him so fascinating from the start.

"I'm surprised you'd even ask that," he said. "Did you really think I wouldn't realize how thoroughly you deceived us? It took less than a day for me to put the pieces together, in case you wondered."

The corner of my lips quirked up. "Less than a day after I'd already left. Not less than a day after the scheme began."

"Fair." He nudged his beer mug but appeared to decide against trying to drink any more of it. "You pulled off a crime under our noses and escaped with the spoils. You couldn't expect me to ignore that."

I shrugged. "There isn't much else you *can* do about it. You can't even prove I did it in any way a court of law will accept."

"I don't understand why you did it at all." His gaze searched mine even more intently than before. "That piece you took was valued at a few thousand dollars. Hardly worth the lengths you went to in order to obtain it. Unless you have some personal stake in it."

The piece I'd taken was now part of a gold cuff, etched with mathematical patterns that were punctuated by perfectly symmetrical gemstones, currently wrapped around the middle of my right thigh as it had been since I'd snapped it into place right after the heist. Thinking about it, I had the urge to rub the spot on the back of my neck where the ghostly fiend I'd bartered my soul to years ago had marked me.

The gold cuff was the only thing keeping me out of that fiend's maw. I'd made the deal with it for reasons Sherlock could never have understood. He'd never have believed the shrouded folk with their haunting visages and unsettling powers even existed.

"I can't see that there's any benefit in discussing that," I said.

"How about something even more basic: who exactly *are* you?"

I brushed off the question with a wave of my hand. "The same answer applies."

Sherlock didn't look perturbed. "The benefit is that if

I'm satisfied with your answers, I'll go home. Whatever schemes you're attempting to enact here, I assure you I can be very disruptive."

I didn't doubt it. "Hasn't the greatest consulting detective in the world got better things to do with his time than dog one woman over a single theft you admit wasn't that shocking in value?"

"No," Sherlock said. "Because everything I know about you tells me it's impossible you *aren't* carrying out other schemes of one sort or another. The one I do know about involved at least one man's death. I wouldn't be surprised if you're the greatest danger the world currently faces."

Ha. Let me introduce him to the shrouded folk and see what he thought then. They ate his version of dangerous for breakfast. There was one still hoping to eat *me*.

"So, you're going to follow me around until the end of time?" I said. "That sounds rather tedious."

He gave me his first real smile of the conversation. "I'm counting on it being considerably more tedious for you than for me."

He was very pleased with himself to have found me at all, wasn't he? That would have been amusing to see if it hadn't been equally annoying that he was here at all. I wet my lips, and Sherlock shifted an inch toward me. His voice dropped.

"Jemma, you'll notice I didn't say I'm *sure* you're the greatest danger the world faces. The pieces of the puzzle I do have make me wonder if you weren't in some kind of trouble back in London. Have you escaped it yet?"

A chill tickled over my skin, seeping deep enough to make my fingers itch for one of the sugar cubes I kept in my purse. He did notice more than any man had a right to. Did he think I'd turn to *him* for help if I needed it?

I pulled back and took a swallow of my drink. When I answered, I kept my voice as bland as possible.

"I can assure you that I'm perfectly fine."

Right now, it wasn't even a lie. Sherlock looked skeptical, though. "And how long can that last? One trinket won't hold off a debt collector in perpetuity."

It could if it was more than a simple trinket. But at that moment, the chill that had washed over me a moment ago condensed around my thigh—around the gold cuff. An icy tingling shot through my nerves from around the metal surface.

The cuff had set off that sensation a few times in the last couple weeks. I'd tried not to make much of it. This time the tingling quivered right up into my chest. I inhaled, and the scents of the pub turned frigid in my lungs. Cold fingers squeezed around my gut.

For an instant, everything inside me felt frozen, like the instant when I'd peeked out from my hiding place on that high plateau near the cult commune where I'd grown up and discovered what happened to kids like me. Kids who impressed the shrouded folk with their drive and their wildness year after year, spurred on by our parents to prove their loyalty to the creatures they worshipped. The "lucky" ones like that boy just a couple years older than me were chosen—chosen to be swallowed screaming into the fathomless mists of the creatures' mouths.

His screams had gone on for the longest time after he'd disappeared down the shrouded one's gullet, growing fainter as if spiraling into the distance, with hitches and tremors that suggested something inside the fiend was ripping him apart piece by tiny piece. It was the most horrible sound I'd ever heard then or since.

"Jemma?" Sherlock said.

I wrenched myself back to the present. The icy tingling had faded, and the world's most brilliant detective was watching me with eyes that saw too much. I shook off the last of the chill and gathered my ample composure.

"I'm fine," I said, "and I expect to remain fine for the foreseeable future. I don't owe any debts." That deserved to be paid, at least.

Maybe it was time to turn this scenario more in my favor. My trio was here and insistent on staying. Why shouldn't I make use of them?

CHAPTER TWO

Garrett

Normally I found John's easy-going demeanor much more enjoyable to be around than Sherlock's arrogant intensity. But as we waited, watching the pub the consulting detective had headed into after Jemma, the doctor's apparent lack of concern was becoming incredibly irritating.

"I wonder why Croatia?" he said in an offhand way, swiveling the handle of his walking stick where we were standing a little back from the front window of an electronics shop.

Of the questions I'd like answers to, that was pretty far down the list.

I shoved my hands in my pockets to stop them from fidgeting. I'd have taken out my notepad and jotted down observations of the road if that wouldn't have made it even more obvious to the store's staff that we weren't actually browsing their merchandise. It was a good thing they were mostly occupied with the soccer game showing on one of their display TVs. Cheers echoed through the speakers as someone must have scored a goal.

"Why London?" I said. "Why Richter? Why string *us* along?"

John shrugged. "She wanted to get that relic for whatever reason. Maybe we should be flattered that she decided we were her best chance at getting to it."

"That's assuming she picked us because of our skills and not our gullibility," I muttered, although to be fair, no one I was aware of had ever accused Sherlock of being gullible.

She'd pulled the wool over *my* eyes easily enough. I'd been starting to care about her, to think about how I might arrange to see her again.

And now she was sitting less than a hundred feet away, doing God knew what. The restless tremor that ran through me carried a jumble of emotions with it. I wanted to see her. I wanted to touch her again. I wanted to demand an explanation for why she'd done it and have her make some kind of amends. I wanted to never have met her in the first place.

Up until now, I'd been so focused on finding her that I guessed I hadn't given myself enough room to sort out my varying reactions.

"That's why we're here, isn't it?" John said, still way too calm about the whole scenario. "To find out what she's up to and what her grand plan is. Sherlock may very well be right that she was under external pressures."

"That doesn't absolve her of the crimes she committed," I said. And I was pretty sure no "external pressures" had forced her to seduce me. But at the same time the thought that she might have been escaping some kind of danger brought a sympathetic twinge into my chest.

I just had to keep reminding myself that the woman I'd met wasn't real. The Jemma Moriarty I'd gotten to know was a figment she'd created to con us. The true Jemma Moriarty—

I hesitated, leaning closer to the glass and narrowing my eyes. The shade of the awning over the pub's window made it possible to see inside, all the way to where the overhead lights gleamed off bright red hair.

The true Jemma Moriarty was sitting on a stool just a couple feet away from Sherlock.

I stiffened. "They're talking to each other. That wasn't the plan. He said he was just going to watch her and see what she did and who she was meeting."

John followed my gaze. His stance didn't change, but his hand tightened around his walking stick. "She must have recognized him. He was so pleased with that disguise too."

"He shouldn't have gotten that close." She hadn't been conning us about how sharp she was, clearly. I shifted my weight from one foot to the other. I couldn't make out much from this distance, but it looked like they were just sitting there chatting. "If she's made him, she'll know we're here too. Why the hell are we hanging around over here like a couple of idiots?"

"Garrett," John said in protest, but I was already heading out the door. Halfway across the sun-drenched road, he caught up with his slightly uneven gait, his stick tapping against the pavement. "I'm not sure this is the best idea."

"I don't want Sherlock doing all the talking for me," I replied. "Especially when he couldn't even manage to keep up his ploy for five minutes. It's about time *we* put some pressure on her."

I had to see her as she really was, face to face, and then maybe any other feelings still lingering would burn away.

That was the plan, anyway. I stepped into the dimmer space of the bar ahead of John, sour and weirdly savory smells washing over me, and Jemma looked up. She smiled.

Just like that, I was seeing double: the woman who'd told me so earnestly how much she appreciated the risks I was taking and what I now recognized as the sly confidence of a master grifter. My feet stalled for a second before I pushed myself onward.

Other than the air of confidence that came across a little more overtly than it had in London, she looked essentially the same. The scarf she'd pulled over her head had fallen to her angular shoulders, exposing her scarlet hair that caught the eye even when pulled back into a braid. The banded light-and-dark gray of her deep-set eyes stood out as starkly as ever against her pale skin.

It didn't matter that the fullness of her lips didn't totally match that pert nose and pointy chin, or that I knew her deceptively slim frame could topple a man twice her size—I couldn't turn off the part of me that sparked to life at the sight of her. That insisted I'd never met another woman quite so appealing.

"Look who's joined the party," Jemma said in her soft but precise voice, sounding unruffled and if anything mildly amused. "Scotland Yard could spare even you, Garrett?"

"These two wouldn't be here either if it wasn't for me," I found myself saying. I snapped my mouth shut before any other careless remarks could slip out. That competitive impulse, the urge to show I was better than my much-celebrated colleagues, was what had made me so vulnerable to her machinations.

I had to be better than that. I'd thought I was better, at least enough to put the past behind me, until six weeks ago.

Jemma arched an eyebrow at Sherlock, who was still wearing his wig and his droopy moustache.

He raised his shoulder in a light shrug. "Garrett found one of the key pieces of info that allowed us to narrow down your location. It wouldn't have been fair to exclude him from the expedition."

His tone made it clear that he would probably have excluded me if given the option. Sherlock might have preferred to work with me above any of my police colleagues, but mostly he preferred to work alone.

"You don't need to worry about me," I allowed myself to add. "I had plenty of vacation days saved up."

The chief hadn't minded me taking off on a vacation of indeterminate length in large part because of my role in bringing down Stefan Richter. He didn't know that Jemma had handed the international menace to us on a silver platter. The fact that I couldn't really take credit for even that victory niggled at me too.

We needed to sort things out with her, figure out how much of a threat she was and deal with any other crimes she was involved in, and then I could go home and put her behind me like I had all the transgressions of my youth.

"I'd still like to know what the three of you are hoping to accomplish by dropping in on me." Jemma cocked her head. "You have no legal footing to arrest me. If you were hoping to carry out a less official sort of revenge, I should mention that I have a colleague with a pistol watching right now to make sure nothing happens to me."

Sherlock's gaze darted to the back of the pub. A curtain hung over the doorway there, just enough ajar that someone could have gotten a clear shot at any of us if they'd wanted to.

I couldn't make out any figure standing in the shadows there, but a prickle quivered through my nerves. I didn't think she was lying.

"Do you really think I'd come here to rough you up?" Sherlock said incredulously. Revulsion at the idea congealed in my stomach, but it sat uneasily next to the churn of my anger.

"We don't really know each other all that well, do we?" Jemma took a sip of her drink. "I've already told you I've got nothing to discuss with you."

Sherlock shook his head. "That's not a good enough answer."

"*You* involved us," John said. "We need to know exactly what you've gotten us mixed up in."

She flicked her hand dismissively. "Your part in any of my plans is completely behind us. I know you're smart enough to understand what already happened."

As if it were that simple. As if she couldn't have taped our conversations or gathered other evidence of the crime we'd committed—as if all our livelihoods might not rest on whether or not she decided to dabble in blackmail sometime in the future. Did she really think we could forget about that looming possibility?

Did she really think we could just shrug off the way she'd used us, pretend it hadn't mattered at all?

Jemma's eyes found mine as if she'd read my thoughts. Her expression wasn't quite the same as when she'd glanced at me as I'd come in; something more studied and pensive had come into it. Her gaze stayed on me even when Sherlock spoke again.

"I think you're smart enough to know we won't be shaken that easily."

"Well, if you're going to insist on sticking around…" She slid off the stool and slung her purse over her shoulder. "I'll have to get on with my responsibilities as if you're not here. Do whatever you want in Zagreb. It's a lovely city. Just keep away from Pametno Pohranjivanje."

She turned to head out the back. To simply walk away from us after we'd spent six weeks chasing her down. My gut twisted, and my body moved, stepping forward so I could catch her arm.

Jemma's slim forearm was warm against my hand. She stopped and studied me. "I wasn't bluffing about my friend with the gun. What do you think you're going to do with me, Garrett?"

I couldn't have said there was anything suggestive in her voice, but somehow just those words sent my thoughts spinning back to the things we'd done together before—in my hotel room, up against the desk with her legs splayed around me and her gasps in my ear. A different sort of heat flooded me from the groin up.

Before I could figure out how to answer her, she swiveled her arm in my grasp, curling her fingers around my wrist in turn. With a little tug, she leaned in to speak close to my ear.

"You've got nothing here to prove," she murmured. "I've known from the start that the work matters more to you than it does to those two adventurers."

That wasn't at all what I'd been thinking about, and yet somehow the words cut straight to my core. "Jemma," I said, still groping for that perfect verbal blow to knock her down, to shake her confidence the way she'd just shaken me.

She slipped my hold and strode past the curtain with an insistent swish of fabric.

"What was that about?" John asked behind me.

I jerked back around. "Nothing. More of her games." Telling me what she'd managed to determine was exactly what I needed to hear. "Are we just going to let her leave?"

Sherlock showed no sign of concern. He motioned for us to follow him out to the road. On the sidewalk, he glanced around and spoke in a low voice.

"I've seen to it that we'll know if she leaves the city—but I very much got the impression that she has unfinished business she needs to attend to here. I'd like to know what it is. It may provide us with the leverage we need to get our answers."

"She warned us away from Pametno Pohranjivanje," Watson said, his Croatian pronunciation much more badly accented than Jemma's had been.

"That's obviously a ploy," I said. "She *wants* us to look into them for whatever reason. She wouldn't give away a detail that specific otherwise."

Sherlock nodded. "Garrett has it exactly right. Unfortunately, it's for that exact reason I think we should investigate. Not because we assume she doesn't want us to, but to determine why she'd have wanted to point us in that direction. It's a lead in its own way."

I couldn't deny with the logic of that. "What about keeping an eye on her?"

A smile crept across Sherlock's face. "I have a few ideas, one of which is already in motion. But if we do our work right, next time she'll be the one coming to us."

CHAPTER THREE

Jemma

The helicopter jerked with a gust of wind as the pilot guided it along the mountain's slope. "This is as close as we can safely get," he hollered back to Bash and me over the stuttered roar of the whirling blades.

"I guess we don't have to worry about those three Londoners trailing you up here," Bash said dryly, his light green eyes trained on the treetops beneath us. They formed a blanket of green across the range we were cruising over, only a few peaks of pale gray rock poking up through the vegetation. Not even hikers came out to this isolated stretch.

"I gave them something to keep them busy." A smile curled my lips at the thought of Sherlock and the others grappling with the piece of information I'd so blatantly handed them. They wouldn't trust it, but they wouldn't be able to stop themselves from investigating either.

"You don't think we need to worry about them making trouble with any of our business?"

"I've always been very careful that nothing can be traced back to me." I turned my smile on him. "Don't tell me you're worried about them after how easily we played them back in London."

"They seem pretty determined to make things more difficult for you, that's all. They're not going to want to head home empty-handed after working so hard to find you."

The evenness of his voice, more careful than it usually sounded, made me wonder if there wasn't more to his concern. He knew I could handle myself.

Back in London, he'd suggested I was starting to like the trio. Was he more worried about what *I'd* do with them around than what they would?

"They can't be more determined to pin something on me than I am to see through this task," I said. "I don't plan on letting anything distract me." My scheme in London had bought me temporary freedom. If I succeeded here, I'd end any connection between me and the shrouded folk completely.

Then I could get on with crushing their misty asses.

"I don't doubt that," Bash said easily enough, so maybe I'd misread his tone with the racket the chopper was making. He cocked his head, still gazing out the window. "What exactly are we looking for down there?"

I leaned close in case I could spot something right now to point out. No luck. "Anything that could indicate human habitation," I said. "There isn't likely to be anything as obvious as smoke from a fire, but a hint of a building between the trees, or a glimpse of a color you wouldn't expect to be there naturally... Anything that looks like more than part of the wilderness."

Bash nodded. We both wore jackets against the cooler air at this elevation, but the warmth of his body seeped through to mine where my shoulder touched his solidly muscled arm. I couldn't linger in it, though. I scooted over to the far seat to peer out the other side.

My colleague hadn't asked why I thought there might be people living secretly on one of these slopes, or what I wanted with them when we found them. That was the simple unspoken faith he had in me—that I had good reasons, and that when he needed to know, I'd tell him. Just as I had the simple, unspoken faith that when I did need him, he'd act without hesitation.

It was hard to make out anything below through the dense forest. Of course, the people I was looking for would have picked a place with that kind of cover specifically for that reason. That was probably why they'd settled in a country where most of the mountain ranges didn't tower too high above the tree line in the first place. Those sporadic peaks served the cult's purposes just fine while their communes stayed hidden.

Even if I spotted a hint of their presence, we'd have to proceed carefully. We weren't equipped to storm in just yet. I was hoping a little more research would smooth my way there—the task I'd sent my trio on might help.

The helicopter droned on. Nothing passed by beneath us other than rippling green. My body started to tense.

The pilot had said that with the travel time out to this range and back, he could give us an hour in the air at most. At the slow pace I'd asked him to keep so we could really eyeball the terrain, we wouldn't cover even half of this side of the range.

That was all right. I had time. I'd bought myself that time by stealing the pieces of the gold cuff still clamped around my thigh. And even though I was ever aware of the mark on the back of my neck, it hadn't prickled with Bog's insistent presence since I'd put the cuff on. The shrouded one couldn't reach me as long as I wore it.

Bash tapped his window, but by the time I'd rejoined him, he was shaking his head. "Just a lightning scar on a tree," he said. "Nothing man-made."

As I slid back into my seat, the helicopter veered a little higher. My gaze rose too, over the forest to the rocky ground above. The cult of the shrouded folk wouldn't be so careless as to leave clear evidence out in the open. There was nothing up there but scattered shrubs amid the scree, a few patches of grass, and—

And a sun-scorched slab of stone that would have looked like nothing but naturally bleached rock to anyone normal. Anyone who hadn't seen those specific ragged markings come into being with the blaze of a shrouded one's satisfied hunger, long ago.

My pulse hiccupped. "Can you take us down over there?" I asked the pilot, pointing through the windshield. "As close as you can get to that smooth patch on the slope. I need to take a closer look."

"I'll do my best."

As he took the chopper around in a slow circle, checking for a stable place to land, I studied the forest below the bleached slab. It looked as lonely as the rest of this strip.

The helicopter finally touched down on a flat plateau about a ten-minute walk from the bare stone. I hopped out the second the engine had stopped. At the edge of the plateau, I braced my feet on the rough pebble-strewn ground and pitched my way toward the spot more carefully, one hand clutching my purse strap.

Bash followed with heavier steps, his head swiveling as he scanned our surroundings. "What did you see, Mori?"

"I'm not totally sure yet." The chilly wind tossed my hair into my face, and I swept it back, tugging up my hood. "It might not be anything all that helpful."

As we approached the stone, which pointed like a tongue toward the forest farther down the slope, a deeper chill sank into my skin. The mountain air smelled crisp and clean with a hint of evergreen, but an echo of a memory tainted my senses with dry rot and seared skin. I swallowed hard, but I couldn't clear the awful flavor from my mouth. My hand fumbled in my purse for a sugar cube.

With the pure sweetness melting over my tongue, my chest loosened a little. I inhaled fully as I reached the edge of the stone.

For a second, I doubted my senses. Maybe the sun *did* just happen to hit the rock here at the right angle to make those streaks naturally.

I circled the smooth patch and stopped by a boulder

near the tip of the "tongue." My throat closed up, the last fragments of sugar souring in my mouth.

No, I hadn't seen wrong. From this angle, from nearly the same angle as where I'd crouched all those years ago, I could see how the ritual had played out all too clearly. The memory that had hit me when I'd spoken to Sherlock yesterday swelled up from the back of my mind again. The blaze of supernatural light, the unending scream as the shrouded one had consumed the boy bit by bit…

I shut my eyes. Bash came up beside me, his faint heat cutting through the chill.

"Something happened here," he said. Not a question. I wasn't controlling my reaction as well as I'd have liked. But it was Bash seeing me, and Bash knew enough now that I could be at least partly honest with him.

"Do you remember the story I told you about my sister?" I asked, more rhetorically than anything else. Of course he did. "The monsters that took her—they took someone else right here. Maybe more than one someones. Kids. It's always kids."

My hitman let out a sharp sound and glanced around. "On horror's head horrors accumulate," he murmured in a more serious tone than he usually used when he quoted the Shakespearean dramas he refused to admit he loved. "Do you think those monsters are here? Is *that* what we're looking for?"

The shrouded folk were everywhere and nowhere all at the same time. I didn't see how it'd be helpful to tell him that, though.

"There are people who worship the monsters like gods

in a sort of cult," I said, forcing myself to open my eyes again. To edge farther around the stone, checking the ground for other signs. "My parents were like that. The cult has little communes set up here and there, mostly at high elevations. The things thrive on our sunlight. One of those communes has something I need, and my research suggests they're in this country. That's who we're looking for."

Bash took this information in stride without hesitation, although I noticed his hand came to rest on his hip holster. "The people from the commune would have arranged the… sacrifice? That happened here?"

"Maybe. Or maybe there's more than one group around. And the fact that they held a sacrifice here doesn't necessarily mean they're living anywhere all that nearby."

They liked to give the shrouded folk plenty of room for their feeding. I'd slunk along for five hours following the little procession that had led that boy to his doom.

If the cultists who'd arranged the sacrifice had left any signs of their passage at the time, the weather had washed it all away. I turned rocks with my foot, finding bleached streaks on the bottoms of a few that must have been dislodged since the shrouded one had set off its blaze of energy. My meandering path took me down toward the trees.

A hunched pine had sprung up among the rocks a little higher than the line of the forest, almost directly beneath the sloping stone. I studied it, ducking low to check the branches. A dimpled line across one made me grimace.

"Found something?" Bash asked.

"It looks like there's been at least a couple decades' growth since the last time anyone used this spot." I backed away from the tree. They might not do sacrifices often, or they might have moved farther afield. "We're following an old trail."

"One of your sources was more recent than that, wasn't it?" Bash said. "You were sure they'd still be in the country."

That was true. "They had deep roots here. It'd have been difficult for them to completely move. But I don't think this spot is going to help us find them."

Just in case, I eased several paces into the forest, studying the ground and the vegetation. The place looked undisturbed. Not even an oddly snapped twig or a scuffed footprint in the dirt.

I started back up the slope toward the helicopter. "We'll take the rest of this area even slower than before." I wanted to think this meant we could at least narrow down our area to the highlands on the interior of the country, ignoring the peaks along the coast, but this group had kept themselves hidden around their object of worship for centuries if not millennia. Who knew how far they'd go to obscure their location?

I picked up my pace to get past the horrible memories the slab stirred up—to get on with this search—and my foot came down hard on a jagged edge in the rocky ground. The rock snapped and crumbled under the sole of my boot.

Years of martial arts training had given me excellent

reflexes and even better balance. I half stumbled, half leapt to the side, catching my footing on more stable ground. I was already perfectly steady when Bash touched my arm.

"Just the mountain keeping me on my toes," I said. "I'm okay."

The corner of his mouth quirked up. "Of course you are. When aren't you?"

Standing this close to him, I couldn't help thinking back to the one time recently I hadn't been okay at all. When the shrouded one that had a claim on my soul had filled my head with a hallucination of blood and gore I couldn't shake, and only Bash's presence, Bash's devotion, had driven it back. From the way his gaze strayed for a second to my mouth, I suspected my right-hand man was thinking of the same night.

That night I'd given in to the attraction that had always simmered between us. I'd nearly fucked up all the faith and trust we'd built between us. Even if the memory of the unexpected tenderness he'd shown alongside his strength sent an eager pang through me, I couldn't risk making that mistake again.

I stepped away, maybe a little more abruptly than was natural. Bash's hand fell. The awkwardness my first mistake had already created hung in the air for an instant before I swatted his shoulder.

"I'll beat you to the chopper, hitman."

He laughed. "Only if you watch your footing better, Majesty."

We scrambled up the slope, leaving the traces of the shrouded folk's horror behind us—for now.

CHAPTER FOUR

John

I wouldn't say I was religious, but I experienced a certain awe stepping into a building like Zagreb's famous cathedral. Huge fluted columns rose up to the breathtakingly high vaulted ceiling alongside the rows of dark wooden benches. The midday sun beamed through the stained glass windows around the vast altar, filling the space with a warm glow and rendering the intricate gold chandeliers unnecessary. The scent of the place spoke of history: candle wax and varnished wood.

I kept my walking stick tucked under my arm as I walked slowly and therefore mostly evenly up to the table near the front with its stacks of booklets. The chances that Jemma *wouldn't* notice my presence seemed highly unlikely, but the tap of that stick would be an automatic giveaway I could avoid. Only a tiny bit of pain nibbled at my hip.

Several tourists were perusing the central aisle. More had taken at least a brief seat on the benches' red-padded seats. Jemma sat about halfway down the rows at the far end of her bench, where a marble angel seemed to peer down at her. She'd braided her bright hair again, but it was still easy to pick out the back of her head.

Sherlock had been sure she was going to meet someone here around this time. He hadn't said how he'd determined that, but I'd leave my friend a few secrets since he enjoyed them so much. Clearly his intel had been correct. He hadn't known who she might be planning to see or why, though.

Observe what you can, and if you interrupt the meeting, that's fine too, he'd said when he sent me off. *The sooner she realizes she can't simply ignore us, the sooner we'll get some real answers.*

He and Garrett had gone to look at the main storage warehouse belonging to Pametno Pohranjivanje, which had turned out to be a local storage company. We'd taken a quick look around yesterday under the guise of customers needing a tour, but Sherlock had wanted to return for a more in-depth exploration while they were closed over the weekend.

I was going to look odd if I stayed at this table much longer. I wavered, considering my options. Sit at the back where I wouldn't be as visible but also wouldn't be able to hear any conversations Jemma had, or risk a closer approach?

Well, Sherlock had said it wouldn't be a horrible thing even if I simply interrupted her plans. The spoils rarely went to the cautious. I meandered along the aisle, aiming for the bench two rows behind her.

My gamble didn't even succeed long enough for me to get in place. Jemma's head turned as another gaggle of tourists jostled past me, and her gaze immediately locked with mine. I had the ridiculous urge to duck as if she'd somehow forget she'd seen me if I dropped out of sight.

Her mouth tightened, just for an instant. That was the only sign that my arrival bothered her. Then she raised an eyebrow as if to say, *Are you just going to stand there or what?*

Maybe I could observe something useful even after she'd noticed me. Letting my walking stick touch the floor now that there wasn't any point in attempting subterfuge, I headed over to her bench at a faster pace. She got up at the same time. Meeting me at the edge of the aisle, she tucked her hand around my elbow like she had more than once back in London. Her touch set my pulse off-kilter in a way that was both disturbing and exhilarating.

I shouldn't let myself be affected by her like that. I had no idea whether any part of the woman I'd admired in London was even real. Okay, that wasn't entirely true—she was even *more* brilliant than I'd thought. But the other parts that had drawn me to her: the sense of strength in the face of loss, the easy way she'd shared her feelings with me... Those aspects had been a ploy, at least in part.

So why did a large part of *me* want to go head-to-head —and, ah, other bits to other bits, if I was being totally honest—all over again?

Jemma nudged me toward the altar, and I ambled along at her direction. "Taking in the sights?" she said.

"Sherlock said I shouldn't miss this place."

"Hmm. Another coincidence then." She shook her head and dipped her other hand into her purse. Her phone's screen glowed on for a few seconds as she must have diverted her intended companion. "Do you really think this is the best use of your time—following me around?"

"You could always answer our questions and set our minds at ease," I pointed out.

"That's assuming you'd find the answers I could give you at all reassuring." She flashed me a coy smile. "Are you sure you didn't just want to see me?"

We came to a stop at the foot of the main altar. The candles stood unlit, but a spark lit in my chest as Jemma trailed her fingers over my forearm before releasing me.

"What for?" I asked, keeping my voice steady. "So you can wrap me up in an even crazier scheme? I think the once was enough."

"Do you?" Both eyebrows rose this time. "Let's not pretend you didn't love every minute of that adventure, John. When was the last time you'd had as much fun as you did during that week with me? I gave you a gift."

"I usually like to be aware of any ulterior motives that come with a gift."

She poked my chest lightly with her forefinger. "Oh, really? I'd be willing to bet you're also enjoying the fact that you have no idea how much I'm capable of."

Fucking hell, just those words turned the earlier spark

into a flame. I had to focus on what I was here for. Which wasn't dragging her off into the nearest private room and rediscovering how good her body felt against mine. Definitely not an appropriate line of thinking for our current situation or our current location.

"Why don't you tell me more about it, then?" I suggested. "What other thrilling deeds have you gotten up to?"

"Ah, no. I didn't come here to share stories with you."

"But you were hoping to meet up with someone else."

"Another part of my business I'm not planning to share." She wandered to the other side of the aisle, and I followed. "We had some fun together, and we both got something we wanted. Now we're done."

Every part of me rejected that statement. I grasped her shoulder and waited until she glanced at me again. Her expression stayed mild, but I'd be damned if I couldn't still see that hint of sorrow in her fathomless gray eyes.

"No," I said. "We're not done. I'm not leaving until I understand what it was you got out of that bargain."

She shrugged. "A pretty trinket. Why does it need to have more explanation than that?"

"Because it obviously does. Because it wouldn't make sense otherwise."

"Maybe I'm not the most sensible person in the world." She folded her arms over her chest and looked at me through her eyelashes. "I think you've just been bored since I left town. You're looking for stimulation. Is Sherlock still giving you the cold shoulder?"

That question sent a very different twang of emotion

through me. "We're working together as well as we always have," I said, as if I didn't know what she was talking about.

"Still pretending that kiss didn't happen, then, is he? It amazes me he manages to see as much as he does while purposefully blinding himself."

In the weeks since it'd happened, I'd thought I'd managed to suppress all thought and feeling related to the kiss I'd shared with Sherlock nearly as well as he had. One flippant comment from Jemma brought the tangled mix of desire, uncertainty, and frustration rushing right back to the surface.

It was because of her we'd kissed at all—because of her I'd realized that maybe I'd wanted to for a while and very much wanted to again. After nearly two months of Sherlock studiously avoiding acknowledging the event, *that* revelation didn't feel anything like a gift.

Jemma was smiling at the emotions that must have been playing across my face. "Oh, John," she said. "He's your best friend, isn't he? Where did you get the idea that you don't have the right to ask people for things that you want?"

That question caught me like a swift jab to the gut. *You wouldn't understand. You don't even* ask, *you just take.* But the thought of continuing any conversation on that subject made my stomach clench.

"What does it matter to you anyway?" I said, a little more brusquely than I normally would have spoken. "I thought you were done with us."

Jemma paused. I caught another hint of a deeper emotion that might lie behind the nonchalant airs she was putting on—a twitch of her mouth, there and gone.

No, I didn't believe it. She wasn't as detached as she wanted to seem. Maybe she wasn't the woman I'd found myself so drawn to in London, but she was more than a conniving con artist too.

Which only made her more dangerous. Everything about this talk told me how much I should be on my guard with her.

"Maybe I just think it's a waste, all that pent-up longing with no way to apply it." She brushed her hand over my arm again. "I suppose I might as well get going. Enjoy your sightseeing."

I didn't intend to let her wander off to resume her original plans. I tagged along several feet behind her, watching her braid sway against the thin ivory fabric of her sleeveless blouse, which was only a few shades paler than her lightly freckled shoulders.

Jemma must have heard me behind her, but she didn't glance back. She strode out of the cathedral and through the streets to the tram line. One of the long blue vehicles was just pulling up at the stop.

I got on after her. Jemma saved me from having to decide whether to sit next to her or keep my distance by picking a spot between two other passengers. Ignoring me, she pulled her tablet out of her purse and flicked through something on its screen.

If we could get our hands on that device, we could

find out so much more about what she was up to. I couldn't imagine her making that kind of theft easy, though.

She got off down the road from her hotel and headed straight there. After I watched her disappear inside with a thump of the glass doors, I lingered outside, not entirely sure what to do with myself now. I couldn't pursue her all the way to her room. If I'd tried, I imagined she'd have hotel security on me before I'd so much as crossed the lobby.

My phone vibrated in my pocket. I fished it out.

"How did it go?" Sherlock said without preamble.

I sighed. "She spotted me early on, so I didn't find out much, but I did give her a bit of hassle. It looked like she canceled her meeting. She's gone back to the hotel now."

He made an approving sound. "Can you get over to the warehouse? It appears we have a large job here—your assistance would be appreciated."

"Sure, as long as you don't think I should watch the hotel," I said.

"No," he said immediately. "We've done enough there for now. When you get here, come around to the green door on the side."

I took a taxi most of the way there and walked the last short distance out of practiced caution. The padlock that I assumed had been on the side door now lay broken on the driveway's cracked pavement. Sherlock opened the door at the sound of my footsteps and caught my glance.

"Such a shame," he said with a small grin. "We showed

up and the door had clearly been forced open, so of course we felt compelled to investigate."

"Of course," I said, unable to stop myself from smiling back at his self-satisfied expression. In the middle of a successful enterprise, Sherlock took on a buoyant energy you wouldn't have believed he was capable of from seeing him in his more serious moments. His cool blue eyes twinkled. He spun, beckoning for me to follow him and swiping stray waves of his dark brown hair away from his forehead as he strode down the hall.

If you'd asked me two months ago whether Sherlock was a good-looking man, I'd have told you I hadn't really thought about it, and that would have been true. Now I'd have to admit, *Hell, yes.*

"What's going on?" I asked him.

"It appears my earlier suspicions were correct," Sherlock said, as if he'd bothered to tell me about those earlier suspicions. "We even saw a van bringing around a new lot. This business is a front for a cartel of robbers and black market dealers."

We came out into a wider hall that smelled sharply chalky. Three of the locker doors were open. Garrett was peering into a plastic crate inside one and jotting notes.

"I've matched up items in a few of the lockers with recently reported robberies," Sherlock went on. "We'll notify the local police, naturally. But first I'd like to document exactly what was stolen—and to get that done fast. You can take that locker. Do you have something to write on?"

"I have my case journal."

"Excellent. Make note of everything. Let's see if we can't find a pattern that'll reveal Miss Moriarty's intentions."

CHAPTER FIVE

Jemma

Now that the London trio was in town, I wasn't making much use of the hotel elevators. Taking the stairs down offered a little extra workout, and it meant I could scope out the lobby surreptitiously for anyone who might be keeping an eye on those elevators.

Like today. I spotted the familiar head of short-cropped fawn-brown hair almost instantly. Garrett wasn't making any particular effort to hide where he was leaning against the wall near the front doors, his boyishly handsome face stern with concentration as he jotted something in his ever-present notepad. Every few seconds, he glanced toward the elevators and then around the room with its marble-tiled walls and little burbling fountain.

He was taking this job very seriously. I supposed he had to be to take time off from his actual job to track me across the continent. None of the three were happy with me, but the vibe he'd given off the other day in the pub had been outright angry.

I *had* strung him along a little more than the others, even if I hadn't promised him anything. I'd only led him on as much as was necessary, though. He could keep his hurt feelings, and I'd keep my freedom from being devoured by a shrouded one, thank you.

If he'd been assigned to watch the front entrance, what were the chances no one was staked out in back? I wet my lips, considering. Just then, one of the young porters I'd been paying off, Jakov, pushed a cart stacked with luggage into view.

Perfect. I caught his eye with a quick gesture and waved him over, producing a reasonable tip in kuna from my wallet.

"Do me a quick favor?" I said, showing him the money. "One of the men who've been hassling me is over near the entrance. You see him, the one with the notepad? I don't want to make a fuss, but if you could push your cart over there and act like you want to help him, ask him if there's anything you can do for him, whatever you can think of to keep him occupied so I have a chance to leave without him bothering me, I'd really appreciate it."

"Of course, Ms. Matthams," Jakov said with a smile, using the name I'd given the hotel. He looked a little guilty taking the money for that bit of work, but he did take it. It was business, after all, whether he totally understood the extent of it or not.

Jakov set off with his cart. The second the stack of suitcases blocked Garrett's view of the lobby, I slipped through the room and out the door. All I heard from the inspector detective was his frazzled voice saying, "No, really, I'm fine right here. I'm just waiting for someone."

I went the wrong way on the street, heading around the next block and doubling back, just to avoid him getting a glimpse of me out the lobby window. No one followed me. I wandered farther until I was sure I wasn't being tailed, and then I plucked my main phone out of my purse.

"Bash," I said, keeping my voice low as I dodged a pack of morning shoppers. "Did you get confirmation?"

"You were right," Bash said on the other end. "A truck came by around two in the morning and unloaded a bunch of boxes. Novak came down to collect them personally. From the way he handled them, they were heavy."

I smiled. "Boxes of books would be." A wealthy collector of rare texts, Mr. Novak placed his hobby over the law. He'd had a hand in funding the syndicate of thieves who'd been breaking into homes and shops all across the city and the surrounding county. They grabbed plenty of valuable items for themselves, but their targets always just happened to have a special book or five that they lifted too. Those never made it to the black market— they were set aside for Novak.

Yesterday the local police had rounded up most of that gang, thanks to the trio's meddling. They'd worked as quickly as I'd hoped. Novak had hidden his recent acquisitions in storage somewhere I hadn't been able to determine, but the arrests had made him nervous, as intended. He'd brought all his precious texts into the safety of his home.

Safe from police confiscation, maybe. Not safe from me.

"Do you need any support on this one?" Bash asked.

"No, I think it's a one-person con," I said. "Keep your phone where you can hear it, just in case."

I tucked mine away with a rush of heightened spirits. The cult of the shrouded folk kept to themselves and rarely let any record slip out of their hands, but they'd been around long enough and orchestrated enough strangeness that accounts of their activity existed here and there. I'd followed a trail of increasingly clearer references from one book to another until I'd been pointed to a book on Croatian myth and superstition of which only a handful of copies had been printed.

The only one of those I'd been able to locate had belonged to a rare books and antiquities shop on the outskirts of Zagreb until Novak's gang had hit it a few months ago. The volume I wanted was one of those reported stolen.

Now I'd just have to steal it back from him. Considering I'd grown up in the damned cult and as far as I could tell he was only a dabbler in the dark arts, I had more of a right to the information than he did anyway. Taking on the commune wasn't going to help me if I didn't know how to use the prize they were protecting.

I stopped at a corner to wait for an approaching tram and take another look around. The Londoners had helped my mission along, but they'd also thrown a spanner or two into the works. Thanks to John's interruption in the cathedral, the woman I'd spent months finding and weeks coaxing into a conversation had gotten gun-shy all over again. From what I could tell from a few vague comments I'd uncovered on the internet, she'd heard stories about the commune directly, but she wasn't willing to discuss the subject in any more depth by email or phone.

If one of my temporary pseudo-colleagues got in my way today, I might lose my chance with Novak too. I still wasn't sure how the trio had figured out I'd be at the cathedral in the first place.

No one else got on the tram when I did. I watched the street behind me as I walked to a seat. They couldn't even know I'd left the hotel. Even three against one, I could out-scheme them any day.

In the middle of a commercial strip, I had to switch tram lines. I let the crowd of other departing passengers hustle on down the street ahead of me, leaving me some breathing room.

As I strode past the darkened windows of a movie theater, a prickling chill raced up and down my thigh where the gold cuff was clamped around it.

The muscle seized. My lungs constricted at the sudden shock of cold. I stumbled, and at the same moment, a gaggle of elementary school-aged kids brushed past me, one of them bumping my shoulder where I'd bent over.

I jerked my purse close to my chest instinctively. The sensation faded like it had before, but more slowly this time. It took me several seconds before I could straighten up and keep walking, and even then my leg wobbled.

It was getting worse. Whoever had constructed the gold cuff had designed its patterns and gems to disrupt the shrouded folk's senses, but they hadn't meant it to be worn for months at a time. I'd already known I didn't want to rely on a piece of metal as a lifelong solution, but clearly I had less time to find a more permanent fix than I'd assumed.

The brush with the kids had left my nerves jangling too. Sherlock had tracked me using his contingent of street youth back in London. What was to stop him from using similar tactics here?

The first chance I got, I ducked into the shadows of a dusty alley where I'd be out of view from the street. First I patted down the pockets on my slacks. Then I riffled through my purse.

There was nothing in there I didn't recognize—not even a spare coin. And I'd done a thorough accounting after that first meeting with Sherlock at Franjo's. I hadn't found anything then either except a stray sugar cube that had escaped its plastic bag...

My shoulders stiffened. It had seemed so innocuous at the time, and I hadn't seen Sherlock get his hands anywhere near my purse besides, but maybe I'd underestimated him.

I pulled out the baggie of sugar cubes and turned it in the thin sunlight that reached into the alley, studying them. I had a couple dozen on hand, all of which had been in my purse for at least a week. The corners of the cubes no longer poked sharply into the plastic but had dulled from scraping against each other.

The corners on all of them, that was, except one that was still as crisply cubic as any popped fresh from the box.

I dug it out and rubbed my thumb against the gritty surface. It didn't crumble the way a regular sugar cube would have. The glinting crystals didn't give way until I scraped them against the brick wall beside me.

I licked the other side and found it tasted as sweet as usual. Whatever substance Sherlock had used to keep the cube intact, it was probably sugar-based too. He'd been prepared that I might try to eat this one.

And if I had, I might very well have simply swallowed the device inside without realizing. The sugar coated a little gelatin pill. I broke it open to find a tiny rectangle of metal that I had to assume was some kind of tracking device.

For a minute, I just stood there staring at it. For fuck's sake. I'd had my purse on me with the bag of sugar cubes in it every time I'd left the hotel since that first meeting with Sherlock. He'd know that I'd gone to rent the helicopter and then taken it out into the mountains. He'd be able to see where I was right now. I'd almost led him straight to Novak.

The balls on that man. I wanted to both scream in frustration and laugh at his genius.

My fingers tensed around the device with the longing to crush it, to destroy his ploy. I held myself back.

No. If the signal cut out, he'd know I was on to him, and he'd turn to other tactics. Tactics I also might not pick up on right away. Better the enemy I knew than one I didn't.

He'd used this trick against me. Now how could I use it against him?

A plan sprang up in my mind from the soil of everything I'd experienced in the last few days.

My time was running out again. I didn't know how much longer I could wear the cuff without it causing me permanent harm, and the second I took it off, Bog would zip straight over to claim the soul I was already late handing over. My own investigations into the commune had been going too slowly—but my trio had just proven that they had the connections and resources to get things done even here in Croatia. Different connections and resources than I had access to. I wouldn't mind borrowing those.

They'd think they were on *my* trail, but instead I'd put them on the trail of the place I wanted to find. Then, when they found it, I'd hop over their heads and be on my way before they knew it, just like before.

I couldn't have managed it by manipulating them to their faces like I had in London. They'd be too skeptical now. But if they thought they were gathering information I didn't want them to know, they'd jump on a new lead without hesitation.

A smile curled my lips. While no doubt applauding his own cleverness, Sherlock had handed me exactly the tool I needed.

How could I point them in the right direction without giving too much away? They should already know I'd been scoping out the mountains for some reason. Ah, yes. That would come together nicely.

I caught another tram, this one traveling in the opposite direction from where I'd originally been heading. In twenty minutes, I was stepping off just down the street from a small moving company with three trucks in its back lot. I circled the place and peered at the trucks for a little while so anyone tracking the device I'd tucked back into my purse had plenty of time to narrow down my location. Then I stepped into the scruffy looking building.

The room inside and the guy behind the counter looked scruffy too. The floor creaked under my feet. The guy pushed himself straighter where he'd been leaning on his elbows reading a magazine.

"Can I help you?" he asked in Croatian.

I was hardly fluent, but I'd made a quick study of the language when it'd become clear this country would be our next destination. Most of the people in the city spoke decent English, but not all, and plenty in the smaller towns relied on their native language.

"Yes, please," I said, smoothing out my accent as much as I could. "I have a somewhat odd question to ask. It needs to be kept discrete—no talk of the job with other people. Is that possible?"

The guy looked a little puzzled and a little curious. "I don't see why not. What's the job?"

I tapped my fingers against the counter, managing not to grimace at the gritty texture. "I want to know if it's possible to transport an entire small community across a fairly significant distance. The contents of several houses and other buildings packed up together. Much of it would need to be moved across some distance by hand. The locations are quite isolated and at a high elevation—the roads won't reach far enough."

The guy's expression shifted all the way to puzzled. "That sounds like a much larger effort than we're equipped to handle. Where is this community?"

"Never mind about it then," I said quickly, taking a step back. "I thought it was worth checking. Do me a favor and forget I asked."

I hustled out of the office with enough speed to hopefully take him from puzzled to suspicious. Suspicious enough to not feel guilty mentioning what I'd asked him to anyone who came calling to inquire about the visit.

Where to now? A few blocks down the street, I came across a little café wafting a sweet scent that made my stomach twinge. I bought myself a piece of custard cream cake and ate it at one of the spindly-legged tables while I contemplated my next move.

The seed I'd just planted wasn't likely to be enough on its own. I didn't want to head to Novak's today now that Sherlock might have tracked me partway there, even if I stopped back at the hotel to leave the tracking device behind. Better to let that trail go colder.

Why not throw out a little more fishing line and see who came to play? I licked my fingers and dug out my phone again.

"Bash—me again. I had a new thought. Meet me at the zoo? I'll explain along the way."

CHAPTER SIX

Jemma

The perfect meeting spot presented itself the moment I came through the zoo's gates. One of the first enclosures stood off to one side, partly hidden by a high stone wall. Just the kind of wall someone could sneak up behind to listen to a conversation unnoticed.

I took my place at the railing along the edge of the enclosure where I'd be in view of anyone coming into the zoo. As I took out my phone, a snow leopard prowled by on the other side of the fence. Another sprawled on a wide boulder, washing its paw and shooting wary glances toward the visitors.

How did they feel about being stuck in that little space instead of having a whole forest to roam around in? The pacing one gave off a restless tension that resonated through me.

Maybe someday you'll get a chance to escape and run free too, I thought at it.

Not that I'd completely shed my wall-less prison yet.

Tourists and maybe a few locals drifted by with a rhythmic shuffling of feet and oohs and ahs. A little boy lost the ice cream off his cone and started sobbing. I popped an undoctored sugar cube into my mouth. As I rolled its sweetness over my tongue, I switched my phone to selfie mode and held it so I could watch the entrance behind me covertly on its screen.

How long would it take Sherlock to send someone to check up on me? John had gotten to the cathedral no more than twenty minutes after I'd arrived. If I hadn't gone early to scope out the layout and reassure my contact that everything looked safe, I might have been able to meet with her. But then, if I hadn't, he might have shown up when I was still talking with her, and that would have compromised my goals so much more.

Maybe Sherlock would come himself this time. I could turn the tables on his ploy right in front of his face.

The thought sent a little thrill through me, but when the sunlight glanced off a strong brow and swept-back blond hair passing the gate, I smiled. John would do just fine too. As far as I could tell from the way he'd responded to me in the cathedral, he wasn't entirely sure whether he should be hunting me or helping me. Of course he'd be the fastest out of the trio to consider forgiving.

I saw him note my presence and then the wall behind me. Faster than anyone who used a walking stick had a right to move, he slipped out of sight. Good man.

He'd be sidling over to the opposite side of that wall right now. I could picture him: his careful steps to avoid alerting me, his hazel eyes lighting up with the excitement of playing spy, like a golden retriever ready to bound after a tossed ball.

Except a golden retriever couldn't batter a thug into running for his life. I'd rather that I never provoked the more ferocious side of Dr. John Watson that he'd shown a couple times in London, but knowing it was there made me enjoy the game even more.

I stepped closer to my side of the wall as if to ease apart from the other zoo-goers. That was Bash's cue to approach. He sauntered around the enclosure a minute later, his eyes shaded by a wig of distinctive bowl-cut black hair and thick sunglasses. Baggy sweats and his loose gait downplayed his muscular frame. He sure as hell wouldn't strike anyone as a former special ops sniper right now.

"Did you have any luck?" I asked him when he reached me, pitching my voice low but keeping it loud enough that I expected someone listening closely by the wall would make out the words.

Bash shook his head. We'd worked out a loose script over the phone on my way here. "It's a big job. Not the kind of thing these companies are used to dealing with—especially the ones we can trust to keep quiet about it."

"Damn it."

"Are you sure we have to move them? They've been running things out of that little village for ages without anyone noticing."

"My 'friends' from London weren't here poking

around before," I said. "If they stumble on the commune, we're screwed. A few dozen people can't support themselves on a mountainside without leaving some kind of trail. Better to relocate them ASAP than wish we had after it's too late."

"I'll start reaching out to possibilities farther afield then," Bash said. "You're sure of where you want to relocate them *to* now?"

"Yeah. Here are the coordinates. I found a good spot. Equally isolated." I crinkled a slip of paper as if I were passing it to him. "We'll need some construction work too to set up new buildings."

"I'll add that to the list." Bash smirked at me, enjoying the con. "Is there anything else you need from me right now?"

"Just lay low. They've been sticking close to me—I'm not sure how they're managing it. I don't even trust my phones anymore. I'll signal you the usual way if we need to talk again."

"It's a pleasure to work with you as always."

He tipped his head to me, and I nodded to give him the go-ahead to leave. As he walked away, I glanced toward the wall.

I *could* wander off myself and let John head back to report on what he'd heard unhindered. But it would be a lot more fun to keep him on his toes. We wouldn't want him to feel he'd gotten what he wanted too easily, would we?

I suppressed a smirk of my own and let out a sigh,

deliberately letting my feet scrape against the ground as I headed around the wall so he'd have a little warning.

John's walking stick knocked the stone in his haste to hustle away. When I came around the wall, he was standing by a map of the park several feet closer to the gate, his face only slightly flushed. Not a bad feint—not bad at all. I pushed my mouth into a frown and marched over.

"Hello again," I said, propping myself against the sign. "I'm starting to think you've signed up as my new shadow. The old one does work just fine."

John blinked at me, doing a decent job of pretending surprise, even if he didn't quite have Sherlock's poker face. He was rather terribly adorable.

"Jemma!" he said. "I was just passing the time while Sherlock's off on some mission he didn't want to explain." He hesitated. "Oh, that's very clever. You followed *me* here and managed to slip in ahead, didn't you?"

He shook his head with a wry smile, and, okay, I could give him credit for an excellent gambit. Spinning the situation so the accuser suddenly became the accused was one of my favorite tactics too.

I raised my eyebrows at him. "Oh, no, don't try to turn this around on me. Why would I need to follow you around when your only business here is messing with me?"

"Maybe it's a real coincidence then," John said, still smiling. "What are you doing here, then? Playing tourist?"

I shrugged. "I like watching animals when I have a spare hour or two. They're so much simpler than human beings. It looks like you just got here. What were you looking to see first?"

He glanced back at the map, which I suspected he hadn't really studied in his hurry to look as if he were studying it and not eavesdropping. "Ah, I've always been fond of the chimps. Mainly because they aren't all that simple."

"I hadn't made it that far yet," I said. "Why don't I join you? And you can buy me an ice cream to make up for acting like a stalker."

"Of course you would want an ice cream," John said, sounding amused, but he was studying me at the same time. Wondering what my intentions were, no doubt. Eager to get back to report to Sherlock, but also probably hoping he might catch me in a tiny slip that would give him even more to report. And he might have another reason or two to like the thought of sticking around.

I wet my lips. "I didn't leave my sweet tooth behind in London. Come on." I gave his arm a gentle shove, and he went, twirling his walking stick before applying it to the ground.

It wasn't far to the nearest ice cream stand. I asked for chocolate and grinned while John dug out the cash to pay. He couldn't quite manage to look disgruntled about it.

He also couldn't quite manage to stop his gaze from twitching to my mouth as I gave the creamy chocolate scoop a generous swipe of my tongue. The flicker of hunger in his eyes was almost as delicious as the treat in my hand.

It might have been too long since I'd gotten to act on

my own carnal appetites. My work over the last several weeks hadn't required any intimate encounters—and, to be honest, the thought of picking up some random man in a bar just to scratch an itch hadn't been all that appealing after the very satisfying time I'd had in London. Where was I going to find anyone with Garrett's passionate determination, or John's earnest enthusiasm, or Sherlock's unplumbed depths of desire?

It wasn't safe to let myself even consider Bash.

Better that I let those memories fade a little longer. As fun as it was to tease, what were the chances any of the trio was going to give me another shot between the sheets now that they had some idea of who I really was?

"So, you like chimps, hmm?" I said as we strolled that way. I slipped my hand around John's elbow and licked the ice cream again, feeling the thump of his pulse under my fingers.

"They say the apes have an almost human-like intelligence," John said, keeping his tone casual enough. "I always wonder what they'd tell us if we could properly communicate."

"Probably to leave them the hell alone already," I remarked, and John chuckled. "Speaking of human intelligence, what *did* Sherlock tell you about this mission he's abandoned you for?"

John's fading chuckle turned into a cough. "I think I'm offended that you figured there was any chance I might answer that."

"Nothing ventured, nothing gained." I patted his arm soothingly. "I have no doubts about your loyalties.

Presumably he's investigating something to do with me, so perhaps if you told me I could offer some assistance."

John outright laughed at that. "Oh, I'm sure you would. Assistance in pointing him in completely the wrong direction."

"I didn't lead you *that* far astray in London, did I? You got your man."

"I guess we did." He stopped at the edge of the path between two of the enclosures and turned to face me. His expression had become abruptly intent. "Who are you really, Jemma? Is this you, the way you're talking with me now, or is it just another mask you're putting on?"

The unexpected question pricked at me. "What makes you think any of it is a mask?" I said tartly. "I was the woman you got to know in London, the one you believed was a 'kindred spirit.' I'm the woman I am now. I'm whoever I need to be as the situation requires it."

He held my gaze as if trying to read more than I'd said from my eyes. "No one's just a collection of appearances. There has to be something you want, something that drives you, beneath all that."

"I never said there wasn't."

He shifted his arm, freeing it from my grasp and cupping my elbow in his own hand. "When we were talking that one night in London, you told me you lost someone important to you a long time ago. That was true, wasn't it?"

An uneasy shiver ran through my chest to my gut. This wasn't where I'd intended this conversation to go. I should never have shared that with him.

"I told you a lot of stories," I said.

"Yes," he said. "But I know what real grief looks like. I lost my older brother, years ago—to carelessness and alcohol, but he used to be the person I looked up to most." He swallowed the roughness from his voice. "The way that feels, I could see in you."

Kindred spirits indeed. Except he'd lost the sibling who should have been protecting him, and I'd lost the one I should have protected.

My stomach had tightened into a ball, but I kept my smile on my face and grasped onto the one thing I could control. I couldn't let him see he'd put me off balance, so I'd have to throw him off just as much. And I knew exactly the way to spin this conversation around.

I rested my hand on his broad chest, lowering my eyes to look at him through my lashes. "Are you trying to turn me into a fair maiden who needs to be rescued, John? You don't need to go to that much trouble. You're sweet, and I do love sweet things. We could go back to wherever you're staying right now, and I'd happily show you how much."

I slicked my tongue over my nearly finished ice cream. A flush raced up John's neck with a slight hitch of his breath. He stepped back, and I let my hand fall.

"I don't think that would be a good idea," he said.

"Maybe not," I said agreeably, already feeling steadier on my feet. "But doesn't that make you want to do it more? What could it hurt, really? You don't honestly think another little dalliance with me would put you in any danger, do you?"

His jaw worked. "I don't know."

"You want to know the truth?" I eased a tad closer and let my voice drop as low as a caress. "I am fucking dangerous. I can kill a man with my bare hands, and I know because I've done it. But I haven't needed to go to those lengths in years, and I'd like to keep it that way for as long as possible. So really, you're perfectly safe."

John's lips parted, but he didn't appear to know what to say. For all his body had tensed, his pupils had dilated while I'd spoken. I'd frightened him a little, and oh, how that turned him on.

He didn't want a damsel half as much as he wanted to tempt peril, and he could see both in me, wrapped up in one neat bow. I'd give him some time to stew on that.

Before he'd recovered himself, I bobbed up to kiss his cheek. "Enjoy the apes. You know where to come looking for me when you make up your mind."

I slipped away and headed for the entrance. If he made any move to follow, it wasn't fast enough. I strode past the gates and on down the street to hail a cab.

I could almost call checkmate. We'd see where the game led next.

Sherlock

"I don't know what this all adds up to other than it's very, very weird." Garrett jabbed his kebab skewer toward the end of the table where I'd laid out a map of the country. He'd brought take-out dinner for the three of us to the two-bedroom suite John and I had managed to obtain across the hall from his own room. The common living-dining space gave us plenty of room to discuss our discoveries and strategy.

The sharp flavor of the meat lingered in my mouth, a little heavier on the spice than I generally preferred, but I didn't see the value in complaining to the inspector detective. He'd been in a rather combative mood since we'd first seen Jemma.

I pressed down on the last bit of tobacco I'd scooped into my pipe and brought the stem to my mouth to take a few puffs while I lit it. The rich earthy smoke filled my lungs and smoothed out my thoughts into clearer lines.

"Perhaps 'weird,' but we can piece together a decent picture from the evidence we've gathered." I tapped the map. "She's gone off surveying the less-traversed areas of the country's mountain ranges. She expressed interest in moving a small community from an isolated spot of high elevation to another. Whatever that community means to her, it's something important and that she believes our involvement would interrupt. I think we can safely assume local law enforcement wouldn't be pleased if they found out either."

"What could she have an entire village doing for her?" John asked, leaning back in his chair. He hadn't completely sat still since he'd returned from his mission to observe Jemma's secretive meeting at the zoo. Normally I wouldn't have paid his restlessness much mind, but it was becoming unusually prolonged.

I studied his expression. "I'd imagine there are any number of illicit ventures she could be involved in. Obviously our next task is to locate this 'commune' before she can relocate their base of operations and determine what work they're doing for her. Did she say anything while you were with her that gave even a small hint?"

"No," my friend said. "Not that I caught on to, anyway. She's very careful about what she says." He paused, rocking the chair's front feet a little off the floor. "It did seem like something had changed since we last talked, though."

Garrett's head jerked up. "In what way?"

John twisted the handle of his walking stick in his grasp, his mouth slanting at an awkward angle. He looked at the map rather than either of us. "When I spoke to her a few days ago at the cathedral, she made a point of saying that we were 'done'—that she wasn't going to have anything more to do with us if she had her way. Today… She suggested I take her back to my room so we could, ah, pick up where we left off."

He'd kept his voice reasonably even, but the tips of his ears had flared. That explained a few things.

It shouldn't have mattered—it didn't matter—and yet a little spark of irritation flickered up inside me. That she was still coming on to him that way? That he had clearly been tempted?

No, it didn't matter *at all*. I snuffed out the spark and made myself chuckle. "She's certainly never been shy."

"But that means something has changed," Garrett said. His shoulders had tensed, but his tone was almost hopeful. He tossed his cleaned skewer onto his plate. "She wants something from us—maybe just to know how close we are on her trail. She's willing to get close to us to accomplish her ends. We could use that willingness, couldn't we?"

I shifted my full attention to him. He hadn't talked quite like that before. "What do you mean?"

He spread his hands. "Turn her tactics around on her. If we can get into *her* room, we'd have a chance at lifting one of those phones or her tablet where she's doing so much of her planning. We might see something useful, or she might give away something in the heat of the moment."

He paused and seemed to notice for the first time that both John and I were staring at him. His mouth tightened. "What? It isn't as if we haven't already crossed a hell of a lot of lines dealing with her. If you don't want to sleep with her, then don't sleep with her. I was just making a point."

"A fair point," I said mildly. "I'm only wondering whether you could be dispassionate enough to come out unscathed. She got under your skin quite a bit on our first run around."

Garrett glowered at me, but he couldn't argue that fact. "I'd know what I'm getting into this time," he insisted.

He'd have to forgive me for not being entirely convinced. "Your line of thinking is solid, all the same," I said. "Putting aside physical intimacy, her overture to John suggests she'll be more open to entertaining conversation—flirting, as it were, with possibilities."

I took another puff on my pipe and nodded to myself. Garrett and John were too romantic by nature to stay detached when Jemma had already stirred up their emotions. What she and I had exchanged had only ever really been a quid pro quo transaction.

I straightened up. "I think it's time I spoke with her directly again. Perhaps I can tease out a few answers—ones she might not even realize she's giving me." A quick check of the tracking app on my phone showed me she was currently at her hotel a quarter mile away.

"You're going now?" John said, looking as if he were about to get up and then catching himself.

"No time like the present. From the conversation you overheard, covering up her activities will be difficult, but she's pursuing the options with some urgency."

Garrett crossed his arms. "And we should just sit around here while you have your chat with her?"

"No," I said. "You can get to work searching for signs of small secluded habitations in Croatia's areas of higher elevation. Between the two of you, you should have enough knowledge and connections to come up with a few avenues of inquiry."

"Sherlock," John started, with a note in his voice that made something twinge low in my gut, like—like a moment it wouldn't do either of us any use to think about. I glanced at him, and he gave me a sheepish smile. "Be careful."

"I think I can hold my own against one woman, brilliant as she may be," I said.

It was hardly worth summoning a taxi when my destination was less than a ten-minute walk away. This section of Zagreb didn't have quite the same austere quality as the streets I'd often roamed through in London while sorting through my thoughts, but stretching my legs as I passed the modern storefronts still brought a certain calm. I tuned out the jangling of the radio playing through an open car window and focused on the task ahead of me.

In Jemma's hotel, I strode up to the front desk with an ingratiating smile. The only time they'd seen me before, I'd been in full disguise—I didn't expect anyone here would recognize me. Thankfully, we'd managed to determine what name Jemma had checked in with through a brief comment overheard.

"One of your guests asked me to have you call up when I'd arrived to meet with her. Ms. Matthams. You can tell her Sherlock Holmes will be waiting for her in the bar."

"Of course, sir," the woman behind the desk said. She looked at her computer and picked up the phone to convey my message. I was trusting that Jemma would be curious enough about my intentions to come down.

"I will. Thank you," the clerk said to whatever Jemma had responded, and hung up. "She says she'll be down shortly, sir."

I tipped my head to her in thanks and headed into the bar. At this time in the evening, the stools along the slick glass counter were mostly taken, no two free side-by-side. I found an empty table in a corner that wasn't too noisy, ordered a martini, and sat back to watch for Jemma's arrival.

Several minutes passed. I sipped my martini and tried not to dwell too much on the growing possibility that she was toying with me. I was ninety-nine percent certain she'd make her appearance. Well, perhaps ninety-five, at this point.

I was down to the vicinity of eighty percent when Jemma's slim form emerged under the bar's glaring lights. The red waves of her hair drifted over her shoulders in stark contrast with the dusty rose hue of her silk blouse. Her slacks looked neatly pressed. She'd changed since this morning's outings. Earlier, or just now, for me?

She wasn't carrying her usual large leather purse but a simple cloth clutch a slightly deeper shade of pink than her blouse. The color in her cheeks as she dropped into the seat across from me suggested she'd rushed some coming down. I certainly didn't imagine the thought of meeting me had provoked that reaction on its own.

"I hope you weren't too bothered by the wait," she said in that sweet yet assured voice of hers. "I was in the middle of something when I got your call."

I'd managed to disrupt her planning again at least somewhat, then, had I? A minor victory in itself.

"I can't complain, knowing how unexpected this visit was," I said easily. "It's good to see you're not having any trouble keeping yourself occupied here."

She made a humming sound, faintly amused. "And I'm sure you'd like to know what I'm occupying myself with. We'll skip that part of the conversation. What did you want, Sherlock?"

"I can't simply stop by to catch up with a friend?"

She cocked her head with a sly glint in her gray eyes, and the curl of her lips brought back a tingle of sensation —the memory of those lips trailing down my neck, the slender hand she was now raising to her chin tracing over my stomach.

"Is that what we are—friends?"

"We could be," I tossed out.

Her smile grew. "I don't think so. I suspect that being merely your friend would be distinctly unsatisfying— possibly for both of us. Well, if that's all you had to say…"

She pushed back her chair, and my pulse stuttered. I'd

expected more time and more interest than that. I opened my mouth, and my mind shot to Garrett's suggestion, wrapped up in the echo of feeling and the suggestive lilt to her words.

"That isn't all," I said. "I wanted to ask you something."

Jemma paused and leaned her arms on the table. The fabric of her blouse slid against the curves of her breasts. I'd never paid much attention to the bodies of the women around me before, but it suddenly struck me as a ridiculous shame that despite the intense physical intimacy we'd shared that one night in London, I hadn't the slightest idea what that part of her felt like or even looked like unclothed.

"Here I am," she said. "Ask away."

A question I hadn't known had been stewing in the back of my head until just now fell from my lips. "What happened between us in London—was that simply a means to an end, or did you actually enjoy it?"

Her eyebrows twitched. I'd managed to surprise her. I'd have had an easier time calling that a victory if the room hadn't turned inexplicably hot at the same time.

"Why does it have to be an *or*?" she asked. "It served my purposes—I won't deny that—but I also enjoyed it. Every moment of it."

Ah. Well, then. I resisted the urge to adjust my collar, as if that would help at all when a significant portion of the heat was being generated within me.

It was an uncomfortable feeling at least in part because it was still so unfamiliar. Jemma Moriarty was the only woman who'd ever provoked this reaction in me. She'd been right at the time, whatever her larger motives—the physical release had cleared my mind and swept lingering tensions away, at least as well as any high I'd ever gotten. She'd promised me that was possible, with the right partner.

I'd tried a couple times since then to recreate the same effect with women who'd appeared to find me attractive in the bars back home. Those efforts had been as unsatisfying as the few forays of my youth.

Perhaps it was simply that whatever differences formed a gulf between us, Jemma had a mind like mine, and she knew how to cater to my needs in a way no one else I'd ever known could. But that meant I should be able to do as much for her, didn't it?

I could learn about her just as she'd studied me and built off my responses. Lull her the way I'd been lulled. Or perhaps I'd discover even that spark was deadened now that the novelty had worn off, and the temptation would die with it.

In a way, this was exactly what I'd come here for.

"Would you like to enjoy it again?" I said.

Jemma ran her thumb over her full lips. I couldn't help tracking the gesture. She beamed at me. "Are you propositioning me, Mr. Holmes?"

"Are you accepting, Miss Moriarty?"

She paused for a moment, just long enough for a pang of disappointment to shoot through me, and then she extended her hand to me. "Why don't we continue this conversation in my room?"

CHAPTER EIGHT

Jemma

Sherlock stopped just behind me at the hotel room door, close enough that a wisp of tobacco scent reached my nose. He'd been smoking his pipe not long before he'd come calling.

Very, very soon I might be tasting that flavor on his skin. The prospect thrilled me enough to swing me right back to caution.

I glanced up at him, seeking out the cool blue eyes that now gleamed with restrained heat. Heat that radiated off every inch of his lanky frame. It took a lot of effort not to lick my lips.

I'd woken up that passion in him. I'd taught him that he could feel it. And he'd come back for more.

"Are you sure about this?" I asked, keeping my tone casual. "I thought you saw me as some incredible threat to the world at large."

His hand came to rest on the small of my back—tentatively, as if he were testing what he wanted, what he was capable of. His voice came out wry. "Are *you* sure about this? The last time we spoke you seemed to think you needed an armed guard to ensure your safety."

"An initial precaution," I said, "as I judged your intentions. While you seem determined to present as much of an obstacle to my work as you can, dragging me off to interrogate me through torture doesn't appear to be your style. Or am I mistaken?"

The corner of his mouth twitched upward. "I can't make any promises about what methods I'd be willing to resort to were they deemed effective, but information obtained through torture is notoriously unreliable."

"Well, that's reassuring." I tipped my head to the side coyly. "Then I don't see why we shouldn't put our differences aside temporarily to fulfill desires we happen to share. A few hours of truce, and then you can go back to making yourself a nuisance."

"And you can go back to your current schemes. At least I can rest easy knowing you aren't committing any crimes during the time we spend together."

I rolled my eyes at him. "It's a deal, then."

I didn't have any illusions that he was going to turn off the analytical side of his brain. No doubt this sudden interest had been sparked by John reporting the come on I'd made to him. Sherlock had realized the avenue might be open to him too. He might want me and the pleasure I'd summoned in him, but he also would be taking in my accommodations, listening for stray comments. Which was why I'd left my purse two floors up in my main room and only brought a few essentials in this clutch.

The lock beeped at my swipe of the keycard. The lights blinked on automatically as we stepped inside. The second hotel room I'd paid for looked lived in enough— I'd left an extra suitcase, closed, against one wall, squeezed some of the toiletries out, and placed some spare change on the top of the dresser. The scarf I'd worn over my hair the first day the trio had found me hung over one of the bed posts. But the detective would observe nothing in here that would tell him about my recent activities.

I'd booked this room the afternoon after they'd arrived, knowing there was a chance I'd have to entertain them here one way or another, wanting a place that could serve as proper neutral ground.

It was a good thing I'd made other preparations tonight as well. When I'd set off from the hotel, leaving Sherlock's tracking device behind upstairs, I'd asked the hotel clerk to call my cell phone if anyone asked for me while I was out. When she'd rung me up, I'd been a five-minute tram ride away, preparing to make another stab at getting that book from Novak.

Based on his tracker, Sherlock would assume I'd been here the whole time, and thankfully I'd still been close enough to return without too much of a delay. He'd managed to be a nuisance already.

Still, having him like this might be the best thing that could have happened. Novak could wait. The questions Sherlock was sure to ask me once he thought my guard was down might tell me all kinds of interesting things about what he'd discovered from the clues I'd doled out.

The door clicked shut. Sherlock swept his hand across his forehead, scattering the messy dark brown waves of his hair, looking abruptly uncertain as he took in the room.

"Cold feet?" I said.

His gaze jerked back to me. "No," he said firmly. His hands rose to his shirt collar. He undid the buttons with deft jerks of his fingers, gradually baring the chest I'd only felt the last time. He'd already made it most of the way down before I caught his hands with mine.

"You know, normally people fool around a little and take their clothes off as it goes rather than stripping right down from the get-go."

Sherlock peered at me. His clear tenor dropped low. "Is that what you want? Something normal?"

If my panties hadn't been melting in anticipation of this encounter already, they would have then. "No," I said. "Not particularly."

He clasped my wrists and tugged me closer, bending to kiss me at the same time. Like before, it came without warning and there wasn't much art to it, but I'd been ready anyway. His lips were a little rough where they collided with mine, the earthy flavor of his tobacco lingering on them, and just like that I was twice as hungry.

I gripped the loose front of his shirt and pressed into him. My mouth slid against his, finding the place where we could fit together perfectly.

Sherlock cupped the back of my head and kissed me harder. Mmm, yes, that was good. He eased me backward, moving us toward the bed. When we reached it, he pulled back with a tight sound as if breaking away from me even for a moment had been a strain.

"Last time you found all the most effective ways to arouse me," he said. "I want to learn what works for you. What *your* body responds to." He touched my cheek and trailed his fingers down the side of my neck. "Will you let me do that?"

How could I resist that offer from this man? "Be my guest," I said.

We eased onto the bed, him looming over me, his gaze traveling over my body still fully clothed. The smile that curved his lips reminded me of his expression when faced with an unsolved case he was sure he could crack open.

"This will be my first real experiment in this domain. I'll endeavor to do well by my subject."

"I have full faith in your investigative abilities," I said, and he kissed me again.

This time he leaned in, shifting the angle of his mouth just slightly, and just slightly again, until my lips parted. His fingers teased down my side to tug my blouse loose from my slacks. I raised my arms to make it easier for him to slide it off me.

He studied me for a second, considering the swell of my breasts filling out the small cups of my bra. My pulse sped up waiting for his next move.

As if deciding we needed to be at an approximately equal state of undress, he plucked the last couple buttons of his shirt free and tossed it aside after mine. My fingers itched to trace the compact muscles etched across his lean torso.

Before I could reach for him, he ducked his head and brought his lips to my neck. With softly peppered kisses, he tested every bit of my skin, pausing when my breath shifted as he grazed a particularly tender spot.

He stayed there and kissed harder. Pleasure tingled over my skin. A flick of his tongue drew an encouraging sound from my throat.

He kissed lower, across my collarbone and down to the edge of my bra. I ran my hands over his shoulders, but before I got any farther, he caught one of my palms and started working his way down the underside of my arm. He hadn't proved all that sensitive to my ministrations there, but the nerves in my arms responded readily. Giddy quivers of sensation ran over my skin.

Sherlock followed the same path I had on him, all the way to my inner elbow. He tested the tips of his teeth there, and my breath outright hitched. A self-satisfied smile crossed his face.

This slow careful seduction was a certain kind of torture when I didn't *need* to be seduced. A needy ache swelled between my thighs. "Come here," I growled, gripping his neck with my free hand, but Sherlock simply caught that wrist instead.

"I intend to be thorough," he said with a mischievous glint in his eyes that made me want him even more. I let out an impatient sound, but I submitted to his attentions down my other arm, settling for stroking my fingers over his taut chest.

I circled my thumb around one of his small nipples and then swept it straight over. The heat of Sherlock's breath trembled against my arm.

"You're distracting me," he murmured.

"But it's a good distraction, isn't it?" I said. "There are plenty of things *I* haven't gotten to try yet. Like this."

I pushed myself upright and gave his neck a teasing caress while I brought my mouth to the same nipple. A hum reverberated through Sherlock's chest as I applied my tongue to the pert nub. He needed more than that, though. He liked a little force.

I swiped my tongue faster, and then I nipped him between my teeth. With a choked noise, Sherlock's fingers tightened where they'd tangled in my hair.

"I wasn't finished yet," he said with a rasp, and tugged my shoulders to turn me around. He pressed a kiss to my shoulder as he unclasped my bra. Sweeping my hair to one side, he charted a path to my neck and then up to my hairline. The pleasure of his touch mingled with a twinge of awareness from Bog's mark.

Before he could reach the signifier of my deal with the shrouded one, I shook my head, letting my hair fall back into place. Sherlock took the rebuff in stride. He slid his hands around to my breasts and cupped them. His long hands covered them completely.

I relaxed into his narrow but solid chest as he explored them, first with broad strokes that sent muted waves of pleasure through my torso, then focusing in on the peaks. He tucked his head over my shoulder to watch my nipples stiffen to meet the careful flicks of his fingers.

He pinched one between his thumb and forefinger, and I let out another growl at the jolt of pleasure. With a soft chuckle, he repeated the gesture on the other side.

I could pay that pleasure back. I tipped to the side and leaned back my head to kiss the spot on his neck where I'd gotten the most reaction before. Then I shifted one hand backward into his lap. His cock jumped at my touch, already hard enough to make my mouth water.

Sherlock stifled a groan. He caught the side of my face and swiveled us enough to recapture my mouth with his. As I stroked him through his pants, his breath broke with a stutter. He kissed me harder, welcoming my tongue, squeezing my breast in an echo of my hand on his cock.

The hunger in me expanded through my whole body. I'd never met anything sexier in the entire world than this analytically detached man turned wild by my touch.

He had some self-control left. "Still. Not. Finished," he muttered against my lips, and managed to tear away from me. He nudged me down on my back, gazing down at me with eyes as bright as blue flames. "Keep your hands to yourself."

"I'll give you five more minutes," I said. "After that, no promises."

He made a faint sound of protest, but his hands leapt to the fly of my slacks at the same time. As he tugged my pants down, he leaned over to suck my nipple into his mouth as I had his.

At the forceful slick of his tongue, a gasp tumbled out of me. My hands moved instinctively, but I drew them back, giving in to the blissful torture. I dug my fingers into the covers instead.

I had to hold on tight. Shivers of pleasure raced to my core as Sherlock experimented with the movement of his tongue and the pressure of his lips and teeth. He might not have been practiced in the ecstatic arts, but he was a quick study in this as with all things. Every eager twitch of my body had him amplifying the gesture that had provoked it.

My hips arched toward him, and he appeared to take the hint that my patience wasn't going to last much longer. He yanked my slacks the rest of the way down and paused for just a moment as his gaze found the gold cuff that circled the middle of my thigh. The gold cuff made in part of the etching I'd stolen out from under his nose.

"Truce," I reminded him. Dear God, he'd better not change his mind now. "We set all those matters aside."

His gaze held as much inquisitiveness as it did lust, but he inclined his head in a slight nod. I didn't doubt there'd be questions about that discovery later, but right now I didn't much care.

He hooked his fingers around the hem of my panties, and I squirmed to help him slide them off. Then he was bending down again to kiss the plane of my stomach, the dip of my belly button, the slope of my hipbones.

His thumb traced over the mound between my thighs. He watched its passage with more intentness than any lover I'd ever taken before. I had to clench my muscles to keep from bucking up to bring his touch to the place I most wanted it.

When he grazed my clit, a blissful tremor raced through me. He looked up to meet my eyes.

"Here?"

"That would be the spot." I couldn't help amusement from creeping into my voice even as longing twanged through my body. "There are men with multitudes of experience who have trouble identifying it that readily."

Sherlock gave me a smile that was a shade shy of a smirk. "I found the opportunity to do some reading after our last encounter."

A laugh spilled out of me. "Of course you did." My voice broke with a moan as he pressed down on that spot with careful precision. My hips jerked up despite my best intentions.

I eased my legs farther apart so Sherlock could kneel between them. My hands balled around the covers. It'd been well over five minutes now, but I was enjoying his "experiment" too much to risk interrupting him.

He worked over my clit slower and faster, softer and harder, taking in every gasp and sigh. Then he lowered his mouth to me. The first swipe of his tongue had me quaking with need.

The kind of whimper I rarely let myself make slipped out of me as he licked and sucked. Pleasure knotted all through my core up into my belly. So close. So fucking close.

"Your fingers," I said raggedly. "Inside me."

Sherlock obliged in an instant. He traced two fingers down over my slit, drenched with my arousal, and eased them inside. Just a few inches of that pressure inside was all I needed to tip me over the edge with the next flick of his tongue.

I arched up with a gasp and a shiver of bliss that wracked my whole body. Sherlock's breath caught audibly. He kissed me again, covering my entire core with his mouth as I rode out the wave. I cried out at the fresh burst of pleasure.

I sagged back into the covers with a near-delirious grin. Sherlock looked at me, his mouth deliciously flushed and his expression tight with desire. His erection strained against his slacks. He hesitated for a second with that rare uncertainty that somehow turned me on twice as much as before.

"Can you—can that happen for you again?" he ventured. "Right away?"

I laughed and shoved myself upright to pull him into a kiss. "Fuck, yes."

My tart flavor mixed with the smokiness that had laced Sherlock's mouth. Between the two of us, we peeled his pants and boxers off in about five seconds flat. I grasped his cock, reveling in the smooth solid length of it, and his mouth crashed into mine again.

I ached to have him in me, now. "Purse," I mumbled in an instant between kisses, groping across the bed. He caught the clutch and passed it to me, and I dug out the condom I always kept in the inner pocket, just in case. I certainly hadn't expected I'd be needing it tonight.

"Right," Sherlock said, taking it from me. "Naturally."

I touched his jaw as he ripped it open, seeking out his gaze. "I normally do," I said. In that moment, it seemed important that he understand this one fact. We might be enemies in essence, but I wouldn't have wanted to strike out at him that way, a careless passing on of some venereal disease. That wasn't how I worked. "Last time—last time was the only time I haven't. Special circumstances."

Some unfamiliar emotion flickered across his face and was gone. He opened his mouth, but words didn't come. Instead he kissed me again. As his mouth melded with mine, he lowered his body to mine. I opened my thighs to welcome him. He thrust into me, finally blissfully pressing his cock into me to the brim.

I was so primed he could have fucked me just about any which way and I'd have come again. But Sherlock was committed to his experiment to the end. As he plunged in and out of me, his hand slid over my ass. He lifted me, fitting me against him until he found the angle that made me not just gasp but sob with the shock of pleasure that hit me.

When I clutched his shoulders and bit his lip, he groaned into my mouth. He drove into me again and again with sharply powerful strokes. The force of his cock sent my head spinning with bliss.

I scraped my fingernails over his back, he tweaked my nipple tightly, and ecstasy flooded me. We toppled together over the edge in a surge of shudders, sweat-slick skin, and broken breath.

After a minute, Sherlock withdrew and eased down onto his side next to me. I glanced over at him, my limbs boneless with release, not possessing the will to send him off quite yet. I really ought to give him a chance to make his informative inquiries, after all. There wasn't anything wrong with basking in the heat of his body in the meantime.

He grazed a fingertip over my ribs just below by breasts where a faint scar marked my skin. "This was a knife," he said. "A few years ago? It looks as though it should fade away completely before much longer."

The thin pale nick was the only remnant of the second to last man I'd killed with my bare hands, four and a half years ago to be exact. The last person other than Bash I'd ever had business dealings with directly, face-to-face. The head of a criminal syndicate had paid him off to take me down. He hadn't stood a chance.

"You've probably faced off against more knives than I have," I said blandly.

Sherlock's hand traveled from my side to my arm between us. His thumb swept over the point of my elbow. "A childhood scrape, deep. You grew up somewhere with a lot of rocky terrain?"

That observation sent a quiver that was uneasy rather than pleasurable through my nerves. "It wasn't a place with no rocks. I'm sure that narrows it down ever so much."

Sherlock smiled faintly. His fingers skimmed up over my shoulder to my neck. He knit his brow. "Did you know you have an imprint just at the top of your spine here? It doesn't have quite the qualities of a birthmark— somewhat closer to a tattoo, but—"

My jaw clenched for a second before I caught my reaction. I'd expected him to be watching for clues, yes— but with the intent to figure out my current plans, not to dredge up my distant past. A sharper sense of nakedness prickled over my body.

There wasn't anything he could really learn from me without my consent. Not when he wouldn't have believed in the things I'd grown up with, the things I'd made deals with and run from.

I rolled onto my side to fully face him and grasped his wrist. As I pushed his hand away from me, I gave him a pointed look. "Was *tonight* just a means to an end, or did you actually enjoy it?"

The corner of his mouth quirked up. "If it could be both for you, can't it be both for me as well?"

Somehow that response made me want to strangle him and also kiss him until he was hard enough to slide inside me again. Either would have shut him up.

"Fine," I said. "But then you've overstayed your welcome."

"And if I don't happen to feel like leaving yet?"

I let out a huff and sat up to shove him off the bed. Sherlock slipped out of my grasp and swung on top of me. Before he could get a good enough grip on my arms to pin me down, I gave him a light knee to the side that pushed him aside enough for me to scoot free. That worked for all of three seconds before he caught me around the waist. He rolled me over him and then rolled back on top of me.

Sherlock grinned down at me, holding my hands above my head and locking my legs under his, clearly having an excellent time. Also clearly not expending *that* much energy. I had to extend a little respect to his physical prowess and to admit it had aroused me all over again, and both of those facts left me disgruntled.

"I could get you off me," I informed him. "I just don't want to hurt you."

He cocked his head with apparently genuine curiosity. "Why not?"

I grimaced at him. The answer that tripped off my tongue was maybe more genuine than I'd have given if he hadn't appeared to truly want to understand. And if he hadn't just given me the most satisfying sexual experience of my life so far.

"Because in spite of you being a meddling, arrogant know-it-all, I like you."

Sherlock blinked at me. *That* comment was apparently enough to shut him up. My throat tightened. After a moment, I added dryly, "That would generally be your cue to tell me you like me too."

He chuckled, his grip loosening as he shifted his weight. "I'm not sure that 'like' is quite the word."

I'd thought we were bantering. I'd never had any intention of caring what this man or any other thought of me. All the same, the answer felt like a slap across the face.

An uncomfortable sort of heat flashed through my chest. I squirmed out from under Sherlock and grabbed my blouse. "Go whenever you like, then."

I pulled the blouse over my head on my way to the bathroom, not entirely sure what I was going to do in there, but there were plenty of possibilities for occupying myself away from the jackass on the bed. Wash my face.

Brush my hair. Run a bath and drown myself in it for my idiocy.

The mattress squeaked as Sherlock righted himself. "Jemma," he said. "Wait."

I stopped, crossed my arms, and turned partway back, looking at him sideways. "What do you want?"

He sat in the middle of the bed without any self-consciousness about his nudity in his posture, though that earlier awkwardness had come back into his expression. His gaze stayed fixed on me, as intent as ever. I didn't know what he was trying to read now.

He inhaled slowly. "Saying that was difficult for you, wasn't it? I didn't realize. I'm sorry."

The great Sherlock Holmes was apologizing for hurting my feelings. Was that a win or a loss? I wasn't totally sure. I didn't answer, just watched him as he was watching me.

His mouth twisted. He set his hand on the covers beside him. "Will you come back here?"

"Why?" I asked.

His lips parted, and he paused. Then he said, a little haltingly, "So I can tell you what I meant."

Well, God damn it, if Sherlock was going to admit he had feelings, I supposed I could acknowledge them. I allowed myself to return to the bed and sat on the corner. "Tell me, then."

He looked far more pleased that I'd come than he had any right to, and the look gave me far more pleasure than *it* had any right to. I clasped my hands in my lap.

"I don't think," he said, "that anyone examining my

thoughts and behavior since I met you would consider 'liking' a potent enough term to encapsulate those. If I'm being purely objective, I'd have to admit that something along the lines of 'fascination' or perhaps even 'obsession' would be more accurate."

The sharp edges that had risen up inside me softened with a flicker of surprise. "Oh," was all I managed to say.

He ran a hand through his now thoroughly mussed hair. "This isn't my forte," he said. "I can analyze people and their motives and all the rest, but when it comes to the interplay between myself and them, absorbing and responding—I've never really known what to do there. So I generally go forth with whatever I was going to do anyway and let whoever's around me make of it what they will."

I shrugged. "Why shouldn't you?"

"Well, exactly. It's served me perfectly well so far. I've accepted it as who I am."

Had it really served him well, though? For a second, looking at him, I imagined I could see through the man to the boy he must have once been—still an arrogant know-it-all, lurking on the fringes of the posh school his well-to-do parents had sent him off to, which I knew from seeing the records. Had he never felt the slightest pang of childhood loneliness?

I had, and I'd grown up in a community where friendship was never more than a means to an end for anyone anyway. I'd had my sister.

"Never underestimate people's capacity to change," I said with half a smile. "Although in my experience, they generally change for the worse. I'm not complaining about who you are."

"You're not," he agreed. He sighed and folded his hands over his raised knee. "I've never met anyone like you, Jemma. Anyone who reminds me so much… of me. I don't know how you spend your time, why you dream up schemes to steal things like that." He motioned to the cuff around my thigh. "But you're clearly not a common criminal."

"You wouldn't be here if you thought I was."

"No. But you are— We are at odds." He met my eyes again. "Is there no middle ground where we could meet beyond this temporary truce? Do your goals *have* to clash with mine? Perhaps if we talked it through…"

I shook my head. "Do *your* goals have to clash with mine?" I asked lightly. "Why not come all the way over to the dark side, Sherlock? You wouldn't, would you, because of the principles that matter to you? I have guiding principles too." Survival. Security. Vengeance. "I can't throw mine away any more than you can yours."

"Then we're at an impasse."

"And when the truce is over, may the best of us win." A strange prickly affection stirred inside me, more thorns than blooming rose. I eased across the bed to join him. His gaze had become wary, but when I raised my hand to stroke my knuckles against the side of his neck, he leaned toward my touch. "Your consolation prize is getting to go up against a worthy opponent."

"There is that." He took my hand in his. "How much longer is this truce designed to last?"

I had to smile. "I'm sure we could stretch it out a *little* longer." I rose up on my knees and kissed him, this man both fascinating and fascinated. Already he knew how to shift instinctively to align our mouths just a little more pleasurably.

But there were other games we could play even while we were pretending to ignore them. I brushed my lips over his cheek and tipped my head toward his ear. "I'm sure you have many more questions clamoring for attention. Ask, and let's see if there are any I'm willing to answer."

Jemma

On my third attempt at retrieving the book I needed from Novak, I finally made it all the way to his street in the falling dusk. And there was Garrett Lestrade, so hidden in the thick shadow of the wall around the house opposite that I only noticed him because I scanned the area with particular care. He stood watching the blocky modern mansion that belonged to my mark, notepad and pen in hand.

I could say one thing in favor of the geometric monstrosities that Zagreb's nouveau rich gravitated to: Their built-up front yards and parking pads offered plenty of shelter. I crept behind a concrete pillar and peered up the street toward the detective inspector.

The streetlamps gave off only a thin glow against the deepening twilight, but there was no way I could walk up to the Novaks' front door and spin out my planned story without Garrett spotting me. Only an occasional car had rumbled by as I'd walked the last couple blocks here. The warm breeze carried the scent of lilies from someone's private garden. It was all very peaceful.

Too peaceful. I needed a distraction.

If I'd managed to get here the first time I'd set out, I might have avoided this problem. The trio wouldn't have connected the crime ring they'd taken down to Novak instantly. He kept himself detached enough from the thieving syndicate that the Londoners probably weren't sure even now; they just wanted to take the lay of the land. I could head back to the hotel empty-handed *again* and give them a few days to give up on him…

No. I was here now. The longer I waited, the more chance there was that Novak would stash some of his collection elsewhere. I'd play with the hand I'd been dealt.

It'd have been easier if I'd had Bash to act as wingman, but he was staked out at the trio's hotel keeping an eye on their comings and goings, ready to jump in if the right opportunity presented itself. I'd simply have to be careful.

Leaning against the post, I took out one of my more disposable phones and tapped in a number I'd memorized weeks ago. Might as well see what kind of mood Garrett was in tonight.

I was far enough away that I only heard the faintest quaver of Garrett's ringtone. He took out his phone, frowned at the caller display that would have told him nothing, and rocked back on his feet as he answered. A stream of lamplight cut across his face, highlighting one eye, a cheek, the corner of his mouth.

"Hello?"

"Hello, Garrett. Is this a good time to talk?"

He stiffened instantly at the sound of my voice. "Jemma. Why are you calling me?"

I didn't want him to think it had anything to do with his current assignment, but it shouldn't be hard to imply that I was simply digging for general information about their investigations. I wet my lips as if I were a little uneasy. "I just wondered what you're up to."

"Wonder away. That doesn't mean I'm going to tell you anything. Fool me once and all that?"

"I didn't give you such a bad time in London, did I? Can't we have a friendly chat for old time's sake?"

He let out a laugh, but he hesitated before he answered. When he spoke again, some of the tension had smoothed from his imposing voice. "All right. Chat away. What are *you* up to?"

"I just got back from dinner," I said. "I had a very good steak at the place next to Franjo's. You should try it sometime. You seem like a steak man."

"Do I? Are you a steak woman?"

"When I'm in the right mood. I wouldn't mind some dessert though. I'm *always* a dessert woman. How'd you like to join me—or are you too busy with whatever you're doing that you don't want to tell me about?"

"Maybe I've just settled into my room and can't be bothered to leave. You've got actual friends here you can call up to invite, don't you?"

He was doing an admirable job of keeping the tone light while insistently turning the conversation back to questioning me. No doubt he'd realized he should use this opportunity to dig for whatever dirt he could. If I hadn't been able to see him, I might have thought he was cool as a cucumber. But right now the metal fixtures on his pen were flashing in and out of the streetlamp light as he spun it with agitated jerks of his fingers.

Just talking to me was hard for him. Apparently my conversation with Sherlock last night had left prickly thorns of affection sprouting in all sorts of unexpected places, because a twinge of regret ran through my chest.

I could have handled Garrett differently. I'd taken the strategy that was easiest for me without worrying about how it would affect him.

And why should I have worried? I had monsters to vanquish and promises to keep, and all that required a whole lot of money and the right sort of connections. I did what I had to do.

It was possible I could do a little more, though, without hindering my work—just for the sake of reducing the inspector detective's vengeful urges. And making this offering might put him off-balance enough to help along the next part of my gambit.

I drew back from the column and ducked down a side street to circle around behind the Novaks' house. "Oh, I have plenty of friends," I said. "But here you are in town, and I feel like we haven't really talked."

"I'm still not sure what you think we'd talk about."

"Maybe what happened in London? I'm sure there are all sorts of things you're dying to say about that. We should hash things out properly sometime, in person. You can tell me how horrible I am to my face in as many ways as you like, and we'll have cleared the air."

He laughed again, more hesitantly. "Sounds wonderful. Not tonight. But... maybe some other time."

"I'll leave you to it, then," I said. "Your Firecracker wishes you good night."

I hung up and picked up my pace. He'd always said the nickname he'd given me with a mix of awe and apprehension, as if he appreciated my gutsiness but was wary of how far I'd take it. Let him think about that, about the intrepid police prodigy he'd thought I was, while I did... this.

I scooped up a polished quartz stone from the base of someone's yard. Just around the corner from Novak's house, I spotted a Mercedes that was guaranteed to have an alarm system. I flung the stone onto the hood.

The alarm blared. I slipped behind a neighbor's shed as Garrett intrepidly loped around the corner. The moment his attention focused in on the source of the noise, I crossed the yard and made for the Novaks' house, slapping a patch on my button-up shirt as I went and pulling a clipboard from my purse.

I rang the doorbell and pasted a smile on my face, trying not to think about the number of seconds it might take for Garrett to decide the possible intruder a few homes away had nothing to do with his mission.

Mr. Novak was out, as he was most evenings—this was literature and academics night at his favorite auction house just outside of town. He went as much to scope out potential scores to send his minions after as to bid on items, I'd bet. It was his wife, nearly twenty years his junior, who answered the door.

"Hello?" she said in Croatian, her brow furrowing.

"Hello, Mrs… Novak?" I said with the most precise accent I could summon, and handed her the card I'd made up a few days ago for this purpose. "So sorry to disturb your evening. I'm with Grand Pest Control, on behalf of the city. It appears there's been an infestation in this part of your neighborhood, and we've been asked to check the surrounding buildings to ensure it doesn't spread farther."

The woman's delicate wan face tensed. "Infestation?"

I nodded briskly. "It shouldn't take more than ten, fifteen minutes to give the house a quick examination. I'll be out of your way in no time, I promise."

"I guess you'd better come in then."

She stepped back, and just like that, I was walking into the house invited.

I paused in the hall with its ornate rug and knocked on the wall beside me. Mrs. Novak went even more rigid. I glanced at her apologetically.

"If the pests have spread this far, sometimes they come right out of the woodwork while I'm searching. They don't like tile, though. If you want to make sure they don't come near you, you'll be safest in the kitchen or perhaps a bathroom."

She nodded with a quick jerk and vanished into a room farther down the hall.

I made a show of working my way through the first floor, murmuring to myself and knocking here and there loud enough that the wife would hear my progress. Despite the modern trappings on the outside of the house, which I supposed was meant to impress the neighbors more than follow Novak's sensibilities, he'd designed the interior with fine hardwood and old-fashioned moldings like a place from earlier times.

I knocked on up to the second floor, where my real goal lay. A solid oak door there led to Mr. Novak's study. I pulled out a couple of lock picks and made short work of the deadbolt, with a couple knocks for good measure along the way.

The smell of aged leather permeated the dark room. I switched on the lamp near the door. Its light glowed across built-in shelves on every wall and a couple of armchairs facing a round wooden table in the center. Every piece of furniture was stacked with old books, even one of the chairs. Here and there between the rare volumes lay other curiosities of the supposedly supernatural variety: an oddly shaped animal skull, a jar of viscous liquid, and a bundle of partly charred twigs tied with a silk ribbon.

Novak was one of the many who helped keep the cult of the shrouded ones in business. He didn't have a clue who they were or what they stood for; he just purchased their objects of pseudo-power through the back channels where they peddled them with enough gravitas to convince an amateur dabbler in the dark arts. I doubted a single item they distributed had a scrap of actual significance.

The books Novak had amassed were another story. The cult wouldn't have liked any outsider having even the small amount of information contained in the text I was looking for.

Several boxes stood in a stack at the back of the room. He hadn't unpacked yet. I hurried over and started sorting through their contents.

My fingers leapt over the spines. It wasn't in this box. No, nothing in this one either. My heart was pounding by the time I set my hand on the title I was looking for in the fifth box I'd checked. I yanked it out.

Pages fifty-six to fifty-eight. I'd committed the numbers to memory. It was possible the treatise on Croatian folklore held a few other useful tidbits mixed in with the rest, but my life would be easier if Novak never realized he'd been robbed.

I tore the two pages from their binding with a wince, stuffed the book back into its spot, and folded the papers so I could tuck them into my purse.

I was just setting the boxes back into their stack when the creak of the stairs reached my ears. Shit.

I dashed out of the study, snapping off the light and jerking the door shut behind me. When Mrs. Novak reached the upstairs hall, I was knocking on the wall a couple doors down.

"Are you almost done?" she asked, with a nervous glance that darted along the baseboards. "Do we have any?"

"It's looking clear," I said with a smile. "I've just finished up."

She led the way back down the stairs.

"You call the number on that card if you notice any worrisome signs in the next few weeks," I told her, and looked around. "Do you have a back fence? I should take a look at that too before I move on."

"Yes, of course," Mrs. Novak said, all hasty relief. I knocked on a few spots on the fence, declared it pest-free too, and gave the woman my thanks as I headed out the back gate, far from Garrett's watching eyes.

My awareness of my prize tingled through me, but I forced myself to wait until I was tucked in the back of a cab before I drew out the pages. My gaze skimmed over the yellowed paper until I found the lines I was looking for.

One of the most obscure legends of this sort I've encountered is that of the shrouded dagger. The few references I've come across claim this magical weapon was a gift from the fae realm into this one, to solidify the association between those beings and their human allies. It is said to imbue the powers of a fae on any person who brandishes it under the right circumstances.

Fae. Ha. If he'd ever met an actual shrouded one, he wouldn't have placed them in the same category as Tinkerbell.

This all fell in line with what I'd already heard. If the dagger could give me the power of a shrouded one, then I could hope it would allow me to sever the pact I'd made with Bog, just as consenting to that deal with him had freed me from my more general bond to the cult and his kind. But what were the "right" damned circumstances?

The author rambled on for a few paragraphs about how much was unknown about this specific "faerie" people and the humans who associated with them, including why the dagger was referred to as "shrouded," before he finally got to the point. My fingers tightened around the paper, my pulse lurching with a bump of the cab's tires over a pothole.

The best understanding I've arrived at is that adherents believed this faerie people derived their power in our world from sunlight. Thus, a human wielder of the shrouded dagger could only take on full fae potential when the powers of the real fae were muted. A couple of references suggest that night or a place in shadow might be enough to evoke the dagger's supposed magic, but this seems overly simplistic considering how easily one could test the possibility.

One account, though brief, strikes me as having the most validity. It claims that tapping into the power can only happen in the moment the sun is abruptly yet fully interrupted by a solar eclipse. This idea has the ring of proper legend to it.

A giddy rush washed over me. Yes. That *felt* right, down to the core of my being where I'd been shaped by the shrouded folk across the first fourteen years of my life. I dug out my phone and tapped out a search for the next full solar eclipse.

It was just a few weeks away, the full effect visible from certain parts of South America. And there wouldn't be another until next year.

The giddiness faded, replaced by a more uneasy sense of anticipation. If I was ready in time, I could sever the contract between Bog and me in less than a month. If I didn't find all the pieces quickly enough… either the cuff around my leg or the shrouded one I'd bound myself to would destroy me before I got another chance to save myself.

CHAPTER TEN

Bash

I was sitting with a book on the bench outside the hotel when two of my targets emerged from the elevator. Adjusting my position just slightly, I pushed a button on the little receiver in my pocket.

John Watson and Garrett Lestrade made an even odder match without Sherlock between them to balance things out. As they headed to the front desk, the doctor's sweep of blond hair hovered nearly half a foot higher than the detective's close-cropped brown, the former's frame as broad as the latter's was wiry. If Watson had stood directly in front of Lestrade, you wouldn't have caught a glimpse of the smaller guy. But even though he was bigger, there was a softness to the way Watson carried himself that matched what Jemma had told me about his personality.

Neither of them looked like a very formidable foe, even taking into account walking stick combat skills.

My earphones crackled as the clerk at the front desk shuffled a few papers. Watson and Lestrade came to a stop there, and the bug I'd planted transmitted the clerk's thin voice into my ear, just a little louder than the growl of the passing traffic.

"How can I help you this morning?"

Watson was looking at something on his phone. Lestrade spoke first, a little too loud, a little too forceful for the situation—the tone of a guy with too much to prove. "We need a couple of taxis."

That was my cue. I left the receiver on as I got up from the bench and crossed the street to the spot where I'd stashed my mocked-up cab.

"Maybe just one," Watson said in his lighter voice. "It looks like the station is on the way to the hospital. We might as well share."

"Well, you'll be the one who ends up paying then."

"I'll have one around for you in just a few minutes," the clerk said.

I had quite a good stash of disguise options in the trunk, many brought with me, a few obtained here in Zagreb. For this… I tugged a stark white prayer cap over my head and fixed a thick beard that was as much gray as black to my jaw. The coarse hair itched at my skin, but the chances Watson would connect me to the bowl-haired man he'd seen briefly talking to Jemma were essentially nil.

The engine sputtered as I reversed out of the tight, secluded nook. It wasn't the finest car I'd ever driven. Jemma would have given me more cash if I'd asked, but a posh new model would have stood out more than I wanted.

I pulled my fake taxi up in front of the hotel less than two minutes after my targets had requested it and got out to beckon them over. "Mr. Watson and Mr. Lestrade?" I asked, putting on a thick Bosnian accent.

I opened the back, and they got in without more than a glance at me. It was almost too easy. I smiled to myself as I got back into the driver's seat.

"We've got two stops," Lestrade said. "The central police station first."

"Not a problem," I said, and gunned the engine before the taxi that had actually been called could arrive.

"It's really not that far," Watson said to his companion.

Through the rearview mirror, I watched Lestrade lean over, presumably to check the other man's phone. He let out a huff of breath. "I could have walked that."

"Maybe it was better to take a taxi anyway. It'll be harder for her to have anyone follow us in a vehicle than on foot."

"True."

I held back a full smirk. They thought they were pretty smart, didn't they? You'd think they'd have realized by now that Jemma would always be at least two steps ahead of them.

She'd started to find the three of them intriguing while she'd conned them in London. Now that she didn't have to play along with their restrictive ideas about morality, it must be so obvious to her that she could outpace them in an instant. Nothing to admire there. She and I controlled the playing field, and they were just dupes fumbling their way across it. Foolish knights that she brought in one night, Shakespeare might have said. He'd have had a field day with this bunch.

"She's certainly holding her cards close," Watson went on. "Sherlock didn't get much out of her the other night."

Lestrade made a snorting sound. "It depends on what he was looking to get. You know he slept with her, don't you?"

My fingers tightened around the steering wheel.

Watson raised his eyebrows at the other man. "What makes you say that?"

"I saw him right after, when he got back to the hotel. He had this energy to him—it wasn't how a man looks when he's just been foiled in a simple conversation, I can tell you that much."

"I suppose it doesn't really matter."

Lestrade slumped down his seat. "No. I just can't help noticing it was *you* she came on to and *me* who suggested using that angle while he dismissed the possibility, and somehow *he's* the one who ended up in her bed."

He was trying to keep his voice nonchalant, but a ripple of jealousy ran through it. I'd have been more amused if a similar prickling hadn't shot up inside me.

It wasn't any of my business how Jemma conducted her personal affairs. She'd gotten plenty of mileage out of her seductive charms in the past. It was all part of the game.

Did it bother me that she'd gone after them at all or that she hadn't mentioned either incident to me—

making a move on Watson, hooking up with Holmes? It wasn't as if she normally gave me a detailed account of her every maneuver… but I suspected she'd made a conscious decision to keep this to herself. I could even understand why. Things hadn't been quite as steady between the two of us since the night *we'd* shared together in London.

It was harder to tamp down desires after they'd had a little room to breathe and grow.

Jemma had made the boundaries of our partnership clear. Any trouble I had with maintaining that distance was on me.

I forced my hands to relax on the wheel. Lestrade was flipping through a notepad.

"You know, we haven't seen any more of those strange light effects around her this time around. What do you make of that?"

Watson cocked his head. "We did conclude they had to be coming from someone other than her. That someone probably stayed in London. Maybe it really was some conference-goer who was envious of the time she was spending with us—nothing to do with her personally at all."

"Maybe," Lestrade said with a frown. I'd have liked to see the look on their faces if they'd had to deal with the actual monsters Jemma was taking on. Maybe the things would eat the two of them, and Holmes too, and save us any more hassle.

The police station came into view up ahead. "Here we are," I said.

"Good luck with the lab coats," Lestrade said to Watson flippantly. The detective inspector climbed out.

Watson leaned forward. "I need to get to the university hospital now."

"Of course."

I pulled back into traffic, needing a few seconds to work out the best route based on my memory of the city maps. The police station had made sense. What information did the Londoners think they were going to get out of the city's main hospital that would help them figure out Jemma's plans?

I'd just have to find out. That was what she needed from me. These three would outlive their usefulness soon enough, and then we could move on completely.

"Are you sick?" I asked. "I have lived here a long time. If there's something specific you need, I might be able to suggest a place not so busy as the hospital."

"That's all right, but thank you," Watson said. "I'm not going for treatment, just to look at some records. I understand the hospital is associated with the Ministry of Health."

"Ah, I see, indeed," I said with an agreeable bob of my head. "Well, if there is anything else you're looking to know—even about areas farther abroad. Before I settled down here, I lived many places around the country."

Watson stayed quiet for long enough that I thought I hadn't hooked him. But he was obviously a little desperate for information. I could only imagine what they'd made of the odd story Jemma had slyly laid out for them.

"Have you always lived in cities?" he asked. "Did you

ever spend much time in the countryside—near the mountains, maybe?"

"Oh, yes. In my younger days I liked to adventure. I've been many places, talked to many people."

He worried at his lower lip for a moment. "Did you ever hear any strange stories—about things happening on or near any of the mountains?"

"Hmm." I sucked in a breath slowly as if thinking it over. I couldn't point him in the right direction since I didn't know what that was. Jemma and I were counting on his bunch figuring that out. I could at least give him an encouraging nudge that there was something to find.

"There was one place, years ago, people in town talked about things disappearing now and then," I said. "They didn't know why. The custom was to say the fae folk from the mountain took it. Silly tales. Not what you're looking for."

"There might be something to it," Watson said, eagerly enough that I had to suppress another smile. "Which town was that?"

"I can't remember for sure. I moved around so much back then. It was very close to the foot of the mountain— that much I can picture."

Watson fell into silent contemplation for the rest of the drive. I stopped at the main hospital building where panes of glass melded with slabs of graying concrete, and he handed me a handful of cash that had a significant tip on top of the amount showing on the price meter I'd rigged. The man wasn't a cheapskate, anyway. One small point in his favor.

As he disappeared through the glass doors, I drove off —around the complex to the first out-of-the-way driveway I could find. I had another disguise that would work in the trunk. Yes, here, one of the lab coats Garrett had poked fun at.

I yanked that on, tugged off the beard, swapped my prayer cap for a tawny brown wig, and magically I was a white guy with a tan instead of a vaguely Middle Eastern-ish immigrant. Many thanks to my ancestors and their diverse tastes in lovers.

I'd shaved close this morning to remove my usual shadow of stubble, but Watson had seen me several times in the last couple months. For extra security, I popped in contacts that were a much brighter green than my natural color and slid on a pair of thick-paned glasses after them.

The main reception area was crowded, voices bouncing off the high ceiling and blurring together. Watson was only just leaving the room, following a young nurse who must have been summoned to assist him. I swiped an ID card from a brown-haired intern I brushed past and clipped it to my pocket. All anyone needed to see was the hospital logo and a picture that looked like a match at a distance.

I ambled behind Watson and his helper at a careful distance, fixing my face in an expression of intense concentration to discourage anyone from bothering me. Let them think I was in the middle of working out the world's first true cure for cancer. Finally, the nurse ushered the visiting doctor into a room. I loped over and caught the door just before it clicked.

The space on the other side held several desks and a row of computer stations along the far wall. The nurse led Watson to one of the computers. As he sat down, I eased inside.

Getting into place unseen was easy. I could sneak up on an enemy target to put a bullet in his head without him knowing I was there until his skull cracked open. I moved to one of the desks without so much as a whisper of sound and positioned myself as if I'd been standing there working all along. Neither Watson nor the nurse looked up.

"These are the main databases here," the nurse was saying. "We have English versions for sharing information internationally. Let me see…" She clicked on a few things and nodded. "That should get you started. Is there anything else I can help with?"

"No, I think I mostly need to browse through the data for a while," Watson said. "Thank you so much for your assistance."

What story had he offered up to convince the hospital staff to give him access to government data? Had word of Sherlock Holmes' exploits with his sidekick spread all the way out here? Maybe he'd played up his medical career and military service. Or maybe he'd spun as much of a story for them as I had for him in the cab.

He and his consulting detective thought they were such paragons of justice, but they broke the rules left and right when they felt like it.

As Watson got to work, I eased open a folder that had been left on the desk. If he did happen to glance over and notice me, I needed to look as though I had actually been working myself. Once I had the chart spread out in front of me though, I mostly watched the other man. What data was he sifting through that he thought would lead him to Jemma's mountain commune?

Half of the left pane of my glasses contained a magnifying lens. When I angled my head, I could make out some of the larger text on John's computer screen. He tapped in one search inquiry and another, scrolling through reams of records, not looking particularly satisfied with any of it. A pattern gradually emerged.

He was looking for evidence of covert medical activity. Stolen supplies, undocumented patients coming in for treatment. It wasn't a bad line of thought. A small secret community would have to find ways to stealthily look after its members' health.

I couldn't follow everything. Watson seemed to go back and forth between different threads without any obvious connection. I'd been standing, watching over him, for nearly two hours—not nearly long enough for my well-trained body to raise any protest—when a smile crossed his lips. I peered closer.

He'd brought up a bunch of figures from coastal communities. Why was he focused on them rather than the mountains on the interior? Had he seen something that had pointed to the coast as the more likely region?

Two hours. Jemma and I had been in the country for nearly a month without narrowing down our search that much. It had simply never occurred to me to check medical records for clues.

A jab of annoyance ran through my gut at Watson's smug smile. In that second, my hand twitched toward my hidden holster. It would be so very easy to shatter *this* man's skull. I could have my pistol out and my finger squeezing the trigger in the space of a heartbeat. He'd never even know he was in the slightest danger.

The impulse only lasted a second, though, followed by a jolt of shame. Who the hell would that help? Not me, not Jemma. I shifted my weight—and in my distraction I didn't hold myself perfectly quiet.

The floor creaked faintly. Watson startled and jerked around. I raised my head as if I were only just looking up at him.

"Are you all right?" I asked him in a bland voice.

He rubbed his face. "My God, I didn't even realize anyone else was in here."

I gave him a small smile. "You looked very absorbed with your work. I didn't want to interrupt you."

"Yes, of course, that's fine." He shook his head at himself with a sheepish expression.

"Have you found everything you were looking for?" I asked.

"I think so. I actually… I'd like to print some of this information off, but I'm not sure how to handle that with this database. Do you have a moment?"

"I can spare one." I came over, adrenaline pulsing through my veins. "Let me see."

With a quick examination, I found the most likely option. Watson didn't need to know that I was guessing as much as he would have been. When I clicked the command, a machine across the room hummed to life.

"Much appreciated," Watson said.

I pretended to go back to my work. He grabbed his papers from the printer and left. As soon as the door had shut behind him, I stalked back to his computer and drew up the print history. I'd take one more set of those pages for me, thank you.

I tucked the print-off under my lab coat and headed out, watching to make sure I didn't accidentally cross paths with Watson again. Near the back exit, I tossed the ID on a trolley. I shed my lab coat as I came up on my car.

Jemma would be happy about this find. As I dropped into the driver's seat, I could already picture the way she'd beam when I gave her the papers.

I grinned at the thought, and the image shifted. She'd been with Holmes the other night—he'd had his hands on her body, his mouth on hers—

I shut my eyes, inhaled, and exhaled slowly. For fuck's sake, Moran, get a grip on yourself.

The fresh flicker of jealousy faded, but my cock had stirred at the same time. I couldn't completely wipe the memories of the scent of her skin, the feel of her against *me*, from my mind.

I'd have to make a stop at my own hotel room before I went to deliver these. Time to burn off some of that libido by hand—if that would even be enough. I'd almost shot a man half out of jealousy a few minutes ago. Soon I was going to need to turn to a more concrete source of satisfaction.

Jemma

My contact, the woman I only knew as Zena67 from her online posts and her email account, was late. We were supposed to meet in one of the display rooms of the city's Museum of Broken Relationships, and I'd been meandering between the bright white walls and display stands for nearly half an hour.

The stories of the various artifacts of love gone wrong weren't exactly dull, but they weren't what I was here for. The faint hum of the many lights was starting to niggle at my nerves.

She might have already come and gone, losing her nerve at the last second. I wouldn't have known her on sight.

I frowned at the chipped garden gnome on the stand in front of me. If anything, this museum stood as a testament to the stupidity of falling in love in the first place. Too much messy emotion, too little self-awareness. If you knew yourself well enough to recognize what you wanted, then you could simply take it, no need for sweeping promises or fanciful dreams.

But then, the only committed romantic relationship I'd ever gotten to see up close was my parents', and most of their adoration had been focused not on each other or even their children but the shrouded folk they worshipped. They got along because they barely had any selves left. That wasn't an example I could apply widely.

I drifted across the room to a pair of red stilettos I couldn't help thinking it was a shame to have shut away here instead of on someone's feet. The scuff of hesitant footsteps reached my ears. I kept my face turned toward the shoes, but I tracked the figure who entered the room from the corner of my eye.

The woman was short and a little plump, with a bob of graying curls that stirred restlessly around her prominent ears. Mid-fifties to early sixties in age. She wore a drab tan tunic that hung nearly to her knees with equally dull gray pants showing underneath, her small feet tucked into flat leather sandals. The sort of person you'd easily glance over and barely notice was there. Which was, based on how she'd interacted with me so far, exactly how she liked it.

She stiffened a little when she looked at me, but she made her way over as if compelled. Coming to a stop beside me, she folded her arms over her low bosom.

"They might as well have gotten a cat," she said quietly. Her English was good, her accent faint. The sentence had been her idea, part of a coded exchange to confirm we had the right person. I suspected Zena67 had watched too many spy movies in her time.

"Two would have been even better," I said on cue. I felt a bit ridiculous, but Zena's stance relaxed.

"Have you seen the other rooms yet?" she asked now that the brief pre-arranged script was done.

"No. Why don't we have a look?"

We wandered past a wall tacked with bras in various colors. Zena swallowed audibly.

"I'm not sure how much I have to tell you," she said, her voice still so low the soft tap of our shoes nearly drowned it out. Her thick rosy perfume trailed off her as she moved. It fit the mood of this place so well I wondered if she'd picked it for thematic resonance. She obviously enjoyed a little drama.

"That's fine," I said. "As I've said, I don't have high expectations. I'll be happy to hear whatever you're able to tell me, even if it isn't a lot."

"You don't have any reason to think you were followed?"

"No. Believe me, I know how to be careful." I glanced sideways at her. "Do you really think someone might hurt you over this?"

Her mouth tightened. "I wish I hadn't even hinted at what happened in those posts. I'd delete them if I could. It'd been so long, and I'd never talked to anyone about it, so it felt good to let a little out, but... I've gotten calls since then, where I pick up and no one answers.

Sometimes I see a man watching me when I'm doing my grocery shopping."

I highly doubted that any of the shrouded folk's minions had tracked this woman down. *I* hadn't even been able to determine her exact location or identity from those few forum posts and her email address. Whatever she'd experienced, it had clearly left her haunted, though. Haunted to the point of paranoia.

"I have people who can look out for you," I said, improvising. "The more you can help me, the more I'll be able to help you." That sounded like a suitably covert thing to say.

"It has been a long time. I'm sure I've forgotten some details."

I softened my tone as much as I could. "Whatever you remember. Whatever you feel comfortable telling me. You can take your time."

Just hurry up and spit it out already.

My fingers curled around the strap of my purse, but I resisted the urge to pop a sugar cube into my mouth. The less strange she thought *I* was, the less hesitant she'd be to share her story of the strangeness that had shaken her. I shouldn't have to worry about the time—I'd left Sherlock's tracker in my hotel room while I slipped out for this meeting—but he'd already proven capable of interfering with my subterfuge without even meaning to.

Even if I had enjoyed his most recent interference quite a bit in the end.

"I guess I should start from the beginning." Zena

dragged in a breath. "It was about thirty-five years ago. I was working in a hospital in Split, just an assistant. A woman came in who wasn't much older than me—definitely not more than thirty—all scraped and scratched up, wearing odd clothes, and in a total panic. She was so weak she could hardly stand up, but she didn't want to sit still. She seemed like she was trying to run away from something."

Split—down near the coast. Some of the cases John had found suspicious had been clustered in that area. I'd have to take another look at the print-out Bash had brought me yesterday.

"That must have been unnerving to see," I prompted with a show of sympathy.

Zena nodded again, her head moving with a sharper jerk this time. She hugged herself tighter. "I was alone in the room with her for a few minutes. She seemed to go… delirious. Saying things that didn't make any sense. But she was obviously scared and in pain—and a little angry too, I thought."

She paused, rubbing her mouth with a nervous hand. I had to ease her along, not scare *her* off. You'd almost have thought that long-ago woman's panic had infected her.

"Were the doctors able to help her?" I asked, even though I already knew the answer to that. If fleeing the cult of the shrouded folk was as simple as running as fast as you could, I'd never have needed to make a bargain for my soul.

Zena's voice dropped to a whisper. "No. She seized up, all of a sudden, clawing at her chest and her throat. It seemed like only a few seconds—I shouted for the doctor, and he hadn't made it yet even though he hurried—and then she was gone. He said her heart stopped."

Everyone in the cult agreed to a sort of contract for the "honor" of living alongside the shrouded folk. My parents had sworn my sister and me into that fealty within hours of our birth. Stray too far from our loyalties, and our own bodies would betray us. Only a contract with a single shrouded one could override that broader pact.

This woman, whoever she'd been, hadn't been sly enough or brave enough—or maybe, from her perspective, stupid enough—to make the necessary trade. She'd taken her chances in a mad dash, and her fate had come chomping at her heels.

Of course, I couldn't really judge. Mine would have chomped me down already if not for the cuff around my leg. I adjusted my purse, the bottom of it brushing the edge of the gold band through my cotton dress.

"She claimed she'd come from a group that worshiped some kind of supernatural beings, from what you wrote," I said. "Something about 'shrouds.'"

"That was something she said. That the shrouds would come for her. That they didn't let anyone go lightly."

That much certainly was true, but it didn't help me. I ambled on toward another display, and Zena trailed behind me. "What else did she say?" I asked when we'd come to a stop. "Even the parts that didn't make sense… They might be useful somehow or other."

"Those are the parts I don't remember all that well, because of how crazed she sounded." Zena exhaled raggedly. "She said something about people searching for her, and about blood, and… tunnels. The tunnels took her almost all the way, but they were still over her when she came out. I couldn't figure out what she meant by that, but she sounded so tortured when she said it, it stuck with me."

My pulse beat a little faster. Tunnels. The woman had escaped from the commune through some sort of tunnels. Which meant I might be able to use the same ones to enter the place without being noticed on the way up.

"It sounds as though she was nearly insensible," I said. "Difficult to know what she could have been talking about without any context."

"She might have imagined it all, for all I know. Hallucinations or what have you. Obviously she wasn't really serving magical creatures." Zena shook her head. "Someone treated her very badly; that's all I know for sure."

I swallowed hard. "Yes."

I took another step through the museum room, and a stabbing sensation shot up through my hip as if I'd been speared by a blade of ice. My foot went numb beneath me. I stumbled and caught one of the display stands for balance with a rasp of breath. Then my whole body froze as I stared at my hand in front of me.

Where my fingers gripped the sleek white surface, the tips of them were fading away. The gleaming white shone right through them as if they'd turned translucent. Pain echoed from my hand all the way to the clamp of the cuff on my thigh.

I jerked my hand back before anyone else could

notice. My fingertips tingled and then steadied against my belly. My thigh throbbed, but the chill was easing back, inch by inch. I managed to recover my balance on my feet, gritting my teeth against the pain.

Zena was staring at me. Her face had blanched. Maybe I hadn't hidden my hand quickly enough.

"Wait a moment," I said as calmly as I could, holding my hand out to her to show her it was perfectly normal now, but she'd been shaky enough already. Without another word, she spun and dashed away, her curls bouncing behind her.

And I was left with the sinking sensation that as far as I'd come, as much knowledge as I'd gathered, I might still be too late.

CHAPTER TWELVE

Jemma

I came back to the hotel the next afternoon with my stomach pleasantly full and my mouth laced with the doughy sweetness of the pastry I'd just eaten. This time I could walk right through the lobby without any subterfuge, because I'd taken Sherlock's tracker out for a walk. I'd rambled around one of the city's larger parks for a couple hours before stopping by Franjo's.

None of the trio had bothered to follow the tracker to see what I was up to, though—or if they had, they'd been stealthier about it than usual. I'd been hoping I might be able to catch one of them in a conversation and find out what else they'd learned, but no dice.

Maybe it was time I moved on to making my own investigations around Split. I had a fair bit of information to work with. The only question was whether I could make the move there without the trio trailing along behind me, their investigation changing from a help to a hindrance.

Jakov hustled over to me as I stopped by the elevators. "Ms. Matthams," he said in a low urgent voice.

Or perhaps I had more business to attend to here. I gave the porter my full attention. "What is it?"

"One of the men you asked me to watch for—the tall one with the dark hair—he came through the hotel this morning. I didn't see exactly where he went, but I thought you'd want to know. You said it was better not to call anymore, or I'd have told you right away."

"That's fine, Jakov," I said despite a prickle of irritation. I hadn't wanted any unexpected phone calls interrupting my various activities, but in this one case, it would have been nice to get the information immediately. "Thank you for telling me now."

What had Sherlock been doing here? A quiver shot through my nerves as the elevator jerked upward. If he'd determined the main room I was staying in…

When I reached the door, I eased it open carefully with a rustle of the Do Not Disturb sign. No prints marked the sprinkling of face powder I'd left on the carpet just inside the door. I exhaled in relief. It looked as though no one had come through here, including any obnoxiously nosy consulting detectives.

I ducked inside anyway, quickly checking over my things. I hadn't been leaving anything in the room when I went out that would be of much use to Sherlock, but I didn't want him meddling in here anyway. Who knew what his penetrating mind might be able to deduce that I wouldn't have expected?

There was no indication anyone had been in here since I'd left, not a thing missing or out of place. Good. I headed out and down to the other room in my name—the one where Sherlock and I had entertained ourselves the other night.

The moment I stepped through that doorway, I knew. He was too careful to leave any obvious sign of his investigation, but I caught the faintest whiff of that sharp aftershave he wore. In another hour or two, it would have faded. I might not have noticed it at all if I hadn't been searching for it.

One of the screws fastening the grill on the air vent showed a tiny scratch that hadn't been there before. He must have opened it up to check for hidden materials. No doubt he'd riffled through my suitcase and the few articles of clothing I'd left around the room too, though he'd managed to put them back exactly as they'd been before.

Had he been able to conclude that I wasn't really staying in this room? I wasn't sure he'd gleaned enough about my usual habits to know what was typical versus uncharacteristically spartan.

The truce was definitely off. My attempt to draw them out this morning hadn't worked. Let's see if I couldn't find a more successful angle for the afternoon.

I sucked my lower lip under my teeth as I sat on the end of the bed. *What's the latest on our friends?* I texted to Bash.

I'm staked out by a government building right now, he

wrote back. *H and W just headed in ten minutes ago. L left the hotel at the same time, in a different direction.*

Good. Let me know when they leave?

On it.

Do you have any more of those audio bugs? I might have the opportunity to place one in a good spot.

In the bag next to the bedside table in my room. Help yourself, Majesty.

The corner of my lips quirked up. Let's see if Sherlock hadn't left me a little more of a reward than I'd given him.

Half an hour later, I got onto the elevator of the trio's hotel next to a cleaning woman and her trolley. With a feigned stumble and a flick of my fingers, I swapped her master keycard for a standard one I'd nabbed off the check-out desk downstairs. When her new one didn't work, she'd just think she'd grabbed the wrong one by mistake.

She got off on the third floor. I continued up to Sherlock and John's suite. The bug Bash had already placed by the front desk had gotten us their exact room number days ago. Reasons to never order in delivery when you're facing off against a criminal mastermind.

I squinted at the edge of the door before I tried it. A tiny scrap of paper showed between the door and the frame, several inches above my line of sight. Did Sherlock really think a gambit like that would escape me?

The door opened with a swipe of the card. I slipped

inside, scanning the floor and the walls for any other subtle protective measures. Then I snatched up the paper that had fluttered to the floor and tucked it back into place so there was no chance of my forgetting to place it in the right spot on my way out.

The earthy smoky smell of Sherlock's tobacco met me as I slunk through the living area. His wooden pipe and tobacco box lay on the coffee table. A few glasses with a ring of amber liquid I'd be willing to bet was sherry, courtesy of John, scattered the full-sized dining room table. Someone had stuffed several take-out containers into a plastic bag by the wall. They'd left the air conditioning on, the unit making a soft whirring sound as it dampened the late spring heat.

That might suggest they hadn't expected their government meeting to take very long. Bash would warn me when they headed back, but I needed to move quickly if I was going to make a thorough search of the place.

I scanned the table, lifting a napkin here and a receipt there to check for handwriting. A map lay on the kitchen counter, but when I unfolded it to the full spread of Croatia, I didn't find any personalized markings. The drawers held only the hotel-standard offerings.

Damn it. They couldn't have left out even one little note about how they were narrowing down their search for my mountain village?

The dining table appeared to be their center of operations. I knelt down and pressed Bash's bug into a nook where one of the legs met the hardwood top. Then I moved to the bedrooms.

The first one I entered was clearly John's—not at all smoky, with a deck of cards sitting on the side table. He'd set a few small rocks of no discernable value on top of the dresser. I studied them for a second and moved on.

The drawers in there turned up a Western novel with a faded cover, a sleep mask, and a prescription bottle of mild pain pills. His hip must still hurt him enough that he needed those now and then to sleep. I set them back carefully.

John's clothes spilled out of his suitcase haphazardly. I sifted through them and turned up nothing of interest except for a torn notepaper in one shirt pocket that said only *Antibiotics—frequency?* and a few numbers with no clear significance. I took a picture of it with my phone just in case it could lead me somewhere, but it didn't look terribly promising.

Sherlock's bedroom was tidy to a fault. His shirts and slacks hung in a well-pressed row in the closet, his sparse toiletries—toothpaste and brush, shaving kit, and a block of soap with a scent as sharp as his aftershave and a London company name printed on it—set in a semi-circle around the sink. John's covers had been tangled; Sherlock's were pulled crisply straight.

Unfortunately he appeared to be equally fastidious about his work paraphernalia. If he'd made any record of his mental workings outside his head, he had those notes with him or had hidden them away somewhere I couldn't see.

I was just about to drag the chair over to start checking out the air vents, since he'd thought that was a worthy consideration in my hotel room, when the lock on the suite door beeped. I froze.

One set of footsteps came in, with a short sigh and a rustle of clothing as the new arrival must have scooped up the paper from the door. The sigh told me why Bash hadn't signaled me. I hadn't been joined by either of the suite's regular inhabitants but by Garrett. They must have given him an extra key card so he could enjoy the larger living space whenever he wanted to.

I crept to Sherlock's bedroom door, which stood a few inches ajar. Garrett was pushing something into the kitchenette's fridge with a clinking of glass. Then he hunkered down at the dining table. He pulled out his notepad and jotted something in it. Frowning, he considered the page.

A tingle of anticipation quivered through my chest. There'd be something useful in that notepad—I'd be willing to bet on that. He had a tendency to hold onto it though, and right now he was sitting between me and my only escape route. I didn't like the odds of surviving a jump down from an eighth-floor window.

So, why not kill two birds with one stone? I'd won Sherlock over enough to get him into my bed. It'd be useful to know whether the detective inspector's new armor had its chinks too.

I'd be highly surprised if it didn't.

A smile curled my lips. I nudged open the door and sauntered across the room as if it were perfectly natural that I should happen to be there.

Garrett startled and bolted out of his chair. "Hello,

Garret," I said, dropping into the seat across from his. "You look like you could use a little company."

He stared at me. "How did *you* get in here?"

I shrugged, leaning my elbows onto the table. "Not so differently, I'd imagine, from however Sherlock got into my room this morning. Since he seemed to consider an uninvited visit fair play, I didn't see why I shouldn't return the favor."

From the tightening of Garrett's mouth, he'd known that Sherlock had searched my room. He didn't have much of a leg to stand on if he wanted to accuse me of shady practices. He stayed standing, his hand clenched around his notepad.

"What do you want?"

"Well, we did discuss the possibility of having a proper conversation, just the two of us. This seems like an excellent time for it, since our paths happened to cross. Why don't you sit down?"

He sat, but he didn't look happy about it. I pretended not to be interested in his notepad as he set it down in front of him. He paused for a moment and then said, "You took me by surprise—that's all. We can talk."

He'd smoothed out most of the tension from his voice, just as he had when we'd spoken on the phone a few days ago. Making a conscious effort to engage with me. That attitude felt different from the brusque energy he'd given off when we'd faced each other in Franjo's that first time since the trio had caught up with me.

Bash had said that Garrett had mentioned something about "using" the fact that I'd propositioned John. Maybe he thought he could get more out of me by playing sweet than Sherlock had. Wouldn't he love that—to score both between the sheets and by outdoing the great consulting detective in their investigation?

He didn't wear the friendlier attitude well, though. Sherlock had been honestly willing to offer the sort-of truce, to indulge his "fascination" despite his wariness. Garrett's uncertainty showed in the flex of his shoulders, in the twitch of his eyes as I gazed back at him. He was holding back a mass of bottled emotion I'd have loved to uncork and drink down.

"I haven't seen much of you since you three showed up in town," I said casually, aiming a subtle jab at his pride. "Are you letting Sherlock and John take the lead?"

Garrett's jaw worked. "We're all contributing the best way we can. You don't need to worry about that."

"Of course not. You aren't really the type to stand back and let others do all the heavy lifting. Very admirable."

"Am I supposed to believe that you admire me?" he said, managing to sound amused.

"Why not? Am I supposed to believe that you *don't* admire me, at least a little bit?" I tapped his calf with my toes under the table. "There's no shame in it. I'm very good at what I do, even if it's not exactly what you thought I did."

He sputtered a laugh. "That's the understatement of the year."

"Which part? That I'm very good?" I touched his leg again, just enough to move the tap to a caress this time.

"Is that what you wanted to talk about?" Garrett

asked. He leaned toward me, with a flicker of hunger in his expression that I didn't think was an act. "How admirable we both are?"

"Well, if you don't want to talk about it, maybe I should see what wonderful things you've been writing about me."

My hand darted across the table to snatch up the notepad. Garrett sprang after it with a noise of protest, too late. I sat back in my chair and flipped through the many marked up pages.

"You do draw a lot too, don't you?" Words and images fluttered past. I stopped on one that showed a woman with long wavy hair from behind, with careful attention to both the hair and the ass. I grinned. "Is this me?"

Garrett came around the table to make a grab at the notepad. I slipped off the other side of my chair. We studied each other from either side of it, shifting weight one way and then the other to feel each other out, his expression lit with determination.

I could have run for the door, but that would have given away that I wanted the notepad for more than just to tease him. I dashed for the kitchenette instead, brandishing it like a trophy. Garrett leapt after me. He caught my arm, and I spun us around with a laugh. Pushing into the turn instead of fighting it, he pinned me against the counter and plucked the pad from my hands.

"That," he said, close enough that his breath grazed my cheek, "is mine."

He shoved it into the pocket of his jeans. His other hand was still gripping my wrist, his arm flush with mine, the rise and fall of his chest echoing into my body where I was trapped between his wiry frame and the counter.

I raised my eyebrows at him as if to ask, *What now?* For an instant, I thought I felt him about to push away from me. Then his dark brown eyes flashed, and he pressed his mouth to mine.

Garrett Lestrade knew how to kiss. *I* knew that because of the intensity with which he'd met that challenge back in London. Now, he nudged a little closer, his hand rising to grasp my shoulder, but his lips moved awkwardly, hard but hesitant. I felt his reluctance all through the set of his shoulders and the tension in his touch. That wasn't at all the emotion I'd wanted to liberate.

I ducked my head, breaking the kiss, and brought my fingers to his cheek to ease him away from me. "No. We're not going there if you don't really want it."

Garrett backed up a step, his arms jerking up to fold over his chest. In that moment, he looked only furious. "Pardon me? Since when have you ever cared what *I* want?"

I straightened up against the counter, a jab of annoyance stiffening my spine. "Are we going to talk about what happened in London, then? Because I gave you exactly what you wanted. You can't pretend I forced you into a single thing we did together."

"I don't really see how that matters when you were lying to me the whole time." He exhaled sharply and dropped his hands to his sides. "Forget it. It's not as if there's any point in discussing it. I—I do still find you attractive, regardless."

He eyed me as if he were trying to figure out just how convincing he had to be about that for me to accept his advances. Or maybe he was trying to figure out whether the plan he'd decided on really was the best idea. I wasn't sure what would play into my hands most effectively. The one clear thing that had rung through his voice in those first forceful remarks was pain.

I'd known he was angry with me from the start, but I'd thought it was wounded pride. I hadn't realized I might have wounded him more deeply than that. My approach might require some recalculations. And perhaps some strategic honesty, if I was going to get what I wanted from him now.

I held his gaze. "Garrett, I can understand why you're pissed off at me. I wouldn't expect anything else. But you know, everything in London—I made the moves that would get me to what I needed. I maneuver people as it suits my ends, and, yes, sometimes I get some gratification out of that. But I'm not some kind of sadist who enjoys tormenting people just for the sake of it. I didn't have anything against *you*."

"I was just in your way?" Garrett supplied.

"More like you *were* the way to get where I needed to go." I wet my lips, and he followed the movement of my tongue. Part of him did still want me despite everything he knew, despite everything I'd just told him, even if a larger part of him was balking. "You were brilliant, you know. I knew you would be. That's why I turned to you. I could have stuck to Sherlock and John, but they wouldn't have been enough."

"Am I supposed to be flattered by that?" he asked, as if I couldn't tell he was.

"If you want to be." I eased half a step toward him, not daring to try to touch him yet. "You were a pretty brilliant fuck too. I'd have done *that* again just for fun, if there'd been the time for it. We could. Why not? You know what you're getting into this time, and it doesn't have to mean anything more than what it is. You almost went for it just now. What's holding you back?"

His gaze slipped back to my mouth. His throat bobbed. "There are a lot of bad choices in the world and not so many good ones. Somehow you make it hard for me to tell which is which."

I had to smile. So, underneath the passionate competitor, Garrett was a moralist. Who would have guessed? Sherlock must have led him down more questionable paths than I had so far, but this wasn't the time to argue about it.

"I happen to think that most choices aren't inherently good or bad," I said, letting my voice drop lower. "It's what you make of them that matters."

His tone softened. "I don't know what to make of you."

"You can make this the first time I've ever been fucked in this suite, even though it's not yours."

He made a tight sound in his throat, but he moved to meet me at the same time, one hand catching my waist, the other tracing my jaw. His mouth claimed mine.

This was the kiss I remembered, so intent it seemed determined to erase every other lover from my mind. I looped my arm around Garrett's neck as I kissed him back, trailing my fingers down his side at the same time. He nudged me back to the counter again, already hard as he pressed against me.

I let my breath stutter over my lips at the feel of him. Garrett kissed me more deeply, his tongue teasing into my mouth, his hand hot on my hip—

And then he was shoving himself back from me with a heave of his chest. He shook his head.

"No. Fucking hell. No. Every fucking time, you bring out the worst in me."

That last comment stung. He hadn't seen anything like the worst yet.

I wiped my mouth and raised my chin. "Then I guess we're done here. I'm sorry you feel that way."

He didn't try to stop me when I headed out the door. I strode to the elevator, my fingers brushing over the notepad I'd freed from his pocket and stuffed into mine.

I'd come out on top. I should be pleased. So why was my gut twisted into a knot that only lurched tighter with the elevator's descent?

CHAPTER THIRTEEN

Garrett

Pebbles rattled in a frenetic rhythm against the undercarriage of the rental car. As usual, John was driving a bit too fast for comfort as he navigated the road between Split and a smaller town further north where Sherlock had decided we should make inquiries. I wondered if I had any chance of taking the wheel on the way back. My stomach would definitely appreciate a less death-defying pace.

"Do you think she's fallen for the trick?" I asked, glancing out the back window as if I might see Jemma speeding along after us.

"I can't imagine her failing to follow up on a lead like the one we gave her," Sherlock said with his usual confident air. "We all played our parts well."

I'd texted John as soon as Jemma had left their suite, and Sherlock had been in full-out precautionary mode when they'd returned. He'd looked a little ridiculous examining every surface in the suite as if it were a crime scene, but his vigilance had rewarded us, because he'd spotted the bug she must have placed before any of us had said anything we wouldn't have wanted her overhearing.

I'd said she must have placed it before I'd gotten to the suite. That had better be true, because if she'd done it under my nose, I'd have to be doubly humiliated. It'd been bad enough forcing myself to admit to the loss of my notepad she must have lifted off me.

I'd had to grit my teeth, but the boy I'd been ten or fifteen years ago would have hidden the mistake automatically, regardless of the damage it could do. I'd grown up. The man I'd become was better than that.

For the most part.

I *hadn't* mentioned how I might have failed to notice her taking the notepad or anything else that had happened between us other than conversation. My bungled attempt at possibly-seducing-or-maybe-being-seduced didn't seem all that relevant to the case. Why bring it up and have them think I was an idiot as much as I did?

I still wasn't completely sure which had been the more idiotic move: going for that last kiss or pulling away from it.

In any case, after he'd discovered the bug, Sherlock had come up with a plan that I had to admit was solid. We'd hashed out our actual findings of the day in my room, which Sherlock had determined was bug-free, and then returned to the suite's living area to discuss a modified version including supposed follow-up plans. Plans which involved driving into Zadar and heading north from there, rather than flying into Split and heading south like we'd actually done.

Sherlock had fully committed to the deception. We'd rented a different car for our supposed road-trip, set off as if for the coast, and then doubled back through a series of hasty maneuvers that John had way too much fun pulling off. He'd parked that car at the Zagreb airport, where we'd caught a flight to Split.

We hadn't seen any hint that we were being followed, but Sherlock took a lot of delight in his precautions, and since he *had* found the bug, I wasn't going to hassle him about it.

If Jemma tried to interfere with our investigations, she'd have her people looking for us many miles distant. Or she might not have bothered, amusing herself thinking that we were on completely the wrong track.

I really shouldn't be imagining her lounging on her hotel bed right now smiling that sly grin of hers. I'd thought a lot about Jemma over the last several weeks, but after kissing her yesterday, after the way she'd talked to me, she kept popping up when I was trying to focus on other things.

"It's quite the view," John remarked, not that he showed any sign of slowing down to take it in. On the left, we sped by pale buildings made out of stone or plaster, surrounded by green shrubs. Gray mountains speckled with vegetation loomed beyond the shallowly slanted rooftops. At our right, blue-green expanse of ocean stretched out toward the horizon. The air that the car's hitching air conditioning system drew in smelled of sand and salt.

"Too bad we're not here to take in the scenery." I stretched my legs as well as I could in the back seat. "We've found plenty of evidence that there's *some* small group of people operating undercover out here, but it's only traces. Do you really think we've got enough to find a community that's been hiding this well for so long?"

"I'd have preferred to wait until we could trace Jemma more directly to them," Sherlock said, "but her recent activities haven't pointed us any closer. We know she means to move them and to cover up their operations here as soon as she can. I have several possibilities for the location, areas away from the usual tourist routes but within a reasonable range for hospital access and the other unusual reports. I expect the locals will be able to give us a good sense of when we're close."

He ordered John off the paved road onto a dirt one that wound through the countryside toward the line of mountains. We stopped at a country house where Sherlock knocked on the door and explained to the owner in rough Croatian that we wanted to explore a nearby section of the mountain despite the lack of paths. When the man responded with brusque enthusiasm, as if he appreciated our daring even if he'd rather we got out of his face, we returned to the car.

Sherlock crossed an item off his list. "He said the local teenagers roam through the woods there all the time. I'm sure a secretive commune would have found some way to discourage that activity."

Three stops later, I was starting to think we were barking up the wrong mountains. No one had appeared at all concerned about our various supposed uphill jaunts. Even Sherlock was getting a grim look I recognized. If we'd been back in London, it would have meant he'd take to his sofa in his house coat for hours examining his ceiling until I turned up with a case intriguing enough to prod him out of his stupor.

We pulled up outside a stone farmhouse at the edge of a few scruffy fields. A tractor puttered in the distance. An elderly woman with her sleeves rolled up over brawny forearms came out and frowned as Sherlock gestured toward the gray peak jutting in the near distance.

"English, yes?" she said when he was about halfway through his usual spiel.

Sherlock paused. "Yes."

"I speak some. Enough." She waved her hand at the mountain. "No. You don't go there."

She turned as if she thought that answer alone would satisfy us. She'd clearly never met Sherlock Holmes before.

"I'm sorry," he said in a conciliatory tone that was ruined somewhat by the eager light that had sparked in his eyes. "Why not? It doesn't look all that dangerous. I don't believe it's private property."

"Bad things happen there," the woman said. "All around. Last month, a farm even closer, they found half their chickens torn to pieces on the roof of the coop. A few years before, a man came up from town with his dog, the dog ran off, next day we find it at the bottom of the mountain, its skin…" She made a folding motion. "Turned inside out."

My stomach clenched. John looked rather green around the gills too. We'd gotten this far based on stolen medications and odd hospital visits, missing equipment and strange deliveries. We hadn't expected stories of mutilated animals.

"There weren't any police reports," I said. "Haven't you told anyone?"

She raised her hands. "What would they do? People don't live too close. The ones with the chickens, they left. Everyone just knows, anything that goes up the mountain there, don't expect to get it back."

A queasy chill pooled in my belly. I didn't want to ask this, but I had to. "There *was* one report. Five years ago, a little boy who was climbing near here fell. Broke his spine. The account said it was an accident?"

The woman pursed her lips. "The city people, they don't want to think it could be more. He went too close. My husband is the one who found him. The way he was twisted up, his waist bent right around… No one could fall like that. They took his eyes and scraped his hair off to his skull. No accident. Don't go there. Leave the mountain alone, or the mountain takes."

We walked back to the car in silence. My stomach kept churning. There hadn't been any pictures of the boy in the report I'd seen, but the woman's words had drawn a clear enough picture. The kid had been only eight years old.

When we reached the car, John looked at Sherlock. "We're going up, aren't we." It wasn't even a question.

Sherlock dropped into the front passenger seat. "We appear to have found the place we were looking for. There's a road farther along that will take us closer. I don't want any locals running after us trying to save us from ourselves now that we've made our intentions known."

"Are you sure this is a good idea?" I said as John started the engine. "Just the three of us? We're talking about people who'd kill and disfigure a *child*. They're not going to hesitate to come after us."

"A child is easier to kill," Sherlock said matter-of-factly. "I have my pistol, and Watson has his. We'll tread carefully, but there was no point in coming out here if we don't investigate the exact location."

My fingers itched for my own police-issue gun, but I'd had to leave that behind in London since I wasn't here on any official business. Just chasing a woman who'd worked her way too far into my head.

That thought brought a fresh wave of nausea. I rubbed my mouth. "We assumed Jemma had to be the one calling the shots with this group—directing whatever they're doing. This isn't about just stealing pretty artifacts or making money. These people are *sick*."

"We don't know exactly how she's involved," John said, but the protest sounded weak.

Sherlock's jaw had set. "Whatever she's had a part in, she'll face the consequences for her crimes."

What did it say about her that she was willing to work with people who'd torment children and animals? God, what if she'd been the one to give *those* orders? The same woman who'd looked me in the eyes yesterday and told me without a hint of guile that everything she did served a purpose, that she never acted purely to cause pain.

I'm not some kind of sadist…

What did it say about me that I'd believed her, at least in part? That I'd wanted to believe her? Because even though she'd wrapped me around her finger and then flicked me aside in London, I couldn't seem to shake the hold she had over me.

Maybe I hadn't left behind the boy I'd been as far as I'd thought. The boy who'd acted out his frustrations through cruelty. With every case solved, with every bid for justice fulfilled, I'd buried my past deeper, but something in me, something strong, found her compelling. She'd drawn that jealous, resentful side of me out with her teasing encouragement as recently as yesterday.

My hands balled where they were resting on my thighs. Now I knew what she really was. I wouldn't forget it. And this was a reminder not to forget who I could be either, as sick as the memories made me feel.

John parked on a grassy shoulder where the road curved to veer past the steeper slope. My feet felt heavy as I clambered out, but I tramped after the other two into the dense forest that hugged the mountain's base. Every snapped twig, every waver of sunlight piercing through the leaves overhead, made my skin twitch.

The ground grew steeper and rockier, pale gray chunks of rock protruding between roots and shrubs. The trees thinned, letting more sunlight stream through to balance out the cooling air. Sweat streaked down my back. John and Sherlock veered to the right, and I followed them automatically.

After several paces, Sherlock stopped abruptly. He peered around himself and backtracked. I moved to follow him, but the impression gripped me that heading upward would be completely the wrong way.

I hesitated, John beside me. His knuckles had blanched where he clutched his walking stick, his blond hair sticking to his sweat-damp forehead. His expression was tight. The hike had been tiring for me—I couldn't imagine how rough it had been on the doctor's shaky constitution.

A short scramble higher up, Sherlock knelt down and prodded a tiny impression in the dirt.

"What is it?" John asked.

"Only the slightest edge of a footprint, but I believe someone has walked here. Heading down from higher above." Sherlock raised his head and then glanced at his partner. "Perhaps you should stay here with Garrett while I continue investigating."

"No," John said firmly. "You're not wandering off on your own to tangle with child murderers. We go together."

I pushed myself after Sherlock. We climbed farther, leaving the trees for ground that was now all rock spotted with pockets of earth that allowed grass, wildflowers, and the occasional coarse bush. Within a minute, the sense hit me even harder that we were heading the wrong way.

I stopped. "This doesn't seem quite right."

"I agree," John said. "I think we've gotten ourselves off course."

Sherlock knit his brow. He scanned the terrain around us. "I am certain," he said, "if a community such as this exists…" He strode up the rocky slope abruptly as if pushing against the same resistance I felt.

I was watching him—I saw it happen. One moment he was marching along in his obstinate way, and the next, with a shiver of the sunlight, his body buckled as if something had battered his abdomen. He tumbled backward, his feet flying out from under him, his arms wheeling.

"Sherlock!" John cried. He threw himself forward with a lurch of his weaker leg.

Sherlock managed to spin himself around to protect his head, but his ankle slammed into a jutting rock just as John reached him. The thump made me shudder as I rushed over too.

John crouched next to his friend. Sherlock shoved himself upright, straightening his left leg. His ankle was already swelling where the leg of his trousers had ridden up. His normally impassive face pinched with pain.

"You've probably sprained it," John said. "Don't put any weight on that foot, or you'll make it worse." Gripping Sherlock's shoulder, he glanced around us, his other hand going to the pistol in his pocket. "It looked like you were pushed, but there's no one around."

"It *felt* as if I was pushed," Sherlock said. "Hard. But I agree—I was looking straight ahead, and nothing moved at me. Perhaps an impactful projectile?"

"I was looking right at you, and I didn't see anything." I paused. "The light moved strangely right when it happened, that's all. Nothing fell with you that could have hit you."

The light. I paused. It hadn't looked like any of the effects I'd seen around Jemma back in London. She wasn't even here—she *couldn't* be, could she?

John handed me his pistol. "Have a look around while I make him a temporary splint so he doesn't hurt himself even more on the way down. Then we're getting out of here."

"John," Sherlock started to protest.

John stared at him defiantly. "If you've ever trusted me for anything, Sherlock, it's my medical opinion. And I'm telling you this investigation is finished for the day."

I scanned the forest below us, but there was no sign of anyone. Still, I didn't like it. I didn't like any of this.

Evening was falling by the time we left the hospital. I walked behind the other two, John with his rhythmic limp, Sherlock hobbling with a brace around his sprained ankle and a single crutch, which was all the assistance he'd been willing to tolerate. As we reached the rental car, I brought up the subject we'd set aside during the wretched climb down the mountain and the bustle of the hospital.

"Now what?"

"We aren't climbing any more mountains, not for a few days at least," John said before Sherlock could answer.

Sherlock's mouth tightened. "Whoever and whatever is up there, they're dangerous," he said. "And they're tied to Jemma. If we can't tackle the mountain, then we'll tackle her. We have to go back to Zagreb."

"And then do what?" I demanded. "We don't have any more evidence of a concrete crime to charge her with than we did before."

"Perhaps we cut her too much slack. Perhaps we were more swayed by her charms than we should have been." He rubbed his jaw. "Anything more she orchestrates under our watch is on our consciences too. We have evidence. We have proof of a relic she stole from a major London art gallery."

"We don't know where it is. We don't even know if she brought it with her to Croatia."

Sherlock's lips curved into a bittersweet smile. "I do."

CHAPTER FOURTEEN

Jemma

I flopped back on my bed with a stifled groan, holding my phone to my ear. "So there's nothing? No sign they were ever anywhere near Zadar?"

"Our contact there had several of his people on it as soon as I gave him the heads up yesterday," Bash said on the other end. "They paid especially close attention to the roads heading into the mountains. Nothing unusual. No sightings of the car the Londoners left in. And there's something else."

At his grim tone, I braced myself. "What?"

"I put some pressure on a guy with access at the airport here. Three men booked tickets together from Zagreb to Split at the last minute yesterday morning. Under different names, but they've used covert tactics in the past. You thought they might be focusing on Split, didn't you?"

"Yes," I muttered. "Before I heard them talking about their travel plans the other night. Fuck. You know what it is? They found the bug, and they decided to jerk us around like we've jerked them."

Garrett's notepad hadn't been specific enough to tip me off. He'd jotted down information that I guessed must have come from conversations with various police officials here, but he'd been looking into thefts and similar crimes all along the coastal mountains. There'd been a few more pages devoted to the Split area than to Zadar, but it hadn't been totally unbelievable they might have found out something else that had tipped them the other way.

I let out a growl of frustration. Bash gave a dry chuckle. "How should we pay them back, Mori?"

"I need to know what they were doing in Split. They might have found the place already. If they stick their noses any more into this situation…"

Bash diplomatically avoided reminding me that I was the one who'd pointed the trio toward a possible mountain-side commune in the first place. "We'll find a way to redirect them."

"Yes, yes." I glared at the ceiling, and the ping of an incoming text on one of my other phones carried from my purse. I reached for it, and my eyebrows jumped up. "Well, isn't this interesting. Inspector Detective Lestrade just reached out. They want me to come by their hotel for a chat."

Bash made a skeptical noise. "I don't like the sound of that. Either they want something out of you, or they think they've got something on you."

"I might as well play ball to see what they're up to. One can hope they'll have their guard down a bit if I seem to be cooperating by coming to them. Are you in your spot near the hotel?"

"I've got eyes on the lobby and the audio coming through."

"All right. I'll tell them I'll meet them in the lobby, and I'll stay close to the windows once I get there. On the off-chance I should need backup, I'll signal you."

"I'll be watching."

I texted Garrett with the lobby suggestion. He agreed readily enough. I studied the phone for a moment longer, debating calling him up just to hear the tone of his voice. The written word was such an opaque medium.

Well, I'd get an even better read on the three of them in person. It wasn't as if they could be arranging to arrest me or anything that involved. Even if they had found the commune of the shrouded dagger, they couldn't have connected the place to anything I'd done, since I'd never been near the place. At this point they might know more about it than I did.

I hadn't even eaten breakfast yet, so I ordered room service and took a quick shower, and then downed eggs and pastries while pulling on a simple smock dress that gave me plenty of room to maneuver. I hadn't made any promises about exactly *when* I'd meet Garrett and the others.

By the time I reached their hotel lobby, the trio was already standing near the elevators. Too tight a spot for my tastes. I ambled along the broad front window where Bash would have a view of us and waited for the three men to come to me.

Sherlock swiveled, revealing a padded plastic brace around his foot and a crutch tucked under his arm. As he made his way over with a swaying gait, something in my chest twisted. Had those perverse bastards managed to hurt him while he was just poking around? I'd wring all their psychopathic necks on my way to that dagger.

But I wasn't supposed to know where they'd been or even that they'd left town. Better to let them think they had me fooled a little longer.

I cocked my head as they reached me. "What happened to you? A little too much breaking and entering?"

Sherlock gave me a thin smile. His expression struck me as cooler than usual. "I never *break* and enter," he said. "It's hardly my fault if a door just happens to open for me."

I restrained myself from rolling my eyes. John looked more tense than usual too, which I'd have put down to concern over Sherlock's injury if it had been the only change. Garrett had his hands slung in his pockets, his mouth set in a scowl, but that was pretty standard from him these days. He probably wasn't all that happy about the stolen notepad.

I glanced around the little semi-circle they'd formed. "I'm here. What important matters did you need to discuss?"

"I think this is the sort of conversation it'd be better

not to have in public," John said. "Come up to our rooms?"

A warning prickle crept up my spine. "No, that's all right, I'm perfectly happy here," I said. "Or we could head down the street to Franjo's. I did just eat, but I can always find room for a little extra dessert."

Sherlock shifted to the side. If he hadn't been on the damned crutch, I might have marked the movement faster, but my first instinct was to assume he was simply adjusting his balance. The next second, the blunt metal muzzle of a gun pressed into my back, just below my shoulder blades. Right where a bullet could shatter through my ribs to puncture my heart.

John rapped his walking stick against the ground in additional warning. Garrett's expression tightened even more.

"We're going to the elevators," Sherlock said in a flat, measured voice that had more steel to it than I'd ever heard before, "or the three of us will be carrying out the rest of this investigation without any assistance from the late Jemma Moriarty. Are we clear?"

My pulse stuttered. I hadn't pictured this possibility, and if I had, I'd have said they'd never have been fully committed, that they'd have been bluffing enough that I could have slipped their grasp with a few well-placed blows and a fast dash.

There was no bluff at all in Sherlock's tone or the others' eyes. No hint of the desire I'd managed to stir in them before. If I played this wrong, the man at my side would kill me, clean and simple.

What the hell had happened yesterday to harden them like this?

It was my fucking fault for underestimating them. I should have watched my back better; I should have read their mood faster. I shouldn't have let myself get so damned cocky.

I wasn't alone, though. I gave a slight nod and turned toward the elevators, splaying my hand against the side of my purse where it'd be visible through the window.

Bash would follow. Between the two of us, we'd get me out of this mess.

"This is a rather different reception than you've generally given me," I said as we marched across the lobby, Garrett falling in behind me to block anyone else from seeing Sherlock's gun. "Would someone like to fill me in on why you feel this is necessary?"

Garrett guffawed roughly. "Give it a little thought, and I'm sure you can think of a few dozen reasons."

His pocket rustled with a metallic rasp. As the elevator door hummed closed, he tugged my arms back behind me.

Panic flashed through me. I dropped my purse and jabbed out with a knee, an elbow, not thinking, just drawing on years of physical training.

Those years might have given me the upper hand against one of those men, but three—it was a desperate gamble. My heel smacked Sherlock's calf just above his ankle brace. He hissed, but he stayed on his feet, shoving me hard against the elevator wall with the muzzle of the gun digging deep. John let out a grunt from the impact of my elbow, but he wrenched my hand back into Garrett's grasp. His walking stick shot up to jab my throat.

The solid bite of a pair of handcuffs clicked around my wrists. I jerked back from John's stick, my throat aching where he'd hit me. "What the *fuck*?" I sputtered.

"We've become better acquainted with the full extent of your criminal activities," Sherlock said. "I'm afraid it no longer seems wise to let you roam around freely."

"So, what? You're going to chain me up in your hotel room like a dog?" I summoned the composure I'd momentarily lost and twisted my head to catch Sherlock's gaze. "Maybe you get off on that idea."

A flicker of discomfort crossed his face, but the gun didn't waver. "Believe me, I don't take any pleasure from this at all."

John scooped up my purse as the elevator stopped at their floor. They hustled me off and escorted me straight to their suite.

"I'd still like to know what it is you're expecting to get out of doing this," I said. "You obviously don't have any grounds to arrest me, or you'd be taking me to the police."

Sherlock pushed open the door. "I don't trust the local law enforcement to take a deft enough hand with your dealings. You might improve your situation by talking to us. When we've seen where you stand, you can be assured you'll be delivered to the appropriate authorities."

"For what? What do you think I've done? Isn't there some rule about informing people what you're arresting them for?"

"We're not arresting you," Garrett said. "We're just asking some questions."

John pawed through my purse and came up with a single phone—a new burner I hadn't used yet. I'd at least been wary enough not to cart all my devices to this meeting. "There's nothing on here," he said to Sherlock, who made a dismissive gesture.

They'd been set up for this capture. The three of them ushered me through the living area into Sherlock's bedroom, where a wooden chair was already poised by the foot of the bed. The covers lay neatly tucked and a hint of tobacco laced the air, just like when I'd snuck in here two days ago. Otherwise everything felt totally different. The taste of blood lingered in my mouth, sharp and metallic, from biting my lip when Sherlock had shoved me in the elevator.

Garrett pushed me into the chair. The hard back jarred against my spine. He secured the chain of the handcuffs to a wooden rung with a plastic restraint. I sat there awkwardly, my calves braced against the chair's legs, an uncomfortable burn already pinching the muscles in my shoulders.

I sought out John's eyes. Of the three, he'd always had the softest touch. He'd warmed up to me first and resisted me the least.

"You can't really think this is okay. It's not as if I've hurt anyone." Recently, anyway.

He dropped his gaze. "We don't know that," he said stiffly.

The others had stepped back to stand in a slightly

looser semi-circle than they'd formed around me downstairs. Sherlock stood in the middle, right in front of me, his pistol still clutched in his free hand. He leaned his weight on his crutch. I had the urge to suggest he get himself a chair too, but mouthing off at him in his current state didn't strike me as all that wise.

"The first part is simple," he said. "We've seen indications that you're not working entirely for yourself but under the duress of a higher power. Tell us who has given you orders or directed your activities, however they have, and we may be able to end this unfortunate confrontation right now."

I glared at him. "I don't work for anyone. I don't take orders. When I meet a 'higher power,' I hand it its ass."

"All right. Then what orders have you given to your group operating out of the mountains near Split."

If he expected me to look shocked that he'd figured that out, I didn't see any point in giving him the satisfaction. "I don't know what you're talking about. What are they doing that you're all up in arms about?"

The three men exchanged a glance. Fucking shrouded folk. Fucking cult. The trio had obviously seen or heard *something* out there yesterday that had shifted me in their minds from tempting shades of gray to pure menace to society. What were those deluded assholes up to other than protecting their beloved dagger?

"There's no way she doesn't know," Garrett said.

"I concur." Sherlock shifted his cool blue gaze back to me. "From the time I've spent in your presence, I can't believe you wouldn't be keeping strict control over any operations carried out on your behalf."

If they wouldn't tell me what the problem was, I couldn't explain it away. I might end up telling them more than I wanted to at the same time. I dragged in a breath, and the air conditioner thrummed on. With that sound, the bedroom door eased open just an inch, so smoothly none of the men facing me noticed.

My spirits leapt. Bash had made it. I had to give him an opening, had to turn this situation around so we could break me out of it.

My fingers shifted against the back of the chair, feeling for where I could grip it. Even attached to my rear, it could make an effective weapon if I swung it well. All I needed was to batter my way through the trio to the door, and then it'd be Bash's gun against Sherlock's. A fair stand-off.

"I think you've been talking to the wrong people," I said to buy myself a little more time as I readied for my charge. "I can't think of anything I've done or ordered done that should be such a shock to you after what you already knew. Nothing worse than what you're doing to me right now, so I guess that makes you a bunch of hypocrites."

"Nothing worse—are you joking?" Garrett snapped. He motioned to Sherlock. "She isn't going to say anything. This is pointless. We should just arrange to turn her over and figure out the rest on our own."

"Turn me over?" I said. "I still haven't heard how you're going to accomplish that."

Sherlock stepped closer and crouched down in front of me. Too close for me to whip my chair around without him catching the signs and stopping me before I could land a real blow. My fingers tightened around the rungs I'd gripped. The second he stepped back—

"By proving you're in possession of not one but multiple stolen artifacts," he said, and tugged the skirt of my dress high enough to reveal the gold cuff. He met my eyes pointedly. "I did some more research. You have four major thefts on your rap sheet just with this."

John mumbled a curse behind him. My bared skin tingled with the cooling air. The blood vessels around the cuff showed starkly through my flesh, as if my thigh was starting to turn as translucent as my fingers had the other day.

He reached for it, and my heart stopped.

"Don't touch it!" I said, instinctively jerking back in the chair. The movement sent a pulse of pain up my bound arms.

Sherlock ignored my protest. His fingers slid along the cuff searching for a connective seam. "We need it disassembled so we can confirm each stolen item with the original owners."

My chest constricted so abruptly I couldn't breathe. The second he detached that thing, Bog would sense my presence, no matter where in its world the shrouded one was. It would descend on me like the demonic fiend it was and shred my soul. In one instant, everything I'd done, everything I'd fought for, would shatter.

I whipped up my foot, catching Sherlock in the jaw.

He reeled back, his gun hand jerked up, and in that instant I knew there were two ways this could go. I could die in a pool of blood or a shrouded one's gullet, or I could scream and bring Bash blasting in, taking all three of the men around me down.

My blood or theirs.

My throat clenched around the scream. I didn't want either of those choices. But Bash didn't wait for more than the sounds of scuffle he'd already heard. The door slammed open.

The words broke from my mouth. "No! No, Bash, don't."

My hitman halted on the threshold, his hand quivering as if it'd taken a concentrated effort to hold himself back from squeezing the trigger. Garrett and John jerked out of the way, John fumbling a pistol out of his own pocket. Sherlock's head jerked around to take in the new arrival. He kept his gun aimed at my head.

"I can still take them, Mori," Bash said, his voice raw. "Piece of cake."

"No," I said again. The decision I'd made without much chance to think it over reverberated through me. I dragged in a breath. "I don't want them dead. They're just doing their job." Too fucking well.

He grimaced. "Fine. But if anyone shoots her, she won't be able to tell me to stand down anymore, so you'd better be ready to lose your own life over that choice."

"Who the hell are you?" Garrett said, braced as if he wanted to fight but didn't know how to start. As the only man in the room not holding a firearm, he couldn't be blamed for a little uncertainty.

Bash didn't answer.

"He's the guy who would have killed all three of you if I hadn't stopped him," I said, managing to keep my voice steady. "That's not how I want to leave this room. Please don't make me regret it."

Garrett let out a choked sound. "So you'll kill kids, but we're somehow exempt?"

"Who said anything about killing *kids*?" I said, my gut wrenching, and then I knew with a punch of cold right through my chest. The shrouded folk and their brutal rituals, their sadistic ideas of fun. They hadn't been quite discrete enough down near Split.

My whole body tensed. I'd like to strangle the fiends— and then rip their misty heads from their bodies and dropkick them off a cliff.

Too bad that might not even hurt them.

Sherlock looked back at me, at the rage that must have crossed my face, and his own cold expression faltered with a hint of uncertainty. His hand adjusted its grip on the gun, and Bash cleared his throat.

"Get that thing away from her head, *now*."

Sherlock eased back, groping for the crutch he'd set down. My gaze slid from him to Garrett and John standing rigid at opposite ends of the room, then to Bash in the doorway between us. What an epic mess I'd made. And if I didn't want it to still end up with a whole lot of blood on the floor, I was going to have to talk my way out of it.

I'd decided the trio's lives were worth something. Worth enough to trust that they wouldn't take mine. Why should I even care?

Because they were different. Because out of all the people I'd dealt with, bargained with, or conned, they were the only ones I'd ever met who I could believe might put a greater cause than themselves over their own desires when the chips were down. Because the world was already a shitty place, and while I was happy to make use of that, I didn't want to be the one to make it even worse.

Because in their own small ways, they'd made me happy.

They'd found the commune anyway. It wasn't as if they could screw me over *more* than they were right now.

"You found a group of people in the mountains near Split yesterday," I said. "They seem to be associated with some kids dying?"

The trio didn't react. Sherlock straightened up with his crutch, his gun partly lowered but still at the ready.

"You think I orchestrated that somehow," I went on. "And that's fair. I *wanted* you to think the commune was part of my business. I wanted you to find them, because it was taking me too damn long to do it myself. I don't work with them. I'm planning on stopping them. I just had to figure out where the hell they were first."

"That's a little difficult to believe," John said quietly.

"Is it?" I focused on Sherlock. "I found your little tracking device, hidden in your doctored sugar cube. I went to that transport company with weird requests on purpose. I 'set up' a meeting for one of you to overhear.

You didn't discover my plans. I fed false ones to you, just like you did to me yesterday with your little trip. Do you have *any* other proof that I'm connected to the commune? You haven't come across a single shred of evidence that I didn't hand to you, have you? Because there isn't any."

I could practically see the gears turning in the detective's head. His gun hand bobbed down a few inches further. "And you handed us that information because you wanted us to find the 'commune' for you?"

"Yes. I'd already been scouting around for them for weeks when you three turned up. I figured with your smarts and resources you could fast-track the process, and then I'd reap the rewards."

"What rewards are those?" Garrett asked, his tone skeptical. "What does it matter to you what these people are doing if you don't have any connection to them?"

I sat up a little straighter in my chair. "I didn't say I'm not connected to them. I know... people like them. They're part of a larger organization—a sort of cult. I know the kind of horrors they celebrate, and it makes me sick. They have something I need, something that'll help me take down not just them but everyone like them."

"So, this is all selfless generosity?" John said with his eyebrow slightly raised.

"No," I admitted. "It's also self-preservation. If I don't get the thing I need from them, I'm probably going to die. Maybe not for another few months, maybe as soon as one. I've got a chain you can't see dragging me down, and they have my only chance at severing it."

Bash's expression tensed where he was still braced in

the doorway. I hadn't told him that much. I'd have delivered the revelation more gently if I'd had the time.

"What is this thing you need?" Sherlock asked.

He'd never believe the story about the dagger. I improvised. "Their people poisoned me with a slow acting toxin. They cultivate an incredibly rare plant there that'll serve as an antidote."

He studied me for a long moment. He'd seen me under the effects of the cuff's powers at least once. I knew from my glance in the mirror this morning that I was looking paler than usual overall. Bog's claim on me and the aura that protected me from the shrouded one might as well have been a poison.

Whatever Sherlock was looking for, my explanation appeared to convince him. He gestured toward the room at large. "Why are you telling us this now?"

"Because it seems to be either that or watch Bash put a bullet in your brain," I said. "And it turns out I like that brain of yours enough that I don't want to see it splattered on a wall. What would be the good in that? We both want those assholes on the mountain to stop all the shit they're up to. I'll get us in there without them killing us first, you take them down, arrest them, shoot them—I don't fucking care—and let me get what I need, and we all come out ahead."

"We don't know that a single word she's saying is true," Garrett protested.

Sherlock sighed. "Yes, we do. I did plant a tracker on her that I contrived to disguise in a sugar cube. We did manage to hear about her plans in very convenient ways.

We haven't seen any evidence that she already knew the whereabouts of this commune, let alone that she had any control over their activities." He paused. "And from the bearing of our friend at the door, I have no doubt we *would* all be dead if Jemma preferred we were out of the way."

The hostility in Garrett's stance deflated.

"As far as I can see it, it's pretty simple," I said. "You can stop them, or you can stop me. If they're the ones you have the bigger problem with…"

Sherlock's mouth twisted. He looked at Bash. "You follow her orders, I take it."

Bash smiled grimly. "Even when it would give me plenty of satisfaction not to."

The detective tossed his gun on the bed. "Then I assume if the three of us retire unarmed to the other room to discuss how we'd like to proceed, we can count on our heads staying intact?"

"Yes," I said firmly, and Bash nodded.

"Sherlock," John said.

His friend motioned to him. "We were mistaken. We need to reevaluate the situation. I think, given the circumstances and the faith shown in us, we can offer faith a little in return."

John hesitated a second longer and then set his gun on the bed next to Sherlock's.

"Phones too," Bash said. "I don't want to see you making any calls to the police."

"Fair enough." Sherlock fished out his and set it down, and the other two followed in turn. Bash stepped to the side so they could file out into the living area. They gathered around the table and started talking in voices too low for me to make out.

Bash stayed on the threshold, his gaze sliding between them and me. "Are you all right?"

"I've been in more comfortable seats in my life, but it appears I'll survive."

He glowered at me. "I don't think you should be joking about that right now."

"Sorry. I should have been more careful in the first place." I paused. "Thank you for coming to my rescue."

The corner of Bash's mouth quirked up at the wry note I'd let creep into my voice. "My pleasure to be of service, Majesty." He eyed the trio again. "Are you really sure we can't just get rid of them?"

"Yes," I said. "As obnoxious as they've been for the last half hour, I was the one who gave them the idea I was in charge of the damned commune in the first place."

"A little personal responsibility never stopped you from clearing the way before," Bash remarked.

Before I could answer that, the trio returned.

"We have a few conditions," Sherlock said. He strode past the bed to his suitcase, where he retrieved what looked like a thin silver bracelet. "Namely, we want some guarantee that you'll keep to your word. An associate of mine at Cambridge designed this. It's a subtle version of ankle monitor. He thought I might have opportunity to try it out. We'll know your whereabouts—or know if you break it to remove it. This goes on, the handcuffs come off."

I could accept that. I shifted my arms. "Well, get on with it then."

"You'll share everything you know about the commune with us?" John said.

"If you're going to use it to take them down, absolutely."

Sherlock snapped the bracelet into place around my wrist, feeding one end into the other until it was tight enough that I couldn't wriggle it off.

Garrett came over and cut the tie holding the handcuffs to the back of the chair. He hesitated beside me as I stood up. "The key for the cuffs is in my room. I'll go—"

"I'll come with you," I interrupted. "And Bash too, to make sure you do find that key." I studied him and then the other two men. "Are you all on board with this temporary alliance? You don't have any lingering doubts that I'm a child-murdering psychopath? I'd rather avoid being shoved around like this again in the near future."

John's gaze settled on my throat. I could tell from the twinge when I swallowed that a bruise was forming where he'd hit me. "I'm sorry," he said. "It was a defensive reflex. I'm all for an alliance if you are."

"It's fine," I told him. "At least you didn't jab a gun into my back."

"That was a reasonable reaction given the information we had at the time," Sherlock said with a lift of his chin. "A reaction I've adjusted in light of new information."

I gave him a thin smile. "I've decided I'll forgive you."

Garrett just stood there with his hands jammed into

his pockets, his gaze wary. He didn't protest the alliance, anyway. I could feel him out one-on-one.

I turned back to Sherlock. "I'm a little shaken up by this whole adventure, and I could use a few hours to assemble the details I have. You know I'm not going far." I tipped my head toward his tracking bracelet. "Meet me at my hotel this afternoon—let's say two—and we'll go over what we all know? Or would you rather talk here?"

"Let's say here," Sherlock said, his eyes glinting. "And I expect you to be prompt."

CHAPTER FIFTEEN

Jemma

On our way out of the suite, I glanced toward the purse John had left on the dining table. "Can you grab that for me, Bash?"

He caught the leather strap without a word. Garrett watched him with particular attention to the pistol still poised in my hitman's grasp.

Bash gave the detective inspector a particularly unfriendly glower. "Let's get on with getting that key."

He held the gun close to his side as we crossed the hall, but no one came out to notice us anyway. My mind flashed back to the massacre I'd pictured in Sherlock's bedroom, and my stomach turned.

If I'd let Bash blow the three of them away, the scene might not have looked so different from the gory hallucination Bog had forced into my head back in London.

Depending on how well the trio played along, my plans might have just become ten times more complicated. I couldn't say I regretted the choice I'd made, though. I was a liar and a criminal, but I wasn't a monster. A person had to have *some* standards.

Garrett's room was a much simpler affair than Sherlock and John's suite: a bed, an armchair, and a dresser that held a small flat screen TV. The accordion blind was pulled down over the window.

He punched a code into the safe in the closet and retrieved a small key. His thumb slid over the inside of my wrist as he moved to unlock the handcuffs, and a shiver traveled up my arm that wasn't entirely unpleasant. I might have suggested he leave the cuffs on a little longer for the conversation we were about to have if I hadn't known there was no way Bash would leave me like that.

The cuffs clicked free. I pulled my arms around in front of me and rubbed the reddened skin. Garrett's mouth slanted in a way that looked vaguely repentant and vaguely disgruntled by that repentance.

"It's all right," I told him. "You did what you had to do."

Bash snorted. "And he can stew about it while you get your bearings again."

He set a protective hand on my upper arm, but I clasped it and eased it away. "I think I should stay and talk with Garrett a bit," I said, holding Bash's gaze. "We have some unfinished business. I'm all right now. You can wait downstairs for me if you want."

Bash frowned. "Mori…" He didn't quite want to

overtly argue with me, but he didn't want to accept the suggestion either.

I turned to Garrett. "Should I be worried for my life or safety in your presence?"

The slant of his mouth shifted into half a smile, even if it was a tight one. "Don't reveal that you're actually a child murderer after all, and I think we'll make it through one conversation unscathed."

Bash exhaled roughly, but he bobbed his head to me and handed me my purse. "You know what you're doing," he said, managing to sound as if he really did mean that without any *I hope* tacked in front.

He went out, his footsteps fading as he headed down the hall. Garrett set the handcuffs on top of the safe. His gaze skimmed over me as if searching for something.

"You're really dying?" he said.

Oh, yes, I had mentioned that, hadn't I? "Not if I have any say in it," I said, spreading my hands. "These people can be vicious, as you've obviously already found out."

"Does it… hurt? The poison?" A flicker of concern passed through his eyes despite his stiff tone.

"A little," I said honestly, other than the fact that the problem wasn't a literal poison. "I'm managing. If we can get to the commune in the next few days, it'll never be more than a little discomfort." Relative to what I'd face if Bog caught up with me, anyway.

That wasn't what I wanted to talk about, though. I reached into my purse, detached the false bottom, and pulled out Garrett's notepad from the narrow compartment there. "I figured I should give this back. Since we're allies and all for now."

"I suppose we are," he said, not sounding all that convinced, but he accepted the pad and flicked through it briefly as if checking to see if I'd defaced it somehow.

"You doodle a lot," I remarked. "I think quite a few of these drawings are me."

That tight smile came back. He tucked the notepad into his pocket. "I think you know you make a striking visual, Jemma. Why did you tell Bash to take off? Do we really need a repeat of the conversation when you stole that?"

"I was hoping for something a little better."

He sat down on the edge of the bed, watching me. "Why don't you start then?"

He might have been a physically smaller man than his two colleagues, but his presence was plenty potent. Garrett Lestrade had worked his way up through the ranks at Scotland Yard faster than any man his age. He'd managed to impress Sherlock despite his adherence, until recently, to the word of the law.

And there was still a little anger burning in those dark brown eyes when he looked at me.

I believed that Sherlock and John would stick to our deal for the next little while, as long as I didn't do anything epically stupid. Garrett, on the other hand... Something in him was still raw and sore. I needed to know that anger wasn't going to spark at the wrong moment and burn me.

It was possible I also wanted to know that I *could*

douse that anger. That he wouldn't always think of me as the woman who'd brought out the worst in him.

I propped myself against the wall a few feet away from him and felt for the right words.

"I'm sorry. I didn't really say that before, did I?"

Surprise darted across Garrett's face—and vanished into suspicion. "Do you mean it?"

"About working that scheme in London? No. But I didn't mean to hurt you as badly as I obviously did, and I don't enjoy seeing it." I couldn't help making a face. "Do I really seem to you like someone who'd kill a child—or ask someone else to?"

"I don't know, Jemma," Garrett said, sounding weary. "We don't really know you at all. For all I can tell, we could be falling deeper into the rabbit hole with this 'alliance' rather than finding our way back out. Hell, Jemma isn't even really your name, is it?"

"Actually, it is. I was born Jemma Marie Moriarty."

He raised his eyebrows at me. "I'm supposed to believe you gave us your real name back when you were only around to con us?"

I shrugged. "I wasn't sure I was going to make it out of London alive. Maybe it was vanity, but I liked the idea that someone other than Bash would know Jemma Moriarty existed—someone who might appreciate how much I'd accomplished even if they didn't approve of it— if my run ended there."

Garrett stared at me for a second. Then he tipped his head back with a groan. "I don't know when to trust my instincts around you. You lied so easily before."

"What reason do I have to lie now?"

"I don't know. Because you want to be sure I won't screw you over?"

That guess was close enough to the truth to make my skin twitch. I wasn't lying, though.

"There are easier stories I could tell you," I said. "Stories you'd be more likely to believe. Stories you'd want to hear more. Would it make you feel better if I said that you were the only one of the three of you it was hard to leave behind?"

A hint of longing crossed his face before he caught it. He studied me again. "You know it would—if *that* was true. But it's not, is it?"

"No," I said. "That's what I mean. I'm trying to make peace with you here, not play a game. If I had a game in mind, this isn't how I'd play it. All right?"

"What is the truth, then? How do you feel about me —about any of us?"

A lump rose in my throat with the words. It felt like cutting open my skin and displaying my nerves, admitting this. But it was what he needed.

"I ended up liking all of you more than I should. More than I've liked just about anyone. Which may not be a lot compared to the average person, but... I should have been annoyed when you three showed up here to get in my way, and I was, but I was also stupidly glad to have you around again, as ridiculous as that might sound."

Garrett's voice dropped. "It doesn't sound all that ridiculous." The skepticism in his eyes hadn't totally faded, though. He curled his fingers around the edge of the bed. "What's one thing you like about me, then?"

That question wasn't at all hard to answer. I smiled as I trailed my hand over the faint rippling of paint on the wall. "You have that drive to be the best—to be better than everyone around you—but you have it under control. You make the urge work *for* you instead of you working for it."

Garrett gave a startled laugh. "Not always. I've let it ride me more times than I'd like to admit. I'm not any paragon of self-control."

I waved his objection away. "When is anyone absolutely perfect at anything? You found a middle ground. You leveraged that drive into being spectacular at your career. I—" I paused. "The way I grew up, we were raised to jockey for a spot at the top, no matter who it hurt. No matter what it cost. You weren't worth anything unless you could prove yourself." Prove that the highest among the shrouded folk would deem you a delectable meal, it'd turned out.

"When I got out of there, I learned pretty quickly that I couldn't trust that impulse in myself," I went on. "I have no sense of when to rein it in. I have to focus on practicalities and numbers and facts, or it'll lead me away from my goals. You turned the same feeling into fuel to get you where you wanted to go. I think I'm allowed to like that."

"I've never really thought about it like that. As something good." Garrett hesitated. "No one pushed me to feel that way when I was a kid, but I had three older brothers who were all 'better' in pretty much every way, and I don't think my parents really knew what to do with me. I did some rotten things when I was younger, thinking I was just evening the playing field. It got… bad. I couldn't stand to keep going like that. I've turned it around as well as I can."

"And look at you now," I said teasingly with a gesture to myself. "Tracking down master criminals all across the world."

The smile he gave me in return was a little more relaxed in its wryness. "Bringing said master criminals to justice is another matter."

"Oh, maybe you'll catch me yet."

Silence settled between us for a moment, me by the wall and him on the bed. Something shifted in his expression.

"I haven't been able to stop thinking about you," he said quietly. "Even after we realized how you played us. It's hard to trust you when I know that I want to in spite of all available evidence."

The admission tugged at some part of my heart I hadn't known still worked. "Maybe you don't have to trust me," I suggested. "Maybe this can just be whatever it is, and if I fuck up enough, you can toss me behind bars and throw away the key, but until then… until then we take what's in each moment as it comes."

"I don't know."

He didn't look angry anymore, but the pain hadn't completely vanished. I didn't know what to do with that. Maybe I'd gotten as far as I could.

I straightened up, nudging myself off the wall. "Look. I have no agenda right now, in this moment. I still owe you a night. We can make it a morning instead if you want. You call the shots. Get me out of your system. It's up to you. I'll walk out of the room while you think about it so you can be sure I'm not working some kind of voodoo on you. Just don't leave me hanging too long or the housekeeping staff will chase me off."

I didn't wait to try to prompt an immediate answer. I grabbed my purse and went right out. In the brighter lights of the hall, with the door clicking shut behind me, my breath came out in a rush.

When was the last time I'd talked that openly with anyone? I wasn't sure I had ever—not since Olivia. Not even with Bash. I hadn't told Garrett anything he could use against me, but waiting to see what he'd do, my innards seemed to have twisted together.

It was all right. Even if this interlude didn't go any farther—it was all right. He wasn't angry anymore, at least.

I was starting to consider that maybe I should just leave when the door jerked open. Garrett blinked at me as if he hadn't really expected me to still be there. He wet his lips. Then he eased back to make room. "Come in?"

My heart thumped with anticipation as I stepped back inside. Garrett flipped the security latch over. He turned to face me, close enough that the heat of his body grazed my skin.

"Just this once," he said with a rasp in his voice. "To get it out of my system."

"Nothing wrong with that," I said.

He touched my cheek, his fingertips gliding over it and into my hair. "How should we do this?"

"You were supposed to get Jemma Moriarty the rising star of the Friesing Police Department. I can give you her if you want."

He shook his head. "I want Jemma Moriarty, criminal mastermind. How does she fuck?"

I grinned. "To tell you the truth, she liked the desk quite a bit. Two thumbs up."

"Well, then…" He led me into the main part of the room. "No desk this time, but there is this handy dresser."

He shoved the TV over to the far end so we had plenty of room and rested his hand on my hip as I hopped up. The way he'd talked, I'd expected a quick wham-bang-thank-you-ma'am, not so different from our first encounter. Instead he leaned in slowly to catch my mouth with his.

He kissed me at a measured pace, not touching me otherwise except the circle of his thumb over my hipbone and his fingers steady in my hair. When I ran my hands down his chest, he deepened the kiss with a pleased hum.

Hunger welled up inside me at the heat of his mouth, the crackling electric smell of him filling my nose. Every lingering shift of his lips, as if he were absorbing all the pleasure he could from each simple sensation, left my nerves quivering eagerly.

I teased my tongue across the seam of his mouth. He nudged closer and tugged me to him at the same time, his groin settling flush between my legs. The bulge of his erection sent a fresh wave of exhilaration through me. I couldn't help rocking into him as he opened his mouth so our tongues could dance.

"You feel so fucking good already, Firecracker," he murmured, ducking his head to kiss my neck next, careful of the forming bruise.

I sighed in agreement, grinding against him harder until he groaned. He slid my dress up my thighs and tugged it over my head, making quick work of my bra while he reclaimed my mouth. Our tongues slicked together as I ran my fingers through his tawny hair. I couldn't hold back the motion of my hips. *That* felt fucking good. The friction of his jeans through my panties already had me soaking.

Garrett caressed my breasts with both hands and then held me more firmly in place to lower his mouth to one. I tipped my head back against the wall as his lips closed around the nipple and sucked hard.

A gasp shuddered out of me. Pleasure raced through my chest with each lap of his tongue. He devoured me with the intentness of a man enjoying his last meal.

Bliss was building between my thighs too. I grasped Garrett's shoulder, lost between his mouth on my breast and his cock still three layers of fabric away from where I wanted it to be. I couldn't remember the last time I'd come from nothing but contact through clothes, but oh —fuck—

The orgasm caught me like a wave from my core. I arched against Garrett, and he yanked my mouth to his again. We kissed and kissed again, until I was losing myself in that sensation too.

My hunger wasn't sated yet, and I couldn't believe he was anywhere close to satisfied either. I fumbled with his shirt, and he yanked it off. We collided again, his bare chest searing hot against mine, the urgency I'd remembered coming back into his kiss.

I flicked open the button of his fly, and he shed his jeans, groaning when I gripped his cock through his boxers. I rubbed it against me as our kisses grew sloppier, our breath ragged.

He wrenched off my panties. I snatched a condom from my purse and shoved it into his hand. With a rough chuckle, he dropped his boxers and prepared himself. Then he kissed me again, stroking my breast, massaging my hip, until I growled insistently.

"You want this?" he said, running the head of his cock over my opening.

"Yes. Please. Fuck me."

The last word had barely left my lips when he thrust inside me. I couldn't hold back a moan.

Maybe that was what he needed to know more than anything else—that I wanted *him*, that this meant at least a little more to me than mashing genitals with any decently good-looking man who happened to be in the vicinity.

"Garrett," I mumbled around a hitch of breath. He plunged into me even deeper, and I dug my fingernails into his shoulder at the burst of pleasure. "Just like that. Please, Garrett."

At the plea and his repeated name, his thrusts turned wilder. His lips pressed against my jaw and then the side of my neck with a nick of teeth. His cock hit the most sensitive spot inside me. I cried out, arching up to meet him. He hammered into me, and I hung on through the surge of ecstasy that swept over me and crashed with a shimmer of stars behind my eyes.

"Jemma," Garrett muttered. He came with a choked sound, holding me tight. Before the impact had even quite rippled from his body, he drew me into one last kiss.

The kiss went on and on, oddly gentle after the last frantic pounding of our coming together, but perfectly sweet. *Just this once*, I found myself thinking. *To get it out of his system.*

I didn't know what to do with the pang of mourning that came with that thought.

CHAPTER SIXTEEN

Jemma

Even though I'd encouraged Bash to pick a hotel as nice as mine, he'd gone with an older, more modest building a couple blocks outside of the downtown core. It had only eight rooms per floor, which meant it wasn't hard to tell that the woman just emerging into the hall was coming out of his.

I paused for a second on the worn carpet outside the elevator and then pushed myself to start walking again. The woman brushed past me without a hint of concern. Her bleached hair hung slightly damp from a recent shower, but the clothes on her skinny frame suggested a walk of shame—a little too rumpled to be fresh. I caught a whiff of orchid-and-amber perfume she must have recently reapplied, no doubt from that massive rhinestone studded purse.

A sharp-edged sensation wound through my gut. I

waited until the woman had vanished onto the elevator before I knocked on Bash's door.

"Just a second," he called, and opened it shirtless with jeans slung low on his hips like he'd barely managed to tug them on. His blasé expression stuttered at the sight of me.

He'd thought the knock was his recent playmate coming back for something she'd forgotten.

"I see you had a good night," I said with a smile that formed a little stiffly. "Now put on a shirt, and we'll get down to work."

It wasn't that I objected to his bare chest per say. Bash's military training and the physical regimen he'd kept up since that time had bulked him out with an impressive array of muscle. The smooth light brown of his skin was broken here and there by darker scars that only added to the visual appeal.

Right now, though, the visual reminded me a little too starkly of running my hands over those muscles while he'd thrust inside me weeks ago. The memory mingling with the sight of the woman in the hall provoked a trickle of nausea.

I shouldn't be bothered by it. We were better as colleagues—*safer* as colleagues, with the rules cut and dried, knowing exactly what we could expect from each other. I'd never had an honest romantic relationship, open and giving without any ulterior motives, with anyone. It wasn't in me. I had no playbook for that.

Still, my gut stayed clenched as I sat down at the table by the window. The warm mid-morning sun streamed across two glasses and an empty bottle of whisky from the mini-bar. Crimson lipstick marked the rim of one of the glasses. I clamped down on the urge to toss it out the window and enjoy the smash of it shattering on the driveway below.

Bash yanked on a T-shirt that only partly disguised his impressive physique and sat down across from me, studying my face with what looked like wariness. "I didn't realize you'd come by this early."

Somehow both the fact that he was apologizing at all and the fact that he was apologizing in such a half-assed way irritated me beyond measure. I shoved the glasses to the side, maybe with a little more force than was necessary, and set my tablet in front of me.

"I'd like to move quickly now that Sherlock and the others know the score. The less time we're reliant on their goodwill, the better. Your contacts here who can get us military-grade equipment are still good, right?"

"Absolutely. I can reach out as soon as I know what we need."

"Good. I've got a list. Feel free to add anything else you think would help with a covert operation. The budget is no object. I'll need to get as close as possible to the village without them knowing I'm there—probably making use of some natural caves—and then I'll need to keep them diverted so I can get what I need."

"Which isn't any special plant," Bash said. "That whole story about you being poisoned—you made that up to get Sherlock off your back."

"Yes," I said. There wasn't any point in mentioning that my life was still on the line here. Bash couldn't do anything about that. "They have a dagger with supposed magical powers… If I'm lucky, it works as advertised. With that, I should be able to sever the pact I made, and none of those monsters will have any claim on me."

"Sounds good to me."

Bash leaned back in his chair. A hint of orchid-and-amber perfume reached my nose, and my gaze slid past him to the bed with its strewn covers. An image popped up in the back of my head of him bending over that woman there, fucking her the way he'd fucked me.

Sleeping next to her the way he'd slept next to me. The way I hadn't slept next to *any* other man I'd ever fucked.

Why should I expect that part to have meant anything to him? Pleasure and proximity and convenience— nothing more.

I jerked my attention back to my tablet. "We're moving to Split as soon as you have the equipment. It'll be easier to plan our approach from closer by. We'll need a truck or a van to transport everything, since we can't take the equipment by plane without raising some eyebrows. I was going to set us up in the same hotel this time for ease of communication, since we'll need to work together closely for most of this." I paused and glanced up at him. "Unless that would cramp your style."

He looked back at me evenly. "I don't think it'll be a problem."

"Good. And I trust you won't allow any of your extracurricular activities to interfere with our plans."

His jaw tightened at that remark. "Of course not. What we're doing is my first priority."

"Glad to hear it." I stood up abruptly. The jagged feeling inside me had twisted around too much. I didn't like it, and I didn't totally trust my own reactions.

More of that orchid-and-amber scent flooded my lungs as I inhaled. It was all too here, too in my face. A little distance, and I'd have my tangled emotions under control.

"I don't think there's anything else we need to talk about right now," I said. "I'll leave you to it—and whatever else you're occupying yourself with."

As I headed for the door, Bash pushed back his chair, its legs scraping against the tiled floor. "Mori."

"You know," I said without looking back, "you should probably stop calling me that. It's hardly professional."

I grasped the handle. Bash caught up with me at the same moment. He leaned his hand against the doorframe, not exactly blocking my exit—I might have taken a shot at breaking his *fingers* if he'd gone that far—but with the clear implication that he didn't want me leaving. "Jemma."

I looked up at him, willing myself not to glare. The only other time he'd used my first name was right before we'd fallen into bed together. "Moriarty works just fine. I'll even still accept 'Majesty' if you insist. I was on my way out."

"I'd rather you didn't leave angry."

"Who says I'm angry?" I said, with an edge creeping into my voice that I couldn't quite rein in.

His gaze bored into me. "We don't normally talk like this. I know you well enough to tell."

I sidestepped, folding my arms over my chest. "Well,

you don't normally act like this." All the tiny details that had been irritating me collided in a surge of—all right, anger. The words burst out.

"I'm not stupid. I know you have your own needs, and I've assumed you fulfill them as it suits you. But in seven years, you've managed to keep that side of your life totally separate from anything we're doing. I've never seen even a hint of a fling. Somehow today, when you knew I'd be coming by, you just *happened* to have someone here, you let her spend the night, leave her scent all over the place, when we just—when I—" I cut myself off, swallowing thickly.

A shadow had crossed Bash's eyes. "You can't act as if I've done something wrong when just yesterday you told me to take a hike so you could put moves on the prince of Scotland Yard," he said. "You didn't hide that. Why the hell should you be jealous now?"

"It's not the same," I said, my throat constricting. "And this isn't about jealousy. Every man I've ever been with, it's been a means to an end, part of the business— except for you. You know that. I *told* you that. And then you… Tell me it's a total coincidence. Tell me you didn't want me to react. Can you? Because as far as I can tell, this wasn't a mistake. It was a low blow from the one person I trusted to have my back."

Bash winced. His hand fell from the doorframe, but I stayed where I was. I needed to hear his answer.

"Maybe you're right," he said after a minute, hoarsely. "I promise you it wasn't something I consciously planned, but I wasn't thinking—if I'd let myself think about it, this wouldn't have happened. I'm sorry. I've been trying not to let what happened between us change anything, but it's changed already, hasn't it?"

"What do you mean?"

"When you told me you wanted things to stay the way they'd been, you said that you didn't trust yourself to have that kind of relationship honestly. Because I meant something to you, and you didn't know how to handle that. But the Londoners, now… It's not just business with them. You have to admit that they mean something too— they mean enough that you risked your whole plan just to keep them alive!"

My chest clenched. "Bash," I started.

He shook his head. "Maybe I've been angry too. Because you're willing to trust yourself with them but not with me, even though I *am* the one who's always had your back. Unless it's really that you don't trust *me*."

I didn't know what to say to that. Part of me screamed to reach out to him, as if the feel of his skin against mine would somehow heal this rift, but the rest of me balked. I'd only end up complicating our relationship even more.

When he met my eyes again, his were less stormy. His voice came out quiet. "They still don't really know you. The first chance they had, they jumped to the worse possible conclusions about you. They're never going to appreciate how fucking brilliantly incredible you are. I do, so it's hard for me to watch, but that's my shit to handle. I'm sorry I let it affect our partnership."

"Okay." I dragged in a breath. "I'm sorry I didn't realize this was hard for you."

"You know that woman, and any others there've been like her, doesn't matter, right? I'd rather it was you."

I'd rather it'd been me too, but that didn't seem like a helpful thing to say when I wasn't going to follow it up by volunteering. "I don't know exactly what's different with Sherlock and the others," I said. "But even if something is —as soon as we're done here, I'm smashing this tracking bracelet and we're moving on without them. We'll cover our tracks even better. They'll give up on trying to follow soon enough. They're not going to matter either."

His lips twitched into a shade of a smile. "I guess I can grit my teeth for another few days then. And—I promise you won't have to see anything from that side of my life again."

I inclined my head in acknowledgment. "I'm sure I can manage to be more discrete too."

"It really isn't— I know you already have—"

"I'll do better," I said firmly. "Are we good?"

Bash nodded. "I am if you are."

"Then we're good," I said, willing that answer to be true. "And we still have work to do."

CHAPTER SEVENTEEN

John

Jemma crouched close to me and peered at the handheld screens I'd propped up in the back of the helicopter. "Are we getting any useful readings yet?" she asked over the roar of the blades.

"We might need to get a little closer," I said. "Are you worried that these people will get suspicious?"

"I think it'll be all right. They don't know anyone's looking for them." She leaned over to give a few instructions to the pilot whose chopper we'd hired and turned back to the screens. One was lighting up with a blotchy rainbow of bright colors; the other showed undulating bands of gray broken by paler lines. "Quite the set-up your army friends arranged for you."

I shifted against the padded but stiff seat to find an angle where I could study both images without my hip starting to ache. The helicopter dipped slightly, making my breath catch.

"I was lucky one of the fellows at the British embassy did time in Iraq," I said. "Although it's hard to say whether that got me the favor as much as the thought of being part of one of Sherlock's investigations. He has become awfully famous even among the expats. I'm not sure what the Croatian army made of the equipment request, but I guess they figured we couldn't do much harm with a couple of scanners."

"Oh, they of little faith," Jemma murmured.

My attention jerked to her face, but she was smiling in what looked like only amusement, nothing more malicious. Her gaze slipped away from the scanners to the landscape beyond the window, and even that faded. For a second, her brow knit. From the distance in her eyes, I didn't think it was anything here that was bothering her. She'd seemed a little distracted ever since she'd come to meet me for this venture.

I couldn't help looking at the bruise at the side of her throat, the previous purple now faded into a dull brown, where I'd smacked her with my walking stick just a few days ago.

It wasn't as if I couldn't do harm too.

"I got the impression you have some connections of your own, considering the haul you brought with you," I said. I hadn't gotten a close look at the contents of the van she'd driven down in with that associate of hers—Moran, he'd told us to call him in a brief exchange after we'd arrived in Split—but from a few of her comments since then, I'd gathered she expected to go into this commune well-equipped.

Jemma's focus came back to me, and she shrugged. "Maybe, with enough lead time, we could have come up with something like this—but close-range scanners wouldn't have done me much good before we had the location narrowed down. It's easier to find the simpler stuff on the black market anyway. There isn't a whole lot of demand for top-of-the-line infrared scanners among criminals like me." She glanced at me as if daring me to be offended, still smiling. "Why do you think I kept you around?"

That intent gaze sent a nervous shiver through my pulse and a jolt of lust to my groin at the same time. I couldn't forget that even if she'd spared our lives after we'd threatened to kill her, even if her intentions appeared to align with ours right now, she'd told me to my face how dangerous she was.

The trouble was, I also couldn't deny that walking the risky line of being around her appealed to me at least as much as it unnerved me.

"And what will you do with me when I outlive my usefulness?" I asked, mostly joking but with maybe a little genuine curiosity.

Her smile widened, and she gave my shoulder a playful shove. "Don't you worry about that. I've decided the world is better off with Dr. John Watson in it, so far be it from me to remove you."

From what she'd said about the poison she needed the antidote to, she might find herself removed from this world if we couldn't pull this mission off. It was becoming hard for me to imagine a world without Jemma Moriarty in it too, even if I wasn't going to admit that right now. Even if it was driving me barmy that she'd refused my offers to look into alternate treatments.

"How incredibly comforting," I said instead.

"Stop worrying about that and focus on all this fancy monitoring equipment." She motioned to the screens. "I get that 'hotter' colors means more heat. That's pretty simple. You said we should be able to use the radar system to figure out where the caves are? Do you even know how to read it?"

I squinted at the screen with the undulating lines. "The tech guy walked me through the basics. I think I should be able to recognize when we pass over any significant underground crevices. Look, right there!"

I waved toward a sharper jump along some of the lines. Jemma cocked her head and then peered out the helicopter window toward the ground. "You can get exact coordinates from that, I assume?"

"Yes, naturally. And I can double-check with someone who has more experience." I clicked a button on one of the controllers to take a screenshot, and another, and another as the helicopter eased up over the forested slope that Sherlock, Garrett, and I had climbed on foot not so long ago. "If I'm reading this right, the caves start pretty close to the foot of the mountain. I'm not sure we'll be able to tell whether they're wide enough to move through all the way up."

"At least one woman managed to come down the

mountain that way." Jemma sucked her lower lip into her mouth, all her attention on the screens now. "If she could do that, I can figure out a way to go up. The most important question is where exactly the people she was running from have set down roots."

"I'm surprised they could live this close to so many towns and tourist areas without anyone stumbling on them," I said. "That one boy aside, they've hardly been murdering trespassers left and right."

"It is a little odd." She paused. "How did you feel when you got higher up the mountain? You said when Sherlock fell, he'd walked up ahead of you and Garrett—why weren't the two of you right there with him?"

I thought back to the moments before Sherlock's tumble. "I'm not sure," I said. "I just had the sense that we weren't heading in the right direction—an instinct, I suppose. Maybe a wrong one, since Sherlock's pointed him differently."

Jemma made a soft humming sound. If she'd made something of that response, she didn't share the significance with me. She took another look out the window and opened the topographical map we'd gotten of the area on her lap.

"The tree line is inconsistent," she said. "You came out here, where there's this secondary peak, but the forest spreads out around that and continues about another half a mile up the mountain before it falls away completely. They'll probably be as high up as they could get while staying sheltered."

"We're coming up over that area now."

"Keep a close eye on the infrared screen." She eased over to say something else to the pilot—asking him to chart a path just below that tree line across the mountain, from the shift in the helicopter's course.

I studied the fuzzy patches of yellows, greens, and blues. If we'd been closer, we might have picked up larger animals as speckles of orange or red, but at this distance the technician who'd prepped me had said we weren't likely to see signs of life unless there were several large bodies in close proximity. These people had to have additional sources of heat too—fires or gas for cooking, battery-powered devices. If more than a couple of them were living together, we should be able to spot them.

Jemma hunkered down on the floor next to the row of seats, leaning her shoulder against my thigh in a companionable way as she watched the shifting colors. The warmth of her body sparked another flash of arousal, but one I could ignore.

For reasons I didn't totally understand, the dynamic between us—between her and our whole group—had felt less fraught since the whole nearly-killing-each-other episode. Less a game of cat-and-mouse and more a simple collaboration.

We knew, in essence, what she was, what she did, and where she drew the line. She was offering enough trust to include us in her scheme rather than weaving it around us. It still left me slightly unbalanced when I considered that we were throwing our lot in with a self-proclaimed criminal who'd no doubt orchestrated plenty more schemes than the ones we were directly aware of, but I'd felt plenty off-balance when we'd been actively at odds too. I'd take this.

Her spine jerked a little straighter as a flutter of orange appeared on the right side of the screen. I inhaled slowly as the patch flowed across the image, dappled with bits of red. A picture—couldn't forget to take a picture to fix the coordinates.

The edges of the shape trembled and blurred. For a second, it contracted, bleeding back into yellow. I hesitated. "Maybe that was just a glitch."

Jemma shook her head. "No. That's them. It has to be. I didn't realize— They must have more ways of disguising themselves than occurred to me before. I wonder if… I found signs of their activity on another mountain across the country. It could be they traveled all the way over there for the event, or maybe there's another settlement over there too, managing to stay hidden." She sucked her lower lip under her teeth in thought, and then looked up at me. "You recorded it?"

"I got the screenshot."

"All right. Let's take a quick scan around to make sure we haven't missed anything, and then we'll head back to earth." Her gray eyes sparkled. "We've got them now."

I took shots of what I believed to be some more cave formations as the helicopter veered back down the mountain, but nothing particularly striking presented itself. Our pilot set down in the parking lot where we'd left my rented pick-up truck. Clouds were starting to roll across the sky overhead, a thicker dampness congealing in the salty air. I had the feeling it was going to be a wet night.

The pilot helped us detach the external scanners from the body of the chopper. I tucked the tarp wrapping that had come with them tightly around them in the truck's bed and pulled the bed's cover into place as well. Sherlock and I were never getting any more technological favors if we returned these pieces ruined.

The helicopter took off with a gust of wind. Jemma helped me snap the cover securely on and then moved toward the passenger door. I was halfway around the driver's side when there was a pained gasp and the thump of knees hitting pavement.

"Jemma?" I hustled around to the other side of the truck with a lurch of my weak hip.

Jemma was crouched on her hands and knees, her fingers tensed against the asphalt, a tremor rippling through her as she got her rasps of breath under control. I knelt down to help her up—or whatever she needed—and my body stiffened.

Her hands were fading away. Literally *fading*, the black of the pavement showing through her pale skin and the flesh beneath. In that moment, in the space of several heartbeats, only the outlines of them and the wan shadows of bones shimmered visibly against the dark surface, all the way up to her wrists.

I blinked and blinked again, but the sight in front of me didn't change. Jemma yanked her hands closer to her, managing to sit up on her knees. She pushed her hair back from her now sallow face and drew in a lungful of air.

When she gripped the side of the truck to heave herself upright, her fingers looked solid again.

"Jemma," I started.

She motioned me away. "Don't. There's no point in going there."

"I think there is. What the hell just happened to you? There isn't any toxin in the world that could affect your hands like that."

"You don't think there are things in this world beyond what you know?"

"I don't think basic human biology and physics could suddenly turn on their heads."

I stared at her, and all the other eerie moments of the last two months came back to me. The invisible shove that had propelled Sherlock down the mountainside. The ghostly figure we'd seen hovering over Jemma in London, and the strange lights that had dogged her before that.

"What are you really mixed up in?" I said. "Who are these people we're after? And don't tell me the same story you already gave us."

Her mouth set in a pained line. "What's the point when there's no way you'd believe me? What I told you was accurate enough. I need something there that'll save my life. Why do you need to know more than that?"

"How about because we're staking our careers and maybe our lives on this scheme too?" I swiveled my walking stick restlessly. "I know something unnatural is going on. I've seen enough strangeness to be convinced it's beyond the realms of science. I can't promise I'll believe everything, but I'll listen with an open mind. Also, we're not leaving this parking lot until you explain something."

She looked at me balefully, and the awareness prickled over me that if she *really* wanted to leave, there wasn't much I'd have been able to do to stop her. On the other hand, if I told Sherlock and Garrett to call off any arrangements we'd made to help her, they'd almost definitely agree. I did have some leverage.

"I told you this commune is part of a larger cult," she said. "They serve beings that live in their own realm alongside ours, but with the right impetus, they can cross over and have their fun here. Like vicious demonic faerie creatures… It sounds crazy. That's why I skipped that part. But you've pretty much seen one—that day in the park in London."

Demonic faerie creatures. The idea sounded so ridiculous I wanted to laugh, but Jemma looked deathly serious, and we never had been able to explain the strange glowing figure we'd all witnessed.

"And one of those things is hurting you?" I ventured.

"In a roundabout way." She swept up her hair with one hand and turned to show me the back of her neck as she lifted it. A jagged white blotch stood out against her skin at the base of her scalp. "I made a contract with one a long time ago. A sort of deal with the devil, if you like."

She dropped her hair and faced me again, hugging herself. "That cuff I made with the gold artifacts—it's the only thing stopping the thing from collecting me, but apparently it wasn't meant to be used for long periods of time. Now the cure is starting to kill me. What I can get in that commune, it'll help me arrange a more permanent solution."

"What happened just now, you think it's because of the gold band around your leg." Poisoning by percutaneous absorption wasn't unheard of. If I thought of it in those terms and didn't focus on the supernatural elements, I felt steadier. "Would you let me examine you? Just your leg? Maybe there's some way I can help."

Jemma's lips quirked upward. "You really want to play doctor, don't you, John?"

"I *am* a doctor, practicing or not. Come on, get in the truck for a little privacy and let me have a look."

She chuckled under her breath, but she took her seat and pushed it as far back as it would go so she had plenty of space. As I slid in on the driver's side, she tugged her loose pantleg up to mid-thigh.

The gold band and the gems imbedded in it gleamed in the dwindling sunlight. The skin around its edges did have an odd pearly quality to it, the blood vessels showing more starkly than they naturally should.

I reached to touch the spot, and Jemma tensed. I remembered how she'd reacted when Sherlock had put his hands on the band the other day.

"I'm not going to take it off," I said. "I just want to check your leg. All right?"

"All right." She tipped her head back against the seat and managed a grin, even if this one was tight. "Have your way with me, Dr. Watson."

I ran my thumb gently over the thigh muscle below and then above the gold band. For a second, when I applied a little more pressure, I thought I could see straight through to her femur. Nausea pinched at my stomach. This thing was definitely affecting her body in some bizarre way.

"Does it hurt?" I asked.

"Not really. Most of the time I don't even think about how it's there. But every now and then—more often, recently—it sets off this overpowering chill… It's supposed to wipe all trace of me from the creatures' senses. I think it's decided to wipe me out completely."

"And you can't take this off?"

"Not unless I want to go in an even more painful fashion."

I had to ask. "Are you going to be okay to see this whole operation through?"

"I'll have to be," she said matter-of-factly, giving me a smile like I'd never seen from her before, sharp and a shade wild. When I raised my hand, she straightened up. "I should be fine for long enough to crash the commune. After that, I won't need the cuff anymore. No problem."

Jemma Moriarty wasn't just the boldly confident woman who never ran out of sly remarks. This was her too —stoic and determined and maybe just a little scared.

"I wish there was something I could do in the meantime," I said. "It might help if you put some material between the gold and your skin… I don't know how the effect functions."

"I don't think that would cut it. But thank you." She pulled her pantleg down. "I know this is probably too much to ask, but if you can bring yourself to keep a secret for a little while, I'd rather you didn't mention this to Sherlock."

I hadn't thought that far ahead. The request automatically made me balk. "Why not?"

Jemma looked at me, her expression both fond and weary. "You know him a lot better than I do, and even I can see he'd sooner eat his own hand than admit to anything supernatural existing. It was convenient when the thing was trying to mess with us in London, but now, not so much. He wouldn't be helping if he thought this was about some 'superstitious nonsense'."

She was quoting a comment I'd recorded in one of my published accounts of the cases Sherlock and I had worked on. And her evaluation of him wasn't *wrong*, exactly.

"He puts proof above everything else," I said. "If you just show him, he'll have to accept it."

"Show him what? Do you really think this is enough to convince him that paranormal beings exist?" She motioned to her thigh.

"No," I had to admit.

"I can't make one of those attacks come on at will to provide a demonstration. The only concrete proof I could give him would be to remove the cuff in front of him and let him watch one of the fiends devour me bit by bit, but unfortunately that would defeat the purpose of proving it."

I didn't know what else to say. I didn't know what to think about the crazier parts of her story. Maybe she was partly insane—maybe there was some other explanation... but with all my medical training, I couldn't think of one.

Did it matter? She'd given me the answers I'd asked for without any obvious guile, simply and straightforwardly. She didn't expect even me to believe them. I could tell that from the set of her jaw. If this was one more deception, I had to think she'd have chosen one easier to swallow.

I wouldn't have thought of Jemma as a woman in need of defending, but a protective urge rose up in me as she waited for me to lay out my judgment. Whatever she'd been through, regardless of what she'd done before or after, it'd been terrible. I could at least believe that right now she was struggling simply to survive.

I could offer her this one small thing. I didn't know what I'd tell Sherlock anyway. Did it make any difference why she wanted access to the commune? He and I were doing this to take down people who'd been involved in the murder of a child, animal mutilations, and who knew what else. That hadn't changed.

"In that case, I think I can manage to keep it to myself for the time being," I said.

Her gaze snapped to me with blatant surprise. "Thank you," she said. Then a hint of her usual slyness came back. "I knew there was some reason I liked you."

I raised my eyebrows at her. "Is that the only one?"

"Of course not."

She raised her hand to trail her fingers down the side of my face, and my heart jumped. I caught her hand, thinking I was going to ease it away, but somehow instead my body leaned in as she moved to meet me.

The soft press of her lips was just as sweet as I remembered, even if she wasn't the woman I'd thought she was the last time I'd experienced it. She kissed me again, a little harder, but then her body tensed.

She pulled back with a squeeze of my hand. "Let's leave it there. I think I've made things complicated enough already."

Even if she was right, I found myself thinking as I started the truck's ignition that I wouldn't have minded another complication or two if they came in the form of Jemma Moriarty.

Jemma

The growl of my car's engine faded out into the whistling of the breeze at the base of the mountain. Bash parked his van next to me. We got out at the same time, him coming around to meet me at the back of the van.

"I could come with you, just to the caves," he said as he pulled open the doors to the storage area.

I shook my head. "The less activity on the ground around here, the better." The gold cuff might be wearing away at my body, but it also meant any shrouded folk keeping watch over the commune wouldn't see I was skulking around. Bash didn't have the same advantage.

They *were* keeping a close eye on this little village—I was sure of it. From what John had told me, they were using their illusory abilities to discourage people from coming too close, giving them the sense that they were going the wrong way. If a shrouded one could make me see, feel, and smell a room drenched in blood like Bog had in London, the occasional nudge of a stray hiker wouldn't be hard at all.

And if that hiker proved as persistent as Sherlock had, the nudge became a heave.

The way the infrared display had fogged confirmed it for me. Maybe the shrouded folk protected all of the cult's communities that way. There could be another out there by that sacrifice spot we'd found in the interior mountains. For all I knew, there could be a dozen settlements just here in Croatia. I'd never needed to think about details like that while I was living in the commune I'd grown up in.

"You're the boss, Majesty," Bash said. He pulled out the climbing gear he'd assembled. "Oversuit so you don't scratch yourself up. Knee and elbow pads. Rubber-soled boots. Helmet with headlamp. Rope. Waist belt with a bottle of water and a spare headlamp in case they mess with your first one." He elbowed me lightly. "I don't want you getting lost in the dark."

"I think I'll manage to find my way." How much equipment had Zena's patient had when she'd made her desperate scramble away from the commune? Probably none.

Having all this stuff almost felt like cheating. But against these fiends and the people who worshiped them, we needed all the advantage we could get.

I pulled on the oversuit, the thick fabric making my skin heat up within seconds, and attached the various accessories. The rope had a hook to attach it to the side of the belt. As I fixed the helmet on my head, its strap bit into the fading bruise on my throat. Bash frowned, looking at it.

"Are you sure Dr. Watson's technician friend gave you the right directions? The Londoners and their people haven't always been all that concerned about accuracy or your safety."

"I was there. I went over all the radar images with them." I touched Bash's arm. "You don't have to worry. This is just a scouting mission. I'm not planning on getting into anything dangerous."

"Only you would say that right before you race off into unmapped caves on a mountain that seems determined to kick people off it," he said dryly, but he couldn't mask the concern in his eyes. He turned to the van and handed me a couple of metal tools about the size of my hand, shaped like blunt knives. "Pitons, in case you have to clamber up any steep parts. Wedge the narrow end into a crack and use them to lever yourself up."

"Excellent." Going up was almost certainly going to be harder than coming down. I stuffed those into the hip pockets of my oversuit.

Bash reached a little farther into the back of the van. "Here, there's something else I picked up for you. I don't know if you'll end up needing it, but it might come in handy."

He drew out a black metal rod about an inch thick and slightly shorter than my forearm. With a flick of his wrist, two extra segments snapped out, nearly tripling its length. Bash made a few quick jabs with it and tossed it to me.

"Collapsible baton," he said. "The most lightweight one I could find that's still high quality. The steel in that will stand up to just about anything. You could say the good doctor inspired me with his walking stick antics."

I twirled the rod in my hand with amusement. "Did you think I was planning on fighting the caves?"

He chuckled. "No, but it'll give you some maneuverability if you do have to fend off an attacker while you're in there, regardless of the range. And it might be useful for climbing too if you can wedge it across a passage you want to scramble up. You can clip it inside your sleeve so you can whip it out in an instant. I know how fast those hands are."

He gave me a teasing wink as he motioned to my arm, but a little ache formed in my chest. I ducked my head as I attached the clip to my sleeve as he'd suggested. With a quick snatch, I could slip it off and extend it in less than a second. I tried the maneuver a few times before I looked at him again.

"Thank you," I said. The weight on my arm was a testament to how determined he was to protect me, even when I insisted on running off into harm's way alone.

How much longer would I have that?

I knew how human emotion worked even if I hadn't experienced a full range all that deeply myself. I'd watched enough people interacting during my business dealings. Even after Bash and I left the London trio behind, the night we'd shared and the fact that I'd refused any further intimacy would be hanging there between us. It had already been gnawing at him, and it'd keep gnawing at him until the downsides of working with me outweighed whatever he liked about the job.

He could say he accepted my decision, but I didn't know if he could really promise he'd always feel that way. I didn't know if I'd have wanted him to promise something like that. If he had to back off, I'd let him go, and then I'd make my own way again like I had before. It was fine. I'd manage.

It was only the thought of getting to that point that sent a brief jab through my gut.

I went back to my car and retrieved my phone and my written coordinates from my purse. "All right. Off I go."

Bash saluted me and got in behind the wheel of the van. He had other business to look into while I was exploring, but I knew he wouldn't leave until he'd made sure I at least got into the forest without incident. With his eyes on my back, I set off into the brush.

Every few minutes, I checked the GPS display on my phone to make sure I was on track. The forest became denser, fallen sticks cracking under my feet. I wasn't too worried about being noticed this far down. Sherlock and the others had made it a lot higher before the shrouded folk had intervened, and they couldn't detect me. I planned on getting as close to the actual human habitation as I could.

When I came for the dagger properly, I'd want to make my approach at night. There'd be less energy for the shrouded folk without immediate sunlight, and more chance that most of the cultists would be sleeping. I'd like to be totally familiar with my route before I navigated it by starlight.

I'd walked for about twenty minutes before I came on the first point where the radar had shown underground passages near the surface. Other than a crack I could barely fit my fingers through in the rocky shell of the ground, it didn't offer any access. I headed on up to the second location, about five minutes farther.

The commune clearly knew about the cave system beneath them. I found a crevice just wide enough for me to slip through—and a bear trap fixed to the rock right in front of it. They might not venture down this far very often themselves, but they didn't want anyone wandering up and finding them either.

I studied the trap. I might have been able to safely spring it with a branch, but then they'd suspect someone had come through if they checked the trap before I returned. There had to be another option.

I eased up over the loose dirt that covered the ground beside the crevice. The opening wasn't very wide, but it was pretty tall. And there was this handy tree looming right over the top…

With a swing of my arm, I tossed my rope over the lowest branch, tied it firmly near the base, and dangled the rest into the crevice, letting the end fall just beyond the trap. Then I gripped it and jumped through the opening.

The momentum carried me past the trap. I loosened my hold and landed on the uneven turf inside, catching the rope before it could smack into the trap. I was going to need it to get back out again.

I wedged part of the rope into a crack in the edge of the crevice, switched on the lamp on my helmet, and set off into the cave.

The bear trap meant there might be other traps—of that sort or other kinds—along the way. I trod carefully over the dry rock, the cool still air grazing my face as I moved. A faint mineral flavor laced my tongue, like a muted version of the ocean's salt. The white glow of the lamp lit up bulges and dips of rock that wound deeper into the mountain's face and then veered upward with the slope.

Despite the cool dry atmosphere, sweat started to bead on my skin from the climb. I ducked under a low chunk of ceiling and at the last second spotted a patch of floor that didn't look quite right. A thin slab of rock sat in the middle of the passage. I nudged the edge with my toe, and a few pebbles crumbled off it.

A pit trap, I'd bet. I backed up a couple steps and dove over it through the cramped space. A jolt of pain ran through my shoulder as I rolled my landing on the uneven rock on the other side, but the trap stayed undisturbed.

A short climb farther, a streak of natural light coursed down from above. A gap in the ceiling emitted the faint shine, wavering with the movement of distant leaves. I eyeballed the space with an idea unfurling in my head. The gap was big enough that there were quite a few things I could shoot through it. I did still need a distraction as part of my plan.

I made a note of the spot in the rough map I'd been sketching on my phone and continued on. When a side passage twisted away from the main cave, I peered down it and decided to skip it—it looked like it fell away deeper into the mountain rather than offering access upward.

The cave I was moving through widened and tightened again. It wound back and forth through the rough stone and then shot up in a passage that was almost totally vertical. I grasped the pitons and drove them into the cracks, bracing myself with my feet and back between each shuffle upward. This part was definitely going to be easier on the way down.

The ponytail I'd pulled my hair into stuck damp to the back of my neck as I emerged. I paused there for a moment to catch my breath and crept on up the steep incline of the cave.

I squeezed through a particularly narrow section and edged across a patch of more level floor. A shuffling sound overhead made me freeze.

It came again. I held my breath, listening as carefully as I could.

I'd swear that was someone dragging something heavy —the rasp of the friction and the thump as they lowered it between heaves. Another sound wavered down with the texture of a voice speaking, even if I couldn't make out a single word. Another warbled in return.

My heart thumped faster. I'd made it to the commune. Or nearly made it. Knowing I was right beneath the settlement didn't do me much good if I couldn't figure out how to get aboveground.

I slunk along the passage, searching the ceiling and the walls for any sort of opening. Around a curve in the cave, my headlamp picked up a jaggedly circular outline where the ceiling dipped to a little lower than my height. It looked as though a huge rock had been set there to cover the entrance.

The boulder would be heavy, but the people up there must still be able to move it if they needed to. If I dragged the right tools up here, I could heave it out of the way.

I eased closer, meaning to test it gently with my hands. My gaze snagged on a thin cable that stretched across the floor just an inch off the ground. I jerked backward, propelling myself away from whatever trap the trip wire activated—and the ground under my heel crumbled.

My heart lurched into my throat as I reeled backward. One clear impression sprang into my mind: the snicker of Bash's baton snapping to full length. I wrenched the tool from my sleeve and whipped it out just as my body dropped through the chasm that had opened in the floor.

The steel bar jarred against both sides of the chasm. I swung my other hand up to grasp it. My feet dangled beneath me for several aching moments, flailing for purchase and finding none, before I managed to yank them up and plant them on one side of the narrow space.

Ignoring the strain in my shoulders, I glanced down. Only darkness met the stream of my headlamp. My breath snagged in my throat.

I'd almost fallen into nothingness.

I would have, if it wasn't for Bash. He'd managed to

have my back even all the way up here, even though I'd pushed him away and denied him my full trust twice now.

The breath in my throat solidified into a lump. I swallowed hard. Flexing my arms, I managed to walk my feet up the side of the chasm and pull my torso higher at the same time. I swung one leg and then the other over the edge onto the cave floor and wrenched the rest of me up to follow them. Then I lay on my back, one hand still clutched around the baton, my pulse thudding with the memory of that fathomless drop.

The next time I came up here, I'd better stick to the right side of the cave. Good to know. I eyed the stone surface that had crumbled so easily, but I couldn't see any way to cover up the hole I'd broken in it. I'd just have to hope that if anyone checked in the next few days, they'd assume it'd given way on its own.

Shoving myself upright, I checked the floor for any marks I might have left that would reveal my presence. I scuffed away the edge of a footprint. After I'd marked the apparent entrance on my digital map, I headed back the way I'd come.

I didn't let go of the baton the whole journey down.

Evening was falling by the time I made it back to my car. I peeled off my equipment, dropped into the driver's seat, and sent a quick text to Bash. *Have returned alive. Located commune.* Then I tipped the seat back to let myself rest for a few minutes before heading back to the city.

My chest still felt tight, even though the scouting mission had gone perfectly. I'd survived. I'd found a route through the caves to the commune. I had a reasonable expectation of breaking my way the rest of the way through when I needed to.

But for some reason a hole almost as deep as that chasm had opened up inside me.

I needed to put that close call behind me. Move forward, move onward. I'd feel better once I got away from this place.

It was full-out night when I reached Split. I slipped between cheerful friends and couples strolling along the sidewalks to grab a seat in the first bar I spotted. The bartender brought me a burger and then a couple of beers with professional politeness. The alcohol added a slight fizz to my thoughts but didn't really dull my uneasiness.

Keep moving. I left the bar and meandered around the downtown strip until I spotted an asshole spewing drunken pick-up lines at every woman who passed him. I sidled over from behind and neatly lifted his wallet.

Looking at the contents around a corner didn't give me even a little spark of satisfaction. Thirty dollars' worth of local currency and a few credit cards I had no real use for. What the fuck was I doing?

Trying to be okay. Trying to walk far enough to walk *away* from things I hadn't wanted to feel.

But I did feel them. They were part of me. What was the point in denying myself something I wanted that I could have? If it crashed and burned, I wouldn't be any worse off than I was right now.

I wove through the streets to my hotel with a knot in my stomach but resolve swelling around it. When I reached my floor, I pulled the second keycard out of my purse. Bash and I had exchanged our extra copies in case we needed quick access to each other's belongings.

I eased his door open to find the room dark, the blackout curtain pulled, and the slow rasp of sleeping breath drifting through the air. With silent footsteps, I crossed the room to the bed.

Bash was sprawled there on his back, a little off to one side, his face tipped to the pillow.

My body balked for a second. Then, ever so carefully, I sat on the opposite edge of the bed and lay down on top of the covers.

Bash stirred and settled. I closed my eyes and dragged in my first truly full breath since my fall in the caves. With the scent of gun oil seeping into my lungs, my limbs relaxed into the bed.

I was here. We could deal with the rest in the morning.

CHAPTER NINETEEN

Jemma

A hitch of the mattress snapped me out of sleep. My head jerked up.

Bash was staring at me, sitting half upright where he must have startled to see me in his bed, the covers sliding down his brawny torso. As the initial surprise faded from his expression, his jaw tightened with concern.

"Are you all right, Mori? If you didn't think you were safe to stay in your room, why didn't you wake me up?"

I stretched and pushed myself upright, yesterday's blouse and pants shifting against my body in their wrinkled state. Last night, coming here had felt so complicated. Now, with Bash's musky scent surrounding me and his instinctive protectiveness immediately on display, all my anxieties seemed ridiculous.

This was Sebastian Moran. I knew him better than I'd ever known anyone, and he knew me like no one else. If I wanted to take this step without it ending in a mess, he was as close as I was going to get to a sure thing.

"There's nothing wrong with my room," I said, meeting his gaze. "I've been thinking about what you said the other morning and how I feel, and I've changed my mind. We should take it slow, but I'd like to give us a try. As lovers."

Bash blinked as he straightened up, but in spite of his apparent bemusement, an eager warmth had lit in his light green eyes. He glanced from me to the door. "And you figured the best way to tell me that was by sneaking into my room in the middle of the night?"

The corner of my lips twitched upward. "I thought I should make some demonstration of being good to my word. I… I haven't trusted anyone enough to sleep next to them in ten years, other than you. And this time I was thinking clearly about it."

He didn't seem to know what to say about that. He edged his hand across the bed to rest at the small of my back, his thumb tracing an arc over my spine. "What changed your mind?"

The lump that had filled my throat yesterday in the caves returned. I willed it down. "I *can* do this alone," I said, because it suddenly felt very important to make that clear. "But I don't want to. Pretending there's nothing more between us than business is just as likely to fuck things up as, well, fucking."

I don't want to lose you. That understanding sat in my gut, too heavy for me to propel into words, but maybe he could hear it in what I did say.

Bash scooted closer to loop his arm right around my waist. "Sounds perfectly reasonable to me."

I raised an eyebrow at him. "Like I said, I want to take things slow. We're not jumping right to the fucking part. I want to be sure my intentions are in the right place when it comes to you. And—if we're doing this, you have to accept that sometimes I'm going to be with other men too, when I need to."

"And when you want to," he said, as a statement of fact rather than a judgment.

My shoulders came up a bit. "Just because I've enjoyed some of those encounters—"

"It's all right," Bash said. He pressed a kiss to the corner of my jaw that sparked desire all through my body. "I'm not saying the jealousy is gone, but I don't know if I'd really want you to restrict yourself like that. I like the energy you get when you've been 'enjoying' yourself with other people. And I'll definitely like knowing that no matter who you play around with, it can be me you come back to, every time. So, if you get the urge to, say, have a last hurrah with the Londoners before we leave them in our dust, just promise me you'll milk them for everything they're worth." He smirked at me.

I grinned back at him. "That's a promise I have no trouble making."

I couldn't have asked for more than what he'd offered in his response. I leaned into him, inhaling the tang of his natural scent. Wanting to taste him. Wanting to throw the principles I'd decided on out the window and explore every inch of his body at my leisure.

But was that an urge born from honest attraction, or an impulse to tie him to me, to lock down his devotion and appease my sense of control? I wasn't sure I could tell the difference, so I held myself back.

Bash was obviously thinking along similar lines. "When you say we'll take it slow, how slow is 'slow'?"

I wet my lips and looked at his. "Well, I'm not saying we should become monks."

I raised my head and he lowered his at the same time. He claimed my mouth with a firm certainty, as if he knew exactly how I'd want to be kissed even though we barely had before this moment.

He did know, though. The heat of his lips flooded me from head to toe, and I shifted even closer, my hand coming to rest on his bare abs.

Bash let out a faint groan, his arm tightening around me. He deepened the kiss until his tongue twined with mine, and a bolt of lust shot to my core. My self-control started to fray.

I eased away from him, breathless. "Maybe we should put a pin in it for now."

Bash laughed, his fingers stroking over my side. "You're going to be the death of me."

I stiffened automatically. Bash's hand stilled, and he pulled back far enough to meet my eyes. "I didn't mean that literally, Mori."

I let out a breath. "No, but you could have. There's a pretty good chance that's true."

"Hey." He touched the side of my face, all his attention focused on me. "I'm fine with that. I've been tempting death my whole life. I'd sure as hell rather it happened at your side, taking on your monsters, than in the army or doing shitty jobs for the random assholes I worked for before you. I'm where I want to be."

"Okay." I believed him, even if the idea of my mission leading him to his death made my stomach clench. I rubbed my mouth. "We're supposed to meet with Sherlock and the others soon. I should shower and get changed into clothes that aren't clearly slept in, or they'll think I'm losing my touch."

Bash snorted and released my waist. I couldn't help turning to plant one more kiss on him. It went on a little longer than I'd been planning before I managed to wrench myself away. I flashed him another grin and hopped off the bed.

"It's going to be *cold* showers around here," he muttered to himself as I slipped out the door, but it was the happiest muttering I'd ever heard.

Our hotel had a few meeting rooms that could be reserved for private use. The trio arrived right on schedule from the place where they were staying down the street. Sherlock strode right in with a thump of his crutch and a dip of his head in acknowledgment, John and Garrett trailing behind him. We sat around the boardroom-sized table, Bash and me on one side and the three of them on the other.

I leaned back in my chair with a faint creak. "On my side of things, I'm basically ready to go. I've planned a route through the cave system, and I have the gear I need.

All we need to figure out is how you're going to put your raid into motion."

"I'm still not entirely sure why you feel you can take on this entire cult group by yourself, but we'll need extensive help," Sherlock said.

"Oh, you're going to help me," I said. "I'm pretty sure I can make it to their stash, but getting off the mountain unscathed would be trickier. That's why I need to be sure you'll come storming into the place not too long after I get there."

"Also," Bash said, "you didn't even make it halfway up that mountain last time without ending up in a cast."

"It's a brace," Sherlock said tartly. "Only a sprain."

"My point stands."

"Unless I've read the situation wrong, you're the muscle here, not the brains. Perhaps you should leave the discussion to the rest of us."

Bash shifted forward in his seat, and I cleared my throat. "I'm sure I don't have to remind you that Bash very considerately did *not* shoot you the other day when you were threatening me at gun point. So maybe we could keep this conversation considerate as well?"

Sherlock looked a tad chagrinned. "Yes. Well. More to the matter at hand, why should you go ahead of us at all? Why not arrive as part of the raid? I'm sure whatever force we can assemble would overlook the lifting of a small item or two."

"Unless there's something else you have planned before we get there," Garrett put in, his gaze suspicious but his tone more curious, as if he couldn't help wondering how I might pull the rug out from under them yet again.

"No," I said honestly. "All I want to do is grab my cure and get the hell out. But I'll be helping you too on my way up. I'll provide a little distraction, get them stirred up about that, and then it'll be easier for you to swarm the place… without any more turned ankles."

"You could do that just as easily with us," Sherlock said.

"No, I couldn't. I know how to get past their warning systems. I'm the only one who can get close enough to cause enough chaos to open the way."

"You *could* share those strategies with the rest of us."

I gave Sherlock a firm look. "Sorry. I can't do that either. There are certain things that can't be taught." Like the power of a gold cuff to hide one's presence from the shrouded folk he'd scoff at the very idea of.

His eyebrows jumped up. "I'd expect you know by now that I can pick up nearly—"

John knuckled his arm. "Sherlock, *we* know that Jemma has a lot more experience with the cult than we do. If she thinks this approach will be safest for all of us, I say we listen. I don't think she protected us four days ago just to get us killed now."

"That might make a very convenient distraction," Garrett remarked.

I glowered at him, but Sherlock's expression softened a little as he looked at John. "Perhaps we should work out the rest of the plan and see if it hangs together before drawing judgments," he allowed.

John smiled, lighting up the way he always did when Sherlock showed how much he valued his opinion. Watching them, a flutter passed through my chest, like an echo of the longing that had brought me to Bash's bed last night.

They'd developed the same understanding and trust that Bash and I had between us, as clear as anything. It really was a shame that Sherlock couldn't seem to wrap his head around seeing anything more than platonic affection from his friend. Would that friction end up breaking their bond apart the same way I'd been worried Bash and I might fall out?

It wasn't my concern, not really. I drew my attention back to our strategizing.

"I know you don't approve of my usual methods," I said, "but I'd like to see you take down those psychopaths as much as you would, so we really do have the same goal here. If you've changed your mind about believing that, then I'll figure out something on my own. The door's right there." I motioned to it.

"No, no," Sherlock said briskly, as if he could speak for all three of them. "Let's carry on."

Garrett tapped the edge of the table. "We don't have the legal authority to do anything about these people anyway, do we? If the idea is to shut down whatever operations they have running and make sure they don't hurt any more kids or animals, we need to get the local police involved."

"Indeed." Sherlock pulled a slight grimace. "I have less faith in them than your Scotland Yard colleagues back home, Garrett, but I don't see how that can be helped."

"They've ignored the situation for years—maybe decades," John pointed out. "They brushed off that boy's death as an accident."

"And we don't have any proof of more recent crimes."

I rested my hands on my stomach, interlacing my fingers. "We don't need a real crime, do we? We just need a story to get them riled up—or at least feeling like they have to act like they are."

The consulting detective hummed to himself. "That's true. I do have a little sway here. We could appeal to the General Police Directorate. If we convinced them that international relations were at stake rather than merely the concerns of a handful of farmers and countryfolk, that should stir them."

"I'm not going to make up an official case," Garret said. "That could come back to bite me too easily."

"Of course not. Don't worry yourself about crossing those lines. We can make it a private matter. It's simple enough. What innocent British citizen might venture up the mountain?"

Sherlock glanced around looking for suggestions like a professor testing his class.

"A tourist?" John said. "There are always adventurous types looking to go off the beaten track."

"Exactly my thought. This imaginary tourist—we'll make her a woman, that always draws more sympathy, no offense meant to present company—"

"None taken," I said with amusement.

"—she mentioned to relatives back home that she was going to attempt a climb of this mountain, and then they never heard from her again." Sherlock spread his hands. "Not having any contacts in the area, they turned to me for my services. And during my investigations here, I discovered a small hidden community engaged in illegal dealings who almost certainly did away with the young lady."

Garrett nodded. "That hangs together pretty well. They might not be too motivated by the concerns of a couple of independent detectives, though." He paused, and a sly glint lit in his dark eyes. "John, it is the sort of case you might decide to write about. You could tell them you're planning on publishing an account."

"That does sound plausible," John said with a grin. "I'll make sure to emphasize how many people enjoy those accounts, to rub it in that their response will be scrutinized by the public eye."

Sherlock snapped his fingers. "Perfect. We'll hit two points of pressure at once. The potential shame of being revealed to have ignored horrific criminal activity going on under their noses, and the ego stroking of being asked for assistance where my means are not enough. Law enforcement officials are so often guided by pride."

I suppressed a smile, and Garrett caught my eye with a glance of conspiratorial exasperation. As if Sherlock wasn't guided equally well by a good ego-stroking.

"That's all very impressive," I said, "but I have to think the Police Directorate has enough common sense to look into your missing persons case before sending a SWAT team up the mountain. Give me the rest of the day, and I'll have a nice trail of online breadcrumbs for you. Articles, a family website asking for help, social media presence for your supposed tourist. We'll want this to look authentic."

"Right," John said. "You can do that?"

I smirked at him. "I convinced you all that a police officer from Friesing named Jemma Moriarty existed, didn't I?"

Next to me, Bash chuckled.

"Fair," Sherlock said. "Fair enough." He looked as though he wasn't sure whether to be impressed or horrified by my professed efficiency. "It would be good to have all our bases covered."

"It sounds like we have a plan, then. You'll find plenty of evidence to place charges once you're in there." Since the cult of the shrouded folk avoided contact with outsiders, I knew from past experience that they didn't take all that much care to hide their activities inside the settlements.

The trio might have been a little unsettled, but as my gaze slid around the table, an air of triumph came over the room. They worked well together—I'd seen that right in front of me many times now—and I worked well with them, didn't I? Putting our minds and our resources together, we were finding a way to unseat the commune so much faster than I could have without them.

The real shame was that we'd only get to do this once, and then we'd be enemies again. I supposed I should enjoy the collaboration while it lasted.

We talked for a while longer, hashing out the details of the missing person story, and then we parted ways. In the elevator, Bash got out his phone. "Should I reach out to Nikolev?"

"Not yet. When I have the materials put together, I'll give you a shout. I don't want him any more involved than he needs to be. In the meantime, I do have a few more things I'd like you to pick up for my next mountain expedition."

He set off to round up the remaining equipment, and I stepped into my room.

The second the door closed behind me, a knife of pain sliced up through my hip and abdomen from my thigh. I staggered, my lungs squeezing tight.

My breath rattled in my throat. My hand, groping along the wall, washed out from the fingers to halfway up my forearm. For a few seconds, even staring at it, I couldn't feel the texture of the plaster beneath my palm.

I closed my eyes, and sensation gradually seeped back through my body. Fuck. I'd had an episode yesterday morning right before I'd left with Bash too. They were coming on more frequently now.

John's question from two days ago came back to me. *Are you going to be okay to see this whole operation through?*

The answer was the same: I had to be.

CHAPTER TWENTY

Sherlock

I opened the door to my hotel room at a knock, expecting to see one of my colleagues. Instead, Jemma stood on the other side, already dressed in cargo pants and a thin tank top as if ready to set off on her mission right now. She placed her hands on her hips.

"Well, are we good to go?"

It took me a moment to recalibrate my reaction. I supposed, in a way—temporarily—this woman *was* one of my colleagues. "You could have simply phoned," I said.

"I wanted to go for a walk anyway." She cocked her head at me. "Should I head back to my hotel and get on my phone if I want an actual answer?"

"No, no, but I'm not sure it's the best subject to be discussing out here in the hall."

I stepped back to let her come in, and my point was proven before she'd even finished entering. John poked his head out of his room next door, clearly having heard her voice.

"Is there news?"

"For you? Not unless Sherlock's been keeping quiet with you too," Jemma called over her shoulder. She sank down on the edge of my bed.

John came over anyway. The last few days, he'd been more attentive of Jemma than he had been even when she'd first charmed him back in London. The change had happened after they'd gone out on that helicopter flight, to be precise. Something must have happened between them then.

I hadn't asked because I suspected it was the sort of thing John would rather keep private. It wasn't as if I could fault him if he'd continued to indulge in her charms, any more than I could deny that I'd gotten more than professional satisfaction out of the recent truce I'd shared with her. All the same, watching his gaze sweep over her body made my skin tighten.

It wasn't so strange that I'd be concerned about him, was it? This woman *had* tricked the three of us into committing a major crime not that long ago. Her current story lined up with the evidence I'd seen with my own eyes, and I hadn't caught any inconsistencies or unusual occurrences to make me question her true situation as I had last time, but she'd proven her wits were as sharp as mine. I couldn't take anything I thought was true for granted.

"We made our arrangements after you sent along your online work," I said. "Garrett went back to speak with one of the police chiefs after lunch to finalize the details of tonight's raid, but they are committed now."

"And very interested in making a heroic showing in my report," John added with a grin.

"All right. That's good." Jemma leaned back on her hands, denting the bedspread I'd pulled flat a few hours ago, but a tension lingered in her shoulders that offset her casual pose and tone. "You'll be able to keep them on a leash until I set off the flare, I assume. That should give me just enough time to take care of my part."

We were bringing two squads of special officers by helicopter to plateaus in the rocky mountainside above the commune's forest location. On that terrain, with the distance we'd have to cover, I expected it'd take us at least twenty minutes to reach the village. The fastest among us, anyway. John had tried to insist that I stay back on account of my ankle, but the sprain was healing quickly. I didn't need the crutch anymore to move around this room.

And I'd be damned if I wasn't there to take responsibility for the mission I'd agreed to orchestrate.

"We've told them we have an associate who's gotten close to the commune to gather evidence, and that you'll signal us when it's the best time to rush in," I said. "I don't think they'll be in any hurry to go charging off into the woods without that confirmation."

"Everything's ready then." She let out a breath and smiled, but the set of her lips looked tense too.

She was still human, after all. In less than twelve hours, she was going up against enemies far more personal to her than to us, enemies who'd already made an attempt at killing her. She'd be going in alone.

I felt reasonably certain I'd survive the night. Jemma might not have the same expectation.

"I know I've said this before," I said, "but are you sure you shouldn't have some sort of backup with you? Can't that Moran fellow follow your lead?" What was she going to do if the entire commune converged on her with assorted weaponry?

"Bash will be waiting to help me get back off the mountain," Jemma said. "Believe me, if I could have him covering me, I would."

I still didn't understand her insistence on going solo, but I'd decided by now there wasn't any benefit in arguing about it. "Well, if there's any additional equipment you think would help your efforts that your own connections haven't been able to provide…"

Amusement glittered in her gray eyes. "Are you worried about me, Mr. Holmes?"

For some reason, her use of my last name sparked a flicker of heat inside me. Perhaps because the only other time she'd used it recently, in the same teasing tone, we'd been talking about propositions.

"Not so much worried as aware of the magnitude of the danger you're insisting on throwing yourself into," I hedged.

A smile curved her lips. She pushed herself off the bed and sauntered up to me where I'd stayed standing not far from the door. Close enough that her coolly sweet scent, like violets blooming by moonlight, reached my nose.

"I'm flattered that I'm worthy of your concern," she said. Then she bobbed up to brush a kiss to my lips, so soft it reminded me of the peck she'd given me right before she took off on us in London. As if she were saying good-bye with it.

The thought made something clench in my chest. She touched my neck to lean into the kiss, letting it linger on longer than that past one. Despite the hunger that stirred in me, my nerves twitched with the awareness that John was standing just a few feet away.

I pulled back. "Perhaps this isn't the time."

Jemma glanced from me to John, who was standing by the narrow desk with his face set in an uncertain expression, and returned her gaze to me with a laugh.

"Do you think John minds? He probably likes watching, and he's welcome to join in if he wants. He'd like to be kissing you too, you know—and everything else from that to fucking."

"Er," John said, his cheeks flushing.

My spine had gone rigid, my thoughts scattering. I managed to say, "Perhaps we should leave behind this subject entirely."

Jemma rolled her eyes. "My God, you are hopeless. You do remember what happened in London, don't you? You recall that you have kissed him before? I'm assuming you haven't really completely erased that moment from your mind."

I'd buried it very, very deep. Even the brief flicker of memory that rose in the back of my head—the firm pressure of his mouth, not at all like Jemma and somehow provoking a reaction so similar—tipped my sense of balance. Suddenly I wished I hadn't left my crutch leaning against the headboard.

"I remember," I said, looking only at her.

She raised her chin impertinently. "Then you might as well put him out of his misery already. Did you run away because it was so horrifyingly unpleasant?"

Heat started to collect around my collar. I didn't know what to make of what I'd felt during that kiss; I didn't want to talk about it at all. It had been so much easier not having to think about it, setting it aside as irrelevant data. A momentary whim spurred on by Jemma's coaxing… Nothing worth shaking the foundations of our partnership —our *friendship*—over.

John was the only bloody friend I'd ever had, if I was being honest. The only person in my life who'd observed my peculiarities and wanted to immerse himself in them rather than backing away. He'd seemed happy enough to set the incident aside too.

He wasn't arguing with her assessment of the situation, though. I might not be ready to meet his eyes, but I could feel him standing there, waiting on my answer as much as she was.

We could end this conversation right now if I said yes, but I wasn't going to tell a lie that might wound him.

"No," I said. "It was not horrifyingly unpleasant."

"How would you describe it, then?" Jemma asked.

I shifted my weight. Standing here still favoring my ankle in its brace was starting to strain my other leg. "I'm going to sit down," I said.

She swept her arm toward the spot on the bed she'd vacated. "Be my guest, as long as you answer the question too."

I settled myself on the covers and braced my hands against the edge of the bed. "I'm not sure how to describe it, because there was rather a lot going on around that moment, and it's difficult to pick apart what—and who—caused which sensations."

"But there wasn't any part of it you found off-putting."

"No," I admitted, and then I finally found the wherewithal to look at John again.

His flush had faded, but his eyes held a slightly feverish light. "It wasn't at all off-putting to me either."

"Wow. Such enthusiastic declarations." Jemma shook her head, her ruddy waves skipping over her shoulders. She paused to consider us both in turn. "I don't suppose you'd like to try it again and see if we can come up with words beyond 'not off-putting'?"

John shifted forward and hesitated. My shoulders tensed.

Jemma sighed. "We can start with this then." She glanced toward John. "Would you like *me* to kiss him?"

Half a smile curled his lips. "Absolutely."

I might have protested that surely I should have some say in the matter, but Jemma had already cupped my jaw and leaned down to make good on that offer. The conversation we'd just had seemed to have stripped my nerves bare. The simple touch of her mouth sent my whole body tingling, in part because of John's gaze on us.

"We'll want to be clear-headed for tonight, don't you

think?" Jemma murmured, her lips still grazing mine. "Are you game?"

My head certainly didn't feel at all clear right now. My cock was already starting to rise. The urge for release twisted through me.

It was a diversion. A way to pass the time somewhat productively while we waited to see our plan through. I could focus on that and not whatever else this might be.

"What did you have in mind?" I asked.

"This is a good start." She looked John's way again. "Feel free to join us whenever the mood strikes you."

She reclaimed my mouth, and this time I met her with equal ardor. I raised my hand to trace my fingers over her scalp, tangling them in her hair. She trailed her thumb along the sensitive path down the side of my neck that she'd gotten such delight out of stimulating. A quiver of pleasure raced over my skin in the wake of her touch.

John had come up behind her. He set his hands on her waist, watching us, and then kissed her spine where the neckline of her tank top dipped low. At her eager sound, he slid his hands higher under the thin fabric.

Jemma's mouth caught mine with a hum and a nip of teeth. My fingers tightened in her hair. We were all one being generating pleasure together, and it felt perfectly natural.

I reached for her breast, wanting to tweak her nipple the way she'd responded so eagerly to during our truce, and my fingers brushed John's. We jerked apart.

Jemma kissed me harder, and the awkwardness melted away. He shifted his attentions to snapping open the back of her bra. I slid my hand under one cup to caress the soft mound that could provoke such thrilling reactions.

Jemma swayed with our attentions. I squeezed her nipple, and she growled against my lips. That sound and the feel of her was enough to harden my cock completely. The crotch of my pants had become uncomfortably tight.

With a pleased sigh, Jemma pulled back and motioned me farther up the bed. She followed, prowling after me with a passionate fierceness I had to admit made me even harder. As she knelt beside me, she ran her hands over my chest. In a few seconds, she'd loosened my trousers.

"A little help?" she said to John, who was still standing by the end of the bed. My mouth went dry as he tugged the pants the rest of the way off.

Then Jemma was bending over me to ease her lips over my cock, and I didn't have the capacity to feel anything but ecstatic. The hot slickness of her mouth and the swirl of her tongue sparked to life places in me I hadn't known existed.

A curse tumbled from my lips. She smiled around me and licked me from base to tip with a force that echoed bliss through every inch of my body.

John came around the bed to stroke Jemma's back and chest again. She practically purred, her breath spilling over my groin in the most exhilarating way. When she eased up, her tongue flicking around the head of my cock, my body screamed for her to take me back down again.

"You could feel even better than this," she said to me with a teasing lilt. "I've gotten to enjoy the benefit of two mouths, two sets of hands. Wouldn't you like to discover that experience, Sherlock?"

My gaze jumped to John's face. He met my eyes, his expression hesitant but… hopeful?

The longing I read in his eyes made my own hesitation seem ridiculous. What was there really to be afraid of here? I was master over my emotions, not the other way around. Why shouldn't I accept what he so clearly wanted to offer and see where it would bring us?

I extended my hand tentatively. If I'd had any doubts about how eager John was, they'd have been erased by the way he beamed in response. He shifted onto the bed, searching my face. My heart thumped faster, but I tipped my head toward him. He bent down and let his mouth come to rest on mine.

Oh, it was good. Awkward but somehow just right, his lips carefully adjusting against mine until my head twitched upward to solidify the kiss, the fervent tremor of his breath in response. His fingers traced along my jaw.

Jemma bowed over me, and my nerves flooded with sensation like a candle burning at both ends. My hips arched up at the swivel of her tongue. My mouth collided with John's again. The pulsing build of my release swelled at the base of my cock.

At the rasp of a zipper, my eyelids fluttered open. Jemma had yanked down the fly of John's khakis. While she teased one hand over my balls, she dipped the other into that opening to grip his erection.

He groaned against my lips, and they parted as if to accept the sound. Our mouths melded together even more avidly than before. It felt *too* good, between him and her —overwhelmingly so. I turned my head to break the kiss, my breath ragged.

Jemma sucked me hard, and I let out a groan of my own. She released me with a rough gasp.

"My turn again. John, my purse—condom."

When he glanced at me as if worried he'd misstepped, I nodded to say we were all right, as coherently as I was able to. Without another second's hesitation, he fumbled for her purse.

I'd seen other men naked before—at the gym, in the sauna—and John was still mostly clothed, but I'd never seen an erect cock other than my own. I couldn't help watching as he unrolled the condom over his rigid length. Then he was yanking Jemma's pants and panties down and tucking his hand between her legs in a way that made her lips squeeze around my own cock. My vision hazed with pleasure.

John closed his eyes as he thrust into her. He pumped in and out with a shaky exhalation, and Jemma rocked with him. The motion rippled into me with the rhythm of her sucking and the swipe of her tongue, as if he were fucking me through her as well.

My balls contracted. I came with a blaze of bliss that seared through all the scattered emotions I'd been grappling with, every bit of concern I might have had about the mission ahead of us. Burning me clean so my thoughts could regather in better order. It was the best kind of high I'd ever felt. Jemma hadn't lied when she'd promised me that all those weeks ago.

She licked me clean as I softened in her mouth and then ducked her head against my thigh with a moan provoked by John's thrusts.

"Fuck," John said hoarsely.

"So close," Jemma muttered, her fingers curling into the bedspread like they had when I'd worked her over last week. A fresh flare of desire shot through me. I could make her release as dazzling as mine had been.

I turned on the bed as swiftly as I could and pulled her into a kiss, ignoring the salty musky flavor that must be mine on her lips. My other hand traveled to fondle her breast exactly the way that had made her moan before. A cry broke from her throat as my thumb swept over the peak. Her lips mashed into mine with the trembling of her own climax.

John's breath hitched, and he bowed over her with a shudder.

Jemma sagged onto the bed, and John sank down so we formed a sort of triangle between us, a careless assortment of limbs. As my breath evened out, my gaze lingered on my friend's face, the fall of his light hair around it, the broad brow and the soft cheekbones I'd seen thousands of times without really paying attention to them. The mouth that had met mine so eagerly.

His gaze lifted and found mine. My throat closed for a second. Then I said, "Come here?"

He eased up on one elbow. "What is it?" His earlier tentativeness had returned.

I licked my lips. His eyes tracked the movement. Fresh heat quivered through me, but I needed to know for sure.

"I'd like to kiss you once with no other variables involved," I said. "To see… to see what it is when it's only us."

Something shifted in his expression. As he swiveled around to face me properly, Jemma eased back, watching us. John definitely looked nervous again. My own body tensed now that the rush of passion had faded.

"You don't have to if—"

"It's all right," he said. "I want to."

He brought his lips to mine like that first gentle kiss. The quiver of heat turned into a wave. I kissed him back, reveling in the unexpected sensation, until we eased apart again.

"Well," I said, "that was definitely not off-putting at all."

Jemma let out a guffaw and sat up, swatting my back. "Hopeless," she said. "Totally hopeless." But she was grinning with an air that I'd have called joy, as if seeing John and I unearth this new possible realm of our partnership gave her genuine satisfaction.

She'd led us to this discovery. Shoved me would really be more accurate. Just for the selfless enjoyment of watching us find our way there.

This woman was a puzzle. A thief. A murderer, if only of other criminals—as far as we knew. The most gifted liar I'd ever met. Yet beyond my fascination with her brilliance, perhaps I was coming to simply *like* her too, for reasons I couldn't argue away.

And tonight, we might lose her.

CHAPTER TWENTY-ONE

Jemma

Technically, the caves weren't any darker at night than they had been when I'd explored them the other afternoon. No sunlight penetrated solid stone either way. They *felt* darker, though—the shadows around the beam of my headlamp denser, the chill in the dry air thicker—as I picked my way toward my destination.

My load definitely weighed heavier on my back. I had to brace my hands against the rough stone walls to keep my balance with the pack Bash had loaded up for me. The sugar cube I'd popped into my mouth at the entrance had long since dissolved, leaving my mouth faintly sticky. I wasn't even halfway to the top yet, and my back was already damp with sweat.

The trio and their band of police should be waiting higher up on the mountain by now. What would they be talking about to pass the time? I distracted myself from the strain of the climb by thinking back to Sherlock and John's fumbling negotiations after our interlude in Sherlock's hotel room.

Just to be clear, I'm not looking to make some big romantic thing out of this, John had said as he'd straightened out his clothes. *It just might be nice to, er, kiss or whatever else fits the occasion, when the right moment comes up.*

Sherlock had managed to look lofty even while he was tucking himself back into his pants. *That sounds like a reasonable proposition.*

I had to smile at the memory. They really were ridiculous. It was a good thing they'd found each other in their roundabout way. I could even take a little pride in having given them a kick on the ass to help them get there.

When I reached the first pit trap, I had to toss my pack over the thin slab of stone before I hurled myself. After I'd heaved the bag back over my shoulders, I had just a brief climb to reach the small gap in the ceiling I'd noted before.

That spot was definitely darker than last time, the hole barely discernible against the dimpled rock even with my headlamp pointing at it.

I pulled the four flare guns out of the pack. The first one was to get the commune's attention. The others were to convince them something major was going on that they'd better investigate—and a backup in case one or another hit a tree branch on the way up.

Positioning myself beneath the gap, I angled my arms so the flare should shoot out at a slight angle and burst even closer to the commune. They had to feel the potential threat was nearby to guarantee that some of them would leave to investigate.

I squeezed the trigger, and the first shot crackled through the air. My ears rang, but I listened as closely as I could. A sound like a thunderclap and a distant blaze of light penetrated the cave through the gap. Grinning, I reached for the next gun.

The second one blasted off without a hitch. With the third, I must have shifted my angle by accident, because all I heard was the thunk of it hitting something above. I adjusted my position again, and the fourth one sparked another stream of light high above.

I tossed the used guns aside. It didn't matter if the commune found them now. Either I'd be long gone with the dagger by the time anyone from the cult had a chance to search around here, or I'd be dead. Simple as that.

The flares were also the signal for the police to start down the mountain toward the commune. I had to make sure I got there first. I scrambled on up through the narrowing passages.

My arms strained to pull me up the particularly steep section. I gritted my teeth and shoved myself onward. A strand of my hair got caught in a jagged bit of rock and yanked out from the roots, leaving me wincing. I rubbed the stinging spot as I hustled along.

The beam of my headlamp bounced over the uneven

walls and ceiling in a way that looked much more eerie than before. I pushed myself faster.

There. My gaze caught on the outline of the wide opening and the boulder sealing it where the cave narrowed to nearly a tunnel up ahead.

I hadn't forgotten my close call the other day. I treaded carefully along the edge of the still partly hidden chasm and stepped gingerly over the tripwire—and another tripwire a few feet after that.

The area right beneath the entrance looked clear. Dragging in a breath, I reached into the pack and took out the rectangular thing Bash had called a "minor explosive." With a wiggle of my hand, I wedged it as far into a crevice between the boulder and the opening as I could. Then I lit the fuse and darted back the way I'd come, shutting off my headlamp.

Even several feet away, I crouched down to shield my body in case the explosive did more than propel the boulder off its seat as Bash had said it would. *This little thing shouldn't do more than crack the ceiling a bit*, he'd told me, but explosives in caves seemed like exactly the right moment for a little extra caution.

The flame hissed up the fuse. Then the explosive blasted apart with a wallop of sound. The rock around me trembled—and the boulder flew off its resting place.

My heart skipped a beat. I leapt forward, covering both trip wires at once, listening for sounds of approach. The whole commune wouldn't have gone down the mountain to check out the flares, and whoever was left here wouldn't ignore a noise like that.

Peeking out through the opening, I found nothing but trees looming all around. The caves must open up beyond the edge of the actual settlement. A few shouts were carrying from somewhere to my right.

With my pulse pounding through my chest and limbs, I hauled myself out through the opening and ducked behind a tree. My hands wrenched the pack open. I grabbed the grenades stashed near the bottom, flicked the pins, and hurled them off into the forest. With the first fiery *boom*, I dashed in the opposite direction through the trees.

Footsteps hammered across the ground and veered to the side to track the impact of the grenades.

"What the hell was *that*?"

"We'll check it out. Shine the lights down there. And keep your guns ready."

I slunk away as they headed deeper into the forest. With a little luck, my gambit would stop them from even noticing the open cave until I'd gotten out of here.

Some of the cultists would be investigating the flares. I'd drawn a few more away with the grenades. Now I just needed to tackle however many had stayed behind to guard their great prize.

I took out my own gun, a light pistol Bash had picked up for me years ago, and kept it raised as I eased toward sparser woods up ahead. More moonlight streaked through the forest there.

The outline of a wooden hut came into view, the roof draped with fresh branches to blend it in with the canopy. Others lay beyond it, scattered haphazardly between the trees. Any sort of pattern to a layout made the shrouded folk uneasy. They liked randomness, wildness, like the flaring of a fire, like the searing of the sun they fed off.

A couple of figures moved between the buildings. I froze, watching them as they peered after the departed cultists. They murmured to each other in voices too low for me to make out.

I peered into the space beyond them. Where would they keep the dagger? Definitely toward the middle of the settlement, so it was protected on all sides. And no doubt they had a few people standing guard right by it at any given time. I wasn't making it to my prize through stealth alone.

Stealth could take me pretty far, though. I slipped behind one of the huts and eased around the back. The scent of the shrouded folk, dry and sour like long-rotted meat, wafted over me.

My stomach turned. I'd gotten several weeks without having to taste that stench since I'd left Bog behind. Now it seemed to pool in my lungs, congealing into bile.

The people around me didn't even notice the stink anymore. When you grew up in it or gave yourself over to it for years on end, it was the fresh air beyond the boundaries of the commune that tasted off. It'd taken me months to totally adapt to the regular scents of human life after I'd escaped my parents' settlement in New Mexico.

I darted from one hut to another. Someone on the other side of those walls was humming to themselves in an erratic rhythm that told me they were probably swaying with periodic jerks in a reverence meditation. Even though I'd fallen into that trace nearly every day until I was fourteen, even though I'd *wanted* to align my soul more closely with the shrouded folk, it'd always unnerved me watching other people at it.

I'd navigated about half of the perimeter before I felt certain of the village's layout. Seventeen huts stood sporadically throughout a rough circle about a quarter of a mile across. One just off-center had even more branches heaped on top of it than the others, and now and then the moonlight caught on random dents and slashes on the walls where they'd been carved in deference to the shrouded folk. The dagger had to be in there.

The doorway was so narrow I'd barely fit without turning sideways, hung with a burlap curtain. Three cultists in brown robes stood just outside it. I had to go through them.

I didn't have much time left. I eased closer, grimacing at the sight of their faces, which were smeared with dark smudges of blood. Possibly their own, possibly that of another person or an animal—one way or another, obtained through pain. The shrouded folk liked that kind of burning too. *By hurting, you make holy*, one of the elders in my settlement used to say.

I guessed they were going to be particularly holy after tonight.

With my fingers tight around the pistol, I braced myself. Then I dashed across the last short distance to fling myself at the guards.

My knee caught the nearest one in the gut before he had a chance to react. He doubled over, and I fired a bullet into the side of his head.

The woman next to him whipped around with a submachine gun. Adrenaline spiked through my veins. I slammed my elbow into her wrist and dispatched her with a shot to the forehead.

As she slumped, I caught her just in time to make her a living shield. The third guard fired a couple shots. I shoved her backward into him and blasted the back of his head off as he stumbled. Before he even hit the ground, I was hurtling through the doorway.

The stink of the shrouded folk hung so thickly in the air inside that I could almost feel its texture, like shreds of dry flesh. The room was empty other than a wooden altar just off-center. The dagger, curved and gleaming silver with pure gold strands randomly crisscrossing its hilt, lay on a pool of white velvet in a bowl of carved moonstone.

Yes. I snatched it up and threw myself back out of the hut, jamming the dagger into the belted pouch at my waist as I went.

The curved metal shape bumped against my belly—and a spear of pain rammed through my chest from the protective cuff around my thigh. The sensation in the lower part of that leg and my forearms numbed. I staggered, falling to my hands and knees on the well-trodden forest floor. A choked croak escaped my lips as I fought to draw breath.

Fuck. I had to get out of here. Figures were racing

through the trees, brought by the gunshots from just a few seconds ago. I heaved forward, swaying back onto my feet.

With my strained attempt at inhaling, only a trickle of air reached my lungs. The worst of the pain was easing back like it always had before, but the numbness was holding on, seeping deeper with a chill I couldn't shake.

A woman charged at me with a knife. I yanked my gun hand up, much slower than it should have moved. Her blade raked through my oversuit and my bicep all the way to the bone before I managed to squeeze the trigger.

Blood soaked down my sleeve with an even sharper pain. My right foot still couldn't quite find purchase on the ground, prickling tingles racing through it. My head was spinning with the lack of oxygen.

I lurched across the village toward the shelter of the thicker forest. Toward Bash waiting for me at the base of the mountain.

I had the dagger. I had my permanent escape, my chance to turn this all around against the shrouded folk and watch *them* burn. No fucking way was I failing this close to my goal.

A shot rang out just as I ducked farther forward. It clipped my shoulder deep enough to make my flesh flare with agony. I gritted my teeth and stumbled onward.

Then a sound I'd never thought I'd welcome rang out from behind me: a voice speaking strident Croatian, raised to a bellow by a megaphone.

"Down on the ground and stay where you are, by the order of the police!"

The beam of a searchlight swept the village grounds. I

was already staggering past the last of the huts into the dense forest that would lead me down to safety.

I made it ten more steps before my half-numbed foot snagged on a root I hadn't seen. I pitched forward into the darkness.

CHAPTER TWENTY-TWO

Jemma

Lights came and went farther up the slope. Voices echoed. Something crashed to the ground. One shot split the air, but I didn't hear any gunfire after that.

The members of the shrouded folk's cult were obsessed, but they'd know when they were outnumbered. When they'd seen the number of police coming at them, their first priority would have been to destroy as much evidence of their activities as they could. I had faith that my trio would ferret out enough to put the cultists they rounded up away for one crime or another even if the police weren't as adept.

I had less faith in my ability to make it down the mountain to Bash. I'd been counting on having two working legs and also two functioning lungs. After my fall, which I believed had left me with many bruises but nothing worse, I'd managed to scoot into a dip sheltered by shrubs to try to recover.

What felt like at least an hour later, my chest still strained to drag in even half a breath. My right leg prickled with rising and ebbing waves of numbness. Despite the strips of cloth I'd torn from my oversuit's sleeves to wrap around my wounds, my head was only getting dizzier from lack of blood.

The gold cuff around my thigh set off periodic jabs of pain. The damned thing that was supposed to be protecting me had fucked me over even worse tonight. I had to assume it was reacting badly to the shrouded dagger, but I couldn't exactly leave that behind.

I couldn't call Bash to come collect me either. My phone had been in the pouch with the dagger, and the fall had crushed the screen against the metal blade.

My best option seemed to be staying huddled there like a wounded deer and hoping the cuff would cut me a break sometime soon. Going down the slope wasn't going to take as much energy as coming up had, but I did need to be able to count on both my legs staying in this realm of existence.

The sharp spruce-like scent of the shrubs tickled my nose. I teased my lower lip under my teeth, wishing I had another sugar cube.

A crunch of footsteps in the brush reached my ears, much closer than any had come before.

I stiffened in the moment before a familiar voice called out, low but loud enough to carry. "Jemma?"

It was Sherlock, a fact confirmed by the shuffling gait

with which he continued to move toward me, back on his crutch under duress but refusing to let that slow him down. A couple other figures moved through the forest with him. I could guess well enough who they were.

I stayed tensed for a few seconds, my heart thudding, debating my options. I'd wanted to be well on my journey away from the London trio by now. I'd expected the interlude in Sherlock's hotel room would be our last hurrah. But he'd clearly picked up on some clue that had suggested to him I needed help, and, frankly, I wanted to get off this fucking mountain. Keeping the rest of my blood in my body would also be nice.

They'd helped me get this far. I could rely on them a tiny bit farther.

Sherlock was only a few feet away now, pausing to crouch down by the ground with a flashlight. I eased myself upright.

"I'm here."

The beam flashed across my face and hit on my shoulder. Someone—I thought Garrett—sucked in a breath. Then John was pushing forward, one hand tight around his walking stick, the other groping into the messenger bag he was carrying.

Sherlock kept his flashlight trained on me as John produced antiseptic ointment and a roll of gauze.

"Well, you didn't do that bad a job bandaging yourself up for someone bleeding out and one-armed," the doctor muttered, packing and binding my wounds with professional efficiency. "Are you hurt anywhere else?"

He could probably tell those injuries weren't enough to

have kept me so close to the village. I caught his eyes. "I fell. Hurt my leg. It's not bleeding or broken, I don't think, just hard to walk on."

From the brief tightening on his face, I could tell he'd followed my hint. He knew what kind of trouble I'd had with my leg before.

"I guess we can thank you for thinning the herd up there before we showed up?" Garrett said, in a tone that suggested he wasn't sure whether to be impressed or horrified by the short work I'd made of however many cultists I'd dispatched. Four? Five?

He grimaced. "Bunch of sick lunatics. I can't believe some of the things they had stashed away."

Good. They'd gotten what they'd come for, then. I glanced at Sherlock, little more than a tall lanky silhouette behind the glow of the flashlight. "How did you know I was here? I'd have thought you had better things to do than track that bracelet."

"I did." He lowered the light enough for me to make out the curl of his lips into a wry smile. "But one distinctive red hair snagged on a twig, an unusual scuffing in the dirt, and a bit of blood told the story well enough."

"Good thing," John said. With his help, I pushed myself onto my feet. The right one met the ground with a sensation as if it was sifting through sand. That wasn't promising at all.

"We could bring you up back to the choppers," Garrett said.

My chest twisted even tighter. I shook my head. "No. Bash is waiting for me. He'll already be worried." I could have asked for one of their phones to relieve a few of those worries, but I didn't want to give them his number. Who knew what information Sherlock could turn up from that.

Besides, the thought of squeezing into a vehicle full of cops and members of the cult I'd spent the last ten years fighting made my skin itch.

John looked to Sherlock. "We could help her make the walk down. It's not that much farther than we came before."

"By daylight," Garrett muttered.

"We wouldn't *all* have to make the trip," Sherlock said, in a tone that placed immediate judgment on anyone unwilling to.

Garrett's jaw clenched. "We're in this together, aren't we? I'll tell the squad leader that we need to meet up with our operative. It'll fit the story we gave them well enough."

He set off toward the village. Sherlock maneuvered down over the rocky ground with swings of his crutch.

I eyed him skeptically. "Are you sure *you* shouldn't be going back for that helicopter ride?"

"I made it this far," Sherlock said. "Between the four of us, we have five good legs. That seems like plenty."

If a fresh burst of pain hadn't flared around my cuff, I would have laughed. As it was, I had to grit my teeth to keep from gasping. My fingers tightened where I was gripping John's elbow. He looked at me in concern.

"I'll be fine," I said. "I just want to get away from this place."

"You found what you needed?" he asked.

"My mission was successful."

Garrett returned a moment later with a flashlight of his own. "All right," he said. "Let's see if we can make it to the bottom without any more injuries."

It was an awkward, rambling descent, veering back and forth as we followed the most even patches of ground. Insects hummed in the brush, and twigs crackled under our feet. My discomfort clung on, but with each step away from the commune, it eased a fraction more. It hadn't been just the dagger but that whole place setting the cuff's effects into overdrive.

John chuckled to himself and glanced at the other men. "Doesn't this remind you of that case where we spent the whole night wandering around the hilly part of Greenwich Park checking the angles of a bike light around the trees?"

"Lord, don't remind me," Garrett said. "At least tonight we know we accomplished something. I swear Sherlock had that case figured out three days before he let the rest of us in on it—he just likes ordering us around."

"We *did* narrow down the suspects with the information we gleaned with that activity," Sherlock reminded them. "It was a lovely night—rather refreshing, as I recall it."

John outright laughed at that, and a moment later Garrett joined in. Sherlock glowered at them, but he couldn't completely suppress a smile.

Their easy comradery flowed around me with a different sort of warmth than I was usually looking to spark. The kind of warmth that made me want to toss in a clever remark of my own, to become a part of that connection.

A pang spread through my chest. I set my jaw against it. It didn't matter if I liked these men. No, that was all the more reason I had to move on. They could accept me for the moment while we had the same goals, but in the long run? Ha. I'd find myself in handcuffs again.

They'd just have to find new ways to entertain themselves without me.

When we finally emerged from the trees near the pull-off where Bash was waiting, he strode to meet us with a ferocity in his eyes I wouldn't have wanted to be at the wrong end of.

"What happened?" he demanded.

"I had an unfortunate encounter with a knife and then a bullet," I said in the most carefree voice I could summon. "My doctor friend patched them up very nicely, though."

Bash studied me. He could probably tell I was suffering more than just that. The long clamber down had left me exhausted on top of everything else. All I wanted to do was fall into the seat of the van and shut my eyes.

"We should get you to the hospital," John said.

I waved him off. "It's nothing a little rest can't cure." And whatever doctors my upcoming travels could provide.

"Jemma," Garrett started.

I fixed him with a firm look. "I know myself better than anyone does. Besides, you've got this big case to assist with now. There are worse things in this world than me."

"That wasn't—"

"Maybe they're right," Bash said, to my surprise. "We still have a few loose ends to tie up. Why don't we see if they can contribute?"

I raised an eyebrow at him. We'd arrived here separately in the van and the car so we'd have two vehicles in case things turned dire, but the plan had been to hop in the van and floor it to the airport the second I showed up. Granted, I had meant to show up a couple hours earlier. That shouldn't change things all that much.

Did he think I wasn't fit to fly? I took a couple steps, if wobbly ones, on my own and moved my arm while restraining a wince. "What's there to contribute to? I'm good. I bounce back fast. Give me my hotel bed, and I'll have all I need."

He gazed back at me steadily. "It seems like you've run into more complications than you expected."

When had I ever not wriggled my way back out of a situation like that? I tapped his chest. "Into the van with you." I turned to the trio and fished the car's keys out of my pocket. "Since I took you away from your chopper, why don't the three of you drive my car back? If there's anything else you think we absolutely *have* to talk about tonight, you can meet us in the lobby. I'll give you ten minutes. You can even have a head start."

My blasé attitude must have been convincing enough. I tossed the keys to John, who snatched them out of the air with a smile. "Don't burn any rubber," I warned him.

"There are a few matters I would like to discuss, if not tonight then in the morning," Sherlock said, but when I nodded, he moved with the others to the car.

I hopped into the van next to Bash. "Let them go first," I said. "I did promise them their head start."

"What are you up to, Mori?"

I watched as the car's headlights blinked on, swept across the dirt road, and pulled ahead of us on their way back to the city. The pang came back, digging deeper. I shook it away.

"As soon as we're close enough to the city, lose them and get us to the airport. We're still flying out tonight."

Bash

It wasn't hard to lose the Londoners. I let the van drift several car lengths back as if by chance so we weren't directly in their rearview mirror. Then, when they turned off the highway into the city, we roared on by.

Jemma had borrowed my phone to check flight times. The electronic light reflected off her face, which was a sicklier shade of pale than I'd seen it any time except that one panicked night in London and the night six years ago when she'd gone to rescue her sister and failed. She didn't look up, but the corner of her mouth tightened as we left the three behind. She was paying attention, even if she didn't want to show it.

"Swing around to head back south as soon as you can," she said. "They'll expect us to head for the local airport or to Zagreb. We're going to Dubrovnik instead. We should get there right in time for the first morning flights. This exit up here should let you loop around fast."

She set down the phone for long enough to saw through the silver tracking bracelet Sherlock had fastened around her wrist. As soon as she'd snapped it free, she tossed it and the little hand-saw out the window. They crunched under the tires of a car the next lane over.

I swerved around at the exit she'd indicated, watching her in moments between watching the road.

It wasn't just her paleness that worried me. Now and then her hand trembled where she'd picked up the phone again. The set of her jaw told me she wasn't just focused but mastering the pain that must still be wracking her shoulder and arm. The pungent scent of the antiseptic Watson had applied tainted the air along with a metallic hint of blood. We had Vicodin in the van, but she'd refused it, saying she wanted her mind sharp.

I was pretty sure she was suffering from more than just the obvious wounds too. It took a lot to shake Jemma Moriarty's composure this clearly. Her confrontation with the cult had hurt her in other ways too, ways I couldn't entirely understand.

Ways I didn't think even she had been prepared for. Would she have made it down the mountain at all if Sherlock hadn't found her? The question sent an uneasy jab through my chest. I'd have gone looking for her eventually, orders be damned, but I couldn't say for sure I'd have found her in time.

"Where are we flying into?" I asked.

"I'll take the earliest one—that'll get me to Dusseldorf.

There's one a little later into Istanbul that we'll put you on. From there, I think our easiest meet-up point will be Paris. Maybe we'll take a day or two there before we embark on our ocean crossing."

"You said we're going to Chile?"

She nodded. "That's the end point. But I'm thinking word will spread about our adventure tonight, and my monsters might figure out what I'm planning. There's going to be a solar eclipse over part of Chile next week—that's what I need to get there for. It's probably better if we don't arrive until just before I can use it."

Lowering the phone into her lap, she closed her eyes. It was just past four in the morning, and she looked as if she needed a few days' worth of sleep. Maybe she could catch a couple hours during the drive to the airport.

Five minutes later, her whole body tensed with a breath sucked through her teeth. I winced, my hands clenching around the steering wheel.

"Mori?"

"It's okay," she said in an unnaturally hollow voice. "It's getting better now that the fucking dagger is stashed in the back."

In the entire seven years I'd worked for and alongside Jemma, I'd never once doubted that she could pull off whatever scheme she set her mind to—not even in those sick-with-anguish moments in the past. Those, she'd barreled through with her usual force of will. Right now, looking at her, hearing her, the suspicion niggled at me that something tonight had attacked her right down to her strength of will.

Whatever she had to do in Chile, it was even more important than this mission tonight had been. She'd just told me she expected the monsters she was battling to track her there. Tonight they hadn't been ready for her. How much worse was the fight going to be when they were?

If she'd been one of my early clients, this would have been the moment where I'd have backed out. A client wavering on the edge put everyone around them at risk. I wasn't in this for thrills. I had no interest in gambling with my life just for a little extra money.

But I hadn't been in this for the money for a long time. The idea of abandoning Jemma didn't even feel like an *idea*, just a concept as bizarre as turning my gun collection into an art installation or running away to join the goddamn circus.

I'd meant it every time I told her I'd have her back through anything. But I'd been saying that to the Jemma I knew, the Jemma who always came out on top. I still meant it now, though, didn't I? Even if she faltered, even if she stumbled right into some monster's maw, I'd be right there with her.

I cared about this woman too fucking much, and I didn't even mind.

I cared about her enough that I couldn't help saying, even though she'd shot down my earlier hints, "Your London friends did end up coming in handy. Are you sure we couldn't put them to some good use overseas?"

Jemma snorted softly. "You should be glad we're rid of them," she teased. "No more competition." Her eyes turned more serious as she contemplated the landscape beyond the window. Dark waves undulated across the moonlit ocean at our right. "Anyway, they're more hassle than they're worth. They might make more of a mess rather than less of one. We can handle this just the two of us."

Did she completely believe that, or was she trying to convince herself as well as me? For just a second, before she rubbed her hand over her face and closed her eyes again, I'd have sworn she looked sad.

"They seemed to handle the mess tonight just fine," I said, because apparently I didn't know when to quit.

Jemma opened her eyes to shoot me a narrow look. "What is it with you right now? You don't even like them."

But you do. And maybe what she'd said about me wasn't entirely true. All three of them could be jackasses in their assorted ways, Sherlock especially, and I wasn't absolving them of dragging her off at gunpoint any time soon, but I'd seen the way they responded to her during our planning. It was hard to completely hate anyone who'd give this woman all the respect she was due, even if they gave it somewhat begrudgingly.

"I know how important this last operation is," I said instead. "Anything that could swing the situation more in our favor sounds good to me. We've gotten a lot of mileage out of them so far."

Jemma smirked for a moment before that good humor faded. "We did. But convincing them to travel halfway across the world and battle monsters is a very different thing. I'm not going to count on that kind of commitment."

Maybe she should, though—or at least give it a shot. If they didn't turn up, we weren't any worse off than otherwise. After everything I'd seen, I couldn't believe she really thought they'd screw things up more than they'd contribute, unwittingly or not.

I drove in silence for a while, mulling that over, trying to find the right words to frame around the growing knot of uneasiness in my chest. Finally, I said, "I've never told you about my father."

"Not enough that I know more than that he was an asshole," Jemma said.

"That would be phrasing it mildly. He put on a good front—had a nice white-collar job, sniveled to his bosses like a loyal lackey—but he hated being ordered around. He got back at them by skimming profits out from under them, and he took out the rest of his frustration by pushing us around—me and my brother and sister, and sometimes my mom too if she tried to stop him."

Those memories didn't bring up any emotion now other than a dull resignation. That was what normal had looked like for the first sixteen years of my existence: cutting insults and barked criticisms, a shove, a smack. And I didn't see any need to think back on the even darker moments when his frustration had tipped over into fury.

Jemma's full attention was on me now. "Well, he sounds like a prime candidate for getting a bullet in the brain."

I had to laugh, without much humor. "That's what I

thought. I got the younger ones out of there to our grandparents when I could, and then I conned my way into army training early. The whole time I was out there in the field, I knew I was coming back for him. It was the only thing I was sure of."

"Then he got what he deserved."

"I think so, but not exactly like that." I paused. "When I went back for him, I hadn't been in touch for years. It turned out my mom had finally kicked him out of the house. He'd gotten caught at his job, fired and blacklisted. He was working at some shitty diner serving coffee and going home alone to a dingy roach-infested apartment. He couldn't have been more miserable. I watched him for a while, and all I could think was, why would I want to put him *out* of his misery? He earned that. Let him stew in it. So, I left with the bullet still in my gun."

Jemma smiled. "My earlier comment still stands, then."

"It does," I agreed. "My point is—I've only spared someone's life once, and that was to leave him worse off than if I'd killed him. I've *never* seen you back down from a necessary hit. But you trusted those three enough that you decided you were better off with them still living, even after what they did to you, even with them being on the other side of the law. It's up to you what we do about them now. I won't bring it up again. I just thought I should point that out."

Jemma was quiet for a long moment. When she spoke again, her voice came out a little stiffly. "I think I'm in the best position to make judgments on how we go forward. The less said about the London trio from here on, the better. Understood?"

I dipped my head, the knot in my chest hardening into something more pointedly uncomfortable. "Understood."

We didn't speak any more after that. She might have slept for a half hour or so as I drove on along the coast. The sun started to rise, streaking pale pink across the scattered clouds in the sky. Jemma shifted and undid her seatbelt as the city came into view up ahead.

"Drive carefully," she said in a wry tone that said we were putting any previous tension behind us. "We're cutting it close for that first flight. I'm going to get changed."

She squeezed into the back and returned in slacks and a loose blouse that covered her bandages. I parked the van in the airport parking lot, and we grabbed our remaining bags from the back. At a kiosk, Jemma picked up the tickets she'd purchased via my phone and handed my boarding pass to me as we hustled toward security.

Just before we reached the line, she stiffened. "Shit, I almost forgot." She turned to me and passed over a plastic bag from her purse. "I didn't want to get rid of these until we were on our way. You know what to do with them."

"Of course."

She smiled up at me, briefly radiant despite her exhaustion. "I'll see you in Paris later this afternoon."

"Enjoy your flight," I said with a crooked smile in

return, avoiding the impulse to tell her to take care of herself as if she wouldn't.

As well as she could. She rose up to kiss me steadily enough, and for the few seconds her lips lingered against mine, it was hard to feel anything but awed that this woman had decided to lower her guard so far for me. But I couldn't miss the wobble she quickly controlled as she walked to the end of the line. I forced myself to turn away as if I had nothing but total confidence that she'd reach our distant meeting point in full health.

The bag contained several burner phones that Jemma had used for various purposes across our stay in Croatia. I ducked into a stall in the restroom and set about disassembling them and crushing the chips that held the information about who they'd been used to contact or what about.

One of the phones I recognized as the silver flip phone she'd texted the Londoners on a few times. I saved that for last. As I curled my fingers around its cool surface, the knot inside me tugged my ribs tight.

I didn't like that Holmes, Watson, and Lestrade had earned some of Jemma's respect in turn. I didn't like that it obviously bothered her to put an end to whatever they'd had. My job was to look out for her, though, not wallow in my own petty feelings. I was important to her… and there was no denying that they'd become important too.

If they were loyal enough to deserve her affection, let them come and prove it. Making sure she made it through the next week alive was a hell of a lot more important to *me* than how pissed off I might make her.

Technically, she'd only told me not to talk *about* them, not *to* them.

I checked that the restroom was otherwise empty, pulled up the text history, and found Sherlock's number. The line rang as I raised the phone to my ear. I'd rather not leave him with a visual record of this conversation—and I wanted him to know for sure the tip had come from a legitimate source.

He picked up on the third ring. "Jemma, what are you up to now?"

"This isn't Jemma," I said quietly. "It's Moran. We're leaving to take on even bigger monsters than you did last night."

Sherlock's tone turned more urgent. "Where are you going?"

"There's an eclipse she needs to use. I'm sure if you care to be there, the three of you can figure out the rest."

I ended the call and crushed that phone's inner workings like I had the others. On my way out of the restroom, I tossed the bag in the garbage bin.

The pressure in my chest had released a little with those few sentences. Not the way I'd felt when I'd walked away from my father with my gun unfired. No, more like when I'd waved good-bye to Mike and Sara while they'd watched from our grandparents' window.

I'd done the right thing by them then. Here was hoping I'd done the right thing by Jemma now.

CHAPTER TWENTY-FOUR

Jemma

"There's one," I said to Bash as we eased through the town marketplace. I gestured surreptitiously to a woman standing by a fruit stand.

He made note of her with a glance. "How can you tell?"

"They stand out in the sun for hours sometimes in meditation—there's a specific pose. I can see it in her posture. The way she lifted her face toward the sky for a second."

I veered away from the cultist toward a stall selling stuffed tomatoes. The smells of grilled meat and vegetables and a cacophony of spices tickled my nose. I'd have enjoyed it if it hadn't been for the hints of the shrouded folk's dryly rancid scent mingling with the local atmosphere. Some of the folk were prowling alongside their sycophants, invisible yet leaving a trace I could recognize.

The street ahead of us sloped slightly downward. I walked carefully, wary of my wobbly right leg, not wanting to draw any attention by falling. This place wasn't exactly the best environment for someone who had enchanted jewelry gradually wearing away at her thigh.

The whole town sprawled across the side of a low mountain, turning into a patchwork of brightly colored buildings when viewed from above. We'd just come down from the open area along the mountain's peak where I'd been scouting out the best spot to complete the bond-breaking ritual during the eclipse. The dagger was supposed to give me the powers of a shrouded one, and the shrouded folk liked to be close to the sky.

Since I wasn't sure if this ritual was going to work at all, I figured I'd better increase the odds as much as I could. All I had to go on in my planning was what I'd observed of Bog when we'd made our pact, the part I'd had to play in it, and the fealty rituals I'd witnessed for the younger cult children.

It was going to be harder getting up to the mountaintop this evening with shrouded folk and their cultists prowling the place. I'd spotted a couple of men who'd rubbed my instincts the wrong way outside a church on our way back into town. Now, ducking past a shoe shop, I noticed another woman, this one swaying in a slight erratic rhythm for a second before she caught herself.

If I'd already seen four on our first real jaunt through

town, how many more were wandering through here? The shrouded folk who'd been hanging around the commune might not have been able to see who'd stolen the dagger, but they'd know someone had and where a person could use it. And if even one of the cultists who'd gotten a glimpse at me had managed to pass on word to another settlement, all of them would know to look for a slim woman with bright red hair.

Which was why I'd picked up a wig on our rambling travels across the last week. I gave the dark strands a brief tug to confirm it was still secure after our hike, wishing I'd gone blond instead of black. The bright sun was turning my head into a sauna. At least it'd keep anyone from noticing me as long as I didn't do anything eye-catching.

Bash leaned close to me as we left the marketplace behind for less crowded streets. "How do they know to look for you here? It's a big country."

"It is, but there's only a narrow strip where the full eclipse will be visible. They're probably watching for me all along that strip, but this is the only town completely centered along the path."

"Are you sure we should do this here, then?"

My mouth tightened grimly. "I need civilization around to blend into as soon as I'm finished. Once I take off the cuff, even after my contract with the monster is severed, they'll be able to sense me again, affect me again, with whatever power the cultists are giving them. On some lonely mountaintop, they'd break my body on the rocks, lickety split. But they're very cautious about revealing themselves to the rest of human society. They'd sooner let me escape than put their magic on display right in the middle of all these people."

Bash nodded, but his forehead was furrowed. I touched his arm, a simple gesture that felt weirdly intimate now that we'd started touching each other in a whole lot of other ways, but it was getting more normal with each passing day.

"I know this is a lot to take in," I said. "You can let me worry about the supernatural stuff. The cultists—they're just regular humans who think they're something special. You won't have any trouble taking them on."

"I'm not worried, Mori," he said. "It's those bastards who should be."

I wished I felt as confident as he sounded. My leg was throbbing from the long walk, even worse today than yesterday, and too many factors drifted beyond my control.

I'd never known anyone who'd challenged the shrouded folk at all, let alone like this. I had no guidelines for the right approach. I was winging it, and I vastly preferred being prepared.

Especially when Bash's life might very well be on the line as much as my soul was.

An icy jolt shot up from my thigh. I stumbled, and Bash caught me around the waist. He dipped his head toward mine at the same time to give the impression he was tugging me close for romantic reasons rather than to stop me from toppling over on the slanted street, in case any suspicious eyes were watching.

"Okay?" he murmured, a much more pleasant heat washing over me where his body pressed against mine.

"Just a minute." I gritted my teeth, willing the pain back. The cuff had been acting up more and more in the week since we'd left Split, hitting me harder at least a few times a day and continuing to jab at me for minutes at a time instead of seconds. If the eclipse had been farther off, I'd have hung in there even if I'd had to crawl my way to the ritual spot. Thank God I didn't have to find out just how bad it could get.

A dog trotted past us down the road—a stray with notched ears and patchy fur. My gaze followed it as it disappeared down a side street. Blood and anguish helped the shrouded folk transition their powers into this world. A creature like Bog would have delighted in having an animal as aware as a dog used in its honor.

My gut twisted, and not from the pain in my leg. It might have been effective to use one of the town's many strays to boost the dagger's magic, but I wasn't going to give the shrouded folk the satisfaction of having turned me into a monster like them. There'd be blood and pain this evening, but it'd all be mine.

Bash's thumb stroked up and down my side. The jagged ache the gold cuff had sent through me gradually retreated. I tested my leg, and we walked on.

We'd rented a second floor apartment in a little house with beaming yellow walls and a crimson roof. I'd paid for a month upfront on a one-year lease even though we'd only arrived here last night and didn't plan on sticking around more than a day. Our enemies—and anyone else who might be trying to track our movements—wouldn't be looking for apparently long-term renters.

Money couldn't fix all one's problems, but it certainly made tackling some of them easier.

We'd spent each night in a different city before arriving here just in time for the eclipse, even making a stop in Naples so Bash could get himself some one hundred percent authentic pizza—after which he'd informed me that he still liked the New York stuff the best. Through a truly valiant effort, I hadn't rolled my eyes.

If the London trio had bothered trying to trace our movements, they'd have had a long trail to unravel. I didn't think they'd make it very far. How far would they really want to chase me at this point?

Before, they'd been confused and uneasy about who I was and why I'd roped them into the heist. Now, they pretty much had their answers. They had the commune to finish dealing with and cases back home in London waiting for them. Our paths might cross if mine took me back to the UK, but I wasn't posing any threat to them at the moment.

Even thinking that, though, I couldn't help scanning the street before we stepped into the house, not just for any cultish figures but for a familiar tall lanky form, head of golden hair, or boyishly handsome face. Even though we had technically been enemies most of the time I'd known them, I'd worked with the three of them more closely than anyone other than Bash. I'd told them things I'd never *told* anyone other than Bash.

Maybe I was just a little uneasy knowing they were roaming around out there in the world with that knowledge, outside my control. Yes, the pinch in my chest couldn't be more than that.

Bash kept his arm around me as we climbed up the stairs. I stepped away from him once we reached our apartment, but only to walk as far as the bedroom. I flopped down on the light duvet with a sigh as the tension in my thigh eased.

Bash sat down on the end of the bed beside me. He rested his hand gently on my knee, bare where my touristy sundress had ridden up a little. "Would a massage help?"

The dip of his voice promised attentions even more enjoyable than just a massage. Desire sparked low in my belly, but I didn't want him seeing my upper leg right now. The flesh around the cuff had become almost completely translucent. I could easily see the outline of my femur through it. I felt nauseated looking at myself like that— not really the reaction I wanted to provoke in my right-hand man turned lover.

"I think it's better just to leave it alone," I said, and sat up to take his hand in mine. I hesitated before tipping my head against his shoulder. So many tiny gestures of affection I'd only ever used as a ploy before.

"Are you ready for tonight?" he asked.

"As much as I can be. It'll mostly be a matter of getting to that spot on the mountain. The cultists are going to be on the alert when it gets close to eclipse time. And they can probably guess I'd head for higher ground."

"I'll have your back all the way there." Bash lifted his

chin toward the bag in the corner that held a rifle, a couple pistols, and plenty of ammunition. "Anyone comes at you, I'll take them down."

Until the shrouded folk realize what you're doing and take you *down*, I thought, my chest clenching. Bullets couldn't hurt those misty fiends.

The shrouded folk would have encouraged their followers to feed their power with everything they could. If their rulers had decided I was fair game for a hunt, then anyone helping me would be too.

"I don't want you sacrificing yourself," I said. "If the odds go against us, you get out of there. If I'm dead, I'm dead anyway, so there's no point in you dying too in the process."

"Mori." Bash touched my jaw and turned my face so he could meet my gaze. "There's no way in hell I'm bailing on you. What kind of asshole would I be if I took off to save my own hide while I might still make a difference? We're breaking this thing's claim on you together. And then you know I'm ready to go tear all the rest of those monsters apart for you."

I couldn't help smiling at his vehemence. "*I'm* going to tear them apart," I corrected him. "But I'll let you help."

The corner of his lips curled up. "Then I'll be there, by my faith and honor."

I poked his chest. "And *then* you can take up your true calling as a Shakespearean actor."

Bash laughed and tugged me closer. We'd explored the uncertain space between us enough that he felt comfortable going straight for a kiss. I kissed him back, letting the heat of his mouth wash away any lingering pain.

That kiss bled into another and another, until all I could smell was his perfect musky scent, until all I could feel was that heat and the flex of his muscular shoulders beneath my roaming hands. He was a perfect pocket of someplace else in the middle of the horrors both behind and ahead of me.

Longing unfurled from my core up through my chest. It hadn't exactly been easy moderating my interludes with Bash over the last week, despite my best intentions. We'd reached the point of getting each other off with a well-placed hand. All that hesitation felt a little silly now.

Since I'd met him, I'd never been closer to dying than I would be tonight. I knew I wasn't seducing him into staying or fulfilling some other selfish need. I just wanted him. I wanted the thrill of his cock inside me, the total release and the sensation of him following me over that edge.

I wanted to have sex with this man clear-headed and open-eyed, for no reason other than because of how much we'd both enjoy it, and this might be my last chance.

I shifted around to settle myself on his lap. Bash scooted back on the bed, one hand coming to rest on my side to steady me. I kissed him again and again as he eased down the flexible straps of my dress.

When he slid his hand beneath the fabric to cup my breast, I made an encouraging sound. My teeth grazed his lower lip, and he pressed his other hand to my back, kissing me harder.

As his thumb flicked over my nipple with increasing pressure, our tongues tangled between our mouths. I rocked against his growing erection, and he groaned. My hands found the bottom hem of his shirt and yanked it up. While I peeled it off of him, he yanked the bodice of my dress all the way down and tossed my bra aside.

For a second, as he palmed both my breasts, I could only gasp. I tilted forward, my lips brushing his cheek.

"I think we've done enough waiting."

He gave a ragged laugh and kissed me before saying, "I couldn't agree more, Majesty." He teased his hands down my torso and back to my breasts, studying my expression. "I don't want to hurt your leg even more than it already is. Is this a good position?"

"Mmm, I think this works just fine." I sank so my core grazed his cock. With him sitting up, supporting part of my weight, I didn't have to flex my thigh too much, and I could keep the skirt of my dress pooled over the unnerving section of flesh around the cuff. Having him on top of me could quickly turn from *ooooh* to *ouch!* "Let's stay right here."

I reached for the fly of his jeans, but he caught my hand and eased me back so he could bring his mouth to my breast. His tongue swiped over the already taut nipple, and a little growl escaped me. My hips rocked impatiently, but his mouth felt so good I couldn't bear to tell him to stop.

Bash took his time, working over one side to send a rush of pleasure through my chest, and then repeating his attentions on the other. My fingernails dug into his shoulders. Need pulsed between my legs. When he finally raised his head, I yanked his mouth back to my lips and jerked open his jeans at the same time.

His cock sprang free with a few tugs. Bash grabbed my purse and retrieved a condom. I bobbed eagerly as he slicked it over his erection. Then I was sinking *all* the way down, whimpering as the head of his cock pushed past my opening, letting out a shaky sigh when he filled me completely with that blissful burn.

"Mori," Bash said softly, touching my cheek. His light green eyes were soft too as he gazed back at me. The tenderness I saw in his expression would have made me retreat any other time. Even now, my lungs started to clench up.

I inhaled slowly, leaning into the feeling. The knowledge that this man cared more about standing by my side than keeping himself alive. The knowledge that I was willing to put my own life at even greater risk if it meant seeing him safely away.

I didn't know if I was capable of the sort of love his Shakespeare wrote about. I'd never felt that strongly about anyone except Olivia. But this was something—something good, something I'd never had before. As I relaxed into the sensation, the pleasure building inside me shimmered giddily.

"Until the end?" I said.

Bash's voice rasped. "Until the end."

His mouth captured mine as he lifted his hips to meet me. A breath shuddered out of me at that first sharper burst of bliss. I ground down against him, and he urged me on with his hand gripping my ass.

You'd have thought I'd gone a year without sex rather than a week. With just a few thrusts, I could already feel my peak on the horizon. A twinge shot through my thigh, but I ignored it, pumping faster over him.

My lips tore from his. He kissed my neck as he fondled my breast with his other hand. His cock plunged into me over and over, so hard and fast and *right*—

I moaned as ecstasy swelled and crashed inside me. Bash's breath spilled harsh against my skin. As I clenched around him, he held me tight and came with a groan that reverberated through us both.

My head dipped to rest on his shoulder. His arms wrapped around me, hugging me to him. As we lingered there in the moment after the first time I'd done anything remotely close to "making love," an ache formed around my heart.

There were so many things I hadn't known I was capable of doing, capable of feeling, before the last few weeks. Before just now. What a shame that unless a whole lot of luck was with me tonight, I'd never get the chance to make the most of them.

CHAPTER TWENTY-FIVE

Jemma

The day had wound down, but the sun still seared along the rooftops across the town. Slowly but surely, the moon edged closer to covering it. From my mountain perch, the eclipse would be completely visible.

And it was going to be a perch in a very literal sense, because I clearly needed to adjust my plans. I hadn't realized how many tourists would come even to this small-ish town, eager just to get a glimpse of the eclipse at its fullest.

Bash and I wove through the growing crowd on the sparsely treed slope above the edge of the town. Groups of people clustered together talking in excited voices and waving their viewing devices.

They gave us cover, and the shrouded folk weren't likely to strike out at us with so many witnesses this close. Unfortunately, the crowd also hid our human enemies.

They might become enemies themselves if they freaked out once I started cutting myself to bring forth the dagger's power. I wasn't going to get through this night if a bunch of good Samaritans jumped in thinking they were saving me from myself.

So, rather than bracing myself on the barren patch right at the peak, where a bunch of locals had set up folding chairs amid the tourists, I was going to make use of the slab of rock that jutted from the slope a little farther down. Its uneven, weed-dotted surface loomed a few feet over the heads of those passing by, and it looked like a tough enough climb to dissuade any adventurers from taking a seat on its narrow top. I could manage it, though.

As long as my leg didn't totally fail me.

A sharp prickling ran through my limb from knee to hip, deepening to a now-constant throbbing around my joints. I had the dagger tucked in my purse, and the cuff's protective magic was working overtime to defend against the shrouded folk's essence imbued in the blade. I'd wrapped the weapon in a silk scarf with a geometric pattern that dulled the affect a little—but not enough to spare me the discomfort.

The hike wasn't too difficult, at least. I'd picked another summery dress so I could snap off the gold cuff beneath it quickly, but I had practical walking shoes on my feet. Among the tourists, I was far from the most haphazardly dressed.

The summer heat was starting to wane, but the wind that licked over the gathered spectators still warmed my skin. At the same time, it chilled my gut. The sour smell of the shrouded folk hung thicker in the air now.

They knew where I was most likely to make my stand. They and their followers would be gathering around this crowd while I moved through it.

I glanced at Bash to indicate the perch I'd chosen. He nodded in return, his face shaded by a red baseball cap. As we meandered toward the slab, his hand hovered close to the holster hidden under his touristy polo shirt. As soon as we'd seen the growing crowd, he'd known he wasn't getting any use out of his rifle, but a pistol could take down any cultist who got too close to me just fine.

The crowd was thinner around my slab, the ground near it rockier and less comfortable for standing. I circled around to the spot where I could most easily clamber up to the top, smiling at people we passed as if I were just another friendly sightseer.

A gasp nearby made my head jerk up, but the sunlight was only just starting to waver as the moon drifted along its path. I checked my watch. We had several minutes left before totality.

When I lowered my eyes, they landed on a head of messy dark waves that stood out in the middle of the shorter figures all around it. My body stiffened for a second before I caught my reaction.

It was Sherlock. He proceeded methodically through the crowd, his piercing blue eyes scanning the faces around him. I shifted on my feet to ease a little farther behind a nearby couple and spotted Garrett prowling along the edge of the spectators on the other side. No doubt John was around here somewhere too, then.

I ducked my head to let the sleek black strands of my wig shield my face. "What is it?" Bash murmured, tensing, and then relaxed a little with a soft chuckle. "They made an appearance after all."

"Just as long as they don't get in my way," I said.

"I'll pull back. I can cover you better from a little farther away anyway, and it might not take them long to recognize me without a full disguise."

I grabbed his hand to squeeze it. "Whatever happens, we've had a good run of it."

He smiled. "Absolutely."

A tugging sensation ran through my chest as he walked away. Not just to stay close to *him*—I had the urge to stride on over to the London trio and ask what exactly they thought they were doing here. To see the interest that would light in their faces no matter how they felt about my giving them the slip last week. To banter with them one last time.

They really might try to get in my way, though. I only had a few minutes left before I made my move. I had to stay here, braced and ready and beyond their notice.

A fresh pain stabbed down to my ankle and up behind my ribs. I sucked in a shallow breath. Yes, I needed every shred of energy and control I had just to get this chance.

The light was dimming faster now. The voices around me quieted to awed murmurs. Through the fall of my false hair, I saw Sherlock's gaze lock on Bash where my hitman had stationed himself in the crowd. The detective tapped something into his phone as he headed that way. Summoning the other members of the trio, I assumed.

If I'd had more time, I might have tried to interfere. But Bash could handle himself—and the moon was creeping toward the far edge of the sun now. Shadows sharpened against the ground.

I couldn't delay any longer. I had to be at the top of that slab by the time the eclipse was complete. The moon's position would only give me one minute to finish my task.

Clenching my jaw against the pain radiating from my thigh, I marched up to the jutting protrusion of rock and leapt to plant my feet on a bulge on its side. A knife of agony speared through me, but I clutched onto the best handholds I could find and hauled myself upward. My elbow scraped against the rough stone.

Shouts rang across the slope. I had to keep all my concentration on the climb, but the rancid scent of the shrouded folk congealed around me as I yanked myself closer to the top of the slab. Scrambling for another foothold, I banged my right knee and bit my lip to hold in a cry as the impact amplified the cuff's painful effect. My fingers caught hold of the slab's upper edge.

Movement flickered at the edges of my vision. Bash's striped shirt flashed in the dwindling light as he threw himself into someone—one of the cultists, I assumed. A length of dark brown that might have been John's walking stick whipped through the air. Someone grunted, someone hollered. I heaved myself onto my perch—and the click of a gun made my blood turn to ice.

I ducked down instinctively. The shot crackled

through the air close enough that the air rippled against my face. Screams echoed across the mountainside. There was a thump, and another shot nowhere near me.

I couldn't wait. The light around us had turned to dusk. With a choked gasp, I shoved myself upright.

My leg wobbled under me but held despite the agony of the climb. Below my perch, the eclipse spectators were milling around, most of them streaming back toward the city's buildings. Well, that would give Bash a clearer shot at any cultist who came at me now. It'd also mean that the shrouded folk could attack with less caution, but I couldn't worry about that yet.

The wind cooled as the moon slid over the last bit of sun. The tone of a sunrise lit the horizon all around me. A tiny line of brilliance shone around the dark circle in the sky.

It was time.

I dug the dagger out of my purse with one hand while I yanked up my dress with the other. My fingers flicked the snaps on the cuff, and the gold pieces dropped onto the stone.

Bog's mark on the back of my neck flared as if prodded with a searing brand. The glimmering streaks that showed at least a dozen shrouded folk wavered into view around me, but whatever energy they'd been fed by their sycophants, their light was dimmed to near transparency with the blocking of the sun.

That didn't stop them from flinging themselves at me.

"Back!" I shouted, and sliced the dagger in two swift strokes across the inside of my elbow and wrist where the flesh was most sensitive. The pain that flared through my arm immediately overtook the throbbing that was fading from my leg.

"I claim this pain, I claim this blood," I called out, brandishing the dagger. "I am shrouded, and you may not touch me."

A wave of power washed over me from the blade, dizzying and vast. The glimmers of the shrouded folk flinched back.

In that instant, the landscape around me dulled like a sepia photo. The sense of an immense space beyond it rang through my body down to the bones—a space that belonged to me. A space from which I could rule.

No, it didn't belong to me. That was the realm of the shrouded folk, and it only belonged to this dagger. The seconds while I could wield its magic were slipping away from me.

"There is no one more powerful than me," I declared, hoping that in this moment while the sun was swallowed, it was true. "I sever the claim of another on this human soul and stake my own claim. She belongs to me."

I wrenched my wig off my coiled hair and brought the dagger to the base of my scalp. Bog's mark was still burning away. I dug the blade into it, splitting the mark with an X. The pain of the cut skin and the dribble of blood wiped away the sear of my former contract.

"I give myself freely to myself," I said, in case that side needed to be covered too. "I accept Jemma Moriarty's claim."

My voice sounded warbled to my own ears, as if I were

falling away from it into that eerily vast space. Another flare of sensation raced over my skin, this one bright and binding. A rush of exhilaration chased after it.

I was mine now. I belonged only to me, for the first time since my birth. None of the shrouded folk could overstep the claim I'd made while I held more power than any of them with this dagger and the dimmed sun.

They couldn't stake a claim, but they could affect me in other ways. As I dropped the dagger onto the wad of silk in my purse, the blade's purpose fulfilled, the moon edged a little away from the sun. Starker beams of light shot from around its edge. The early dusk began to brighten, and the glimmers of light that showed the shrouded folk's presence quivered into clearer focus.

The sense of power slipped away from me, leaving me with only my totally human joy at my victory and the ache spreading from my wounds. I was no longer the creature with the most authority here, and the cultists had made their own sacrifices for their pseudo gods.

I crouched to slide down off the slab—not fast enough. A whirl of bright streaks flung itself at me and slammed into my side with enough force to break a rib. With a hitch of breath, I skidded off the side of the protrusion and plummeted toward the rocky ground below.

CHAPTER TWENTY-SIX

Garrett

We left the Chilean town behind, following the locals and tourists who were spreading out across the mountaintop. There were dozens of people ahead of us, but I didn't catch a single glimpse of Jemma's flaming hair. I glanced at Sherlock as we started up the slope.

"Are you sure she'll be here?"

Sherlock gave me the haughty look that often came over him when anyone questioned his reasoning. "It wasn't as if I needed to consider the entire world or even a large portion of it. Narrowing down my range of inquiry to the path of the eclipse, I should hope I'd be able to locate two reasonably distinctive travelers."

"They're not looking all that distinct to me right now." I eyed the crowd ahead of us. "What the hell would she even be doing here?"

"All her man told you is that she needed to watch the eclipse, right?" John said at Sherlock's other side, leaning a little more than usual on his walking stick as we hit a steeper section.

Sherlock kept a slightly slower pace than usual too, sans ankle brace but wary of turning his recovering foot again. He frowned at John's question.

"That's the gist of it. He didn't say why. And this appears to be the ideal location for those in town to observe. The fact that he shared that information does still concern me, though."

"That and the fact that she left us in the lurch *again* back in Split?" I said.

John's gaze roved over the sightseers nearly as intently as Sherlock's, twitching here and there at sudden movements. What was he worried about?

"It was hardly 'in the lurch'," he said without looking at me. "There was nothing fake about the evidence we found in that commune. If she hadn't looped us in, the cult would have kept up all the torture and the thefts and —everything."

He was right. And it was because of that I couldn't summon any real anger about Jemma's second disappearance. Had I really expected her to sit around and have tea with us after she'd gotten what she needed? She was still an admitted criminal, and we were still men sworn to bring criminals down. Which led me to my main concern.

"All right. Then why are we here at all? To finally bring her in for stealing that relic? Because we don't have evidence of any other crime *she's* committed, and last time I checked, there weren't any laws against watching an eclipse."

John's mouth tightened. "It might be an opportunity for someone to commit a crime *against* her. She said that this cult is widespread. They've already tried to kill her at least once. Whether she put Moran up to the call or he made it of his own accord, it could have been for her protection."

"The whole thing seems too complicated to me," I muttered. Poisonings, psychotic cults, random trips across the ocean… I could have been spending the rest of my vacation on a beach someplace where I wouldn't have to beware of anything worse than a sunburn.

I could have been, but when Sherlock and John had picked up the chase, I'd come here anyway. Maybe it was because when I thought of Jemma, what I remembered first was seeing her huddled weak among the trees outside the commune. And then my mind went to the efforts she'd taken to clear the air between us back in Zagreb.

She'd needed me for her plans in London. I hadn't really served much use in her operations in Croatia— nothing Sherlock or John couldn't have taken over. Nonetheless it had mattered to her to make peace, even after the rough way we'd treated her when we'd assumed she was leading the cult rather than fighting them. Wasn't it all right then for it to matter a little to me what happened to her?

I didn't have a solid answer, but it'd been enough justification to get me on the plane.

That morning with her in my hotel room, she'd suggested I could get her out of my system. Clearly I hadn't managed that yet.

"No matter what her reasons are, we'll be on our guard for whatever comes," Sherlock said. "Come on, let's split up to cover more area at once. Your phones still have a signal? We can alert each other that way if we spot either of them."

Without waiting for our agreement, Sherlock strode off to the right, so I headed left, leaving John to take the middle route. The sightseers looked excited, grins and upbeat chatter all around me. I forced my mouth into a smile so I didn't look too out of place.

Jemma wasn't a stranger to disguises. She could be anywhere here. I eyed every woman—and even some of the men—checking for signs that their appearance was only a front.

My gaze settled on a couple at the edge of the crowd, and my instincts tingled uneasily. They weren't chattering happily, just standing there rather stiffly with their eyes fixed on the crowd. They were looking across the mountainside rather than down toward the dimming sun.

What—or who—were they watching for? What was about to happen here? I couldn't think of any crime it would make sense to commit at this specific moment in the middle of this event.

My phone chimed in my pocket. I glanced up without checking it, my gaze finding Sherlock across the way with no trouble thanks to his height. He was cutting through the crowd with all the intensity of a homing missile.

I managed to follow his gaze to a guy in a baseball cap and polo shirt standing higher up the slope. A guy with enough bulk to fill out that shirt with muscle and a strong tanned jaw beneath the cap's shade. Moran.

My attention skittered across the crowd around him with a lurch of my heart. If he was here, then Jemma almost certainly was. Probably close. But with the sunlight dwindling even more as the moon drifted across it, it was getting harder to make out faces at a distance.

I set off to join Sherlock. He might need backup.

John clearly had the same idea. His bright hair glinted in the lingering sunlight just ahead of me. Then he froze, his head snapping toward a thick spear of rock that thrust up from the earth just below the mountain's peak.

A woman was scrambling up the side of the rock. The wind tossed black hair across her face, and it was so dark now I might not have been able to make out much of her features anyway, but seeing that slim frame move with such strength and speed, I knew it was Jemma just as John must have.

She swayed for a second as her right leg bowed, and a pang of concern shot through my chest. Whatever injuries she'd had before, she hadn't completely recovered.

What the hell was she doing?

I started forward again, and several other figures made a beeline toward her through the crowd at the same time, including the couple I'd seen staring on the fringes. Apprehension prickled down my spine. One of the figures, closer to her than I was, sped up to a run with the flash of something metal in his hand. He raised his weapon as he charged at Jemma.

Moran leapt out of the crowd and tackled the attacker to the ground. "We've got to help her," he shouted. "They'll try to kill her."

We. He was speaking to us. He'd either seen us here or assumed we'd make it.

I didn't have time to think about that. John had hustled ahead of me to the base of the stone. He whacked his walking stick into the gut of a woman who was jumping after Jemma. Jemma was just reaching for the peak of the rock, her face pale and stiff with controlled pain.

As I hurried toward the stone, my gut wrenched between two opposing instincts. She was wounded and under attack yet unwilling to back down, and part of me longed to protect that determined, defiant spirit. But we had no idea about her plans here, who these people were, or what she intended. What if they had a good reason to try to stop her?

I couldn't let my emotions rule my mind yet again.

One thing I was sure of: I had to at least help my friends. John was springing at another guy who'd run at the looming stone. Bash lunged around to punch someone in the face. Sherlock had grabbed a man by the collar. I hustled the rest of the way to John's side, even though he didn't look as if he needed a whole lot of assistance at the moment.

Just as I reached him, a strangled squeak reached my ears. My gaze jerked around.

A man stalking toward me had a furry lump clutched in his hand. A mouse, I realized with a jab of queasiness. He'd crushed it in his grasp. He raised its mangled body toward the sky, blood streaking down his forearm. "For the shrouded folk!"

An invisible force that felt more solid than the wind whipped past me. Streaks of gauzy light that couldn't have come from the nearly covered sun slashed through the air around the rock. And a woman several paces away came to an abrupt halt and raised a pistol toward Jemma.

Resolve hardened in my chest. Whatever Jemma had done, whatever she was doing now, these people were worse than her. I'd never tackled an evil like this. I didn't understand the cult we'd uncovered in Croatia, but these were clearly the same brand of lunatics. If only in this one conflict, Jemma's side was the only side I wanted to be on.

I threw myself at the woman with the gun, wincing as her first shot split the air. She managed to pull the trigger a second time just as I barreled into her. I shoved her to the ground, and the shot went wild. With a kick, I sent the gun spinning from her hand.

The sightseers around us were shrieking and shoving away from us now, scattering across the lower slope. Everyone except the deranged cultists. The man who'd crushed the mouse dove for the gun, and I threw myself at him. As I shouldered him to the side and snatched up the pistol, a billow of filmy light blasted into me, knocking the breath from my lungs. I crashed onto the ground on my back.

I started up at the wavering form descending on me,

and a rush of cold arrived with the fall of an even deeper darkness. The eclipse was full.

Jemma stood at the top of the stone, stabbing a curved silver knife toward the sky. She yanked at something on her leg—the gold cuff—and its pieces clattered onto the rock beneath her feet.

Several of those strange billows of light, fainter now despite the darkness around us, converged on Jemma. The one over me whipped around to follow them. I blinked hard, trying to wrap my head around what I was seeing. When I squinted at them, they looked almost like—like *ghosts*, for fuck's sake. Like that creepy form that had appeared over Jemma in the park back in—

Oh. Ice formed around my stomach. What if that hadn't been a projection from some source we'd never determined. What if… that had been an actual *creature*, appearing and moving by some will of its own, like the patches of hazy light flying toward Jemma were giving every appearance of being?

I didn't believe in ghosts. Since I was ten, I'd rolled my eyes at my gran leaving milk out for the "wee folk." But I couldn't deny that something very real and not of the world I knew had appeared in front of me.

Jemma slashed the curved knife across her arm. I shoved myself back onto my feet, swallowing back queasiness at the sight of blood streaking over her pale skin. I wanted to run to her, to wrench the blade from her hands, but at the same moment the filmy beings that had been racing toward her flinched back.

Her voice rang out, strained but clear. "I claim this

pain; I claim this blood!" Light flared around her, silhouetting her slim form, brighter than the things that circled her. A quivering energy radiated from her perch and washed over my skin. It warbled in my ears so loudly I lost the next few things she said.

Jemma tossed off her wig. The unnatural light burned even sharper around her pinned-up red hair. My stomach lurched as she brought the knife to the back of her neck.

What the *fuck*?

I couldn't help stepping forward, my hands opening and closing, grasping for something to do but not knowing what. As crazy as this situation looked, as unnerving as Jemma's actions were, her voice and her stance spoke of total control.

She knew what she was doing, and I sure as hell didn't.

I couldn't see the back of her neck, but I could tell she'd dug in the blade from the way her jaw clenched. "I give myself freely to myself," she called out. "I accept Jemma Moriarty's claim."

I didn't know what that meant either, but it must have been enough to accomplish her ends. She dropped the knife into her purse.

Daylight glimmered brighter over the mountainside as the moon edged away from the sun. Jemma's glow faded, and the gauzy patches around her shimmered a touch brighter.

They whipped toward her in an instant. She bent down—and a force with a flicker of light rammed into her, sending her tumbling over the side of the stone. Like the wallop that had thrown Sherlock on the mountain near Split.

I ran to her as she hit the ground, her arm braced protectively around her head. Sherlock, John, and Moran dashed over too. Glowing streaks seared the air around her, and she flinched, jabbing out with her hand as if fighting against something.

Another flash of light punched me in the chest. I reeled back for a second and then sprang at her.

The air around Jemma had turned frigid enough to bite into my skin. Her head lolled to the side, a welt from a blow I hadn't seen forming across her forehead.

"We have to get her out of here," Moran said, dropping next to her across from me. "She'll be safe in the town. Those things won't follow us there. Cover me!"

He hauled her up, slinging her quickly but carefully over his shoulder as if she weighed nothing, and launched himself down the slope. The three of us raced after him, Sherlock's expression tight, John wide-eyed and pale.

A shimmering streak battered me to the side, but I shoved back to block it from getting at Moran and Jemma. John flailed his walking stick, the wood reverberating as it struck or was struck by something none of us could see beyond a glimmering patch of air.

My heart pounded hard and heavy in my chest. Another blow smacked me across the face. I swore and jabbed out my elbow instinctively, light sparking around the filmy surface I hit.

Then we were stumbling into the midst of the sightseers who'd congregated at the edge of the town.

Shouts carried after us, but Moran kept hurtling onward with Jemma, and the three of us charged after him.

The air didn't attack me again. The wavering light effects faded away. But my pulse kept thudding and my skin kept crawling as we hustled through the streets.

I didn't know what we'd tangled with on that mountaintop, but clearly the world contained villains more terrifying than I'd ever imagined could exist. And the woman now crumpled on Bash's shoulder not only knew but had dared to stand up to them.

CHAPTER TWENTY-SEVEN

Jemma

I woke up on a soft bed in an unfamiliar room. Sunlight streamed through a wide window, lighting up the pale yellow walls and white furniture. A warm breeze rippled the curtain. A distant jangle of music carried with it, much more perky than I felt.

"Mori!" Bash had been sitting in a wicker chair on the other side of the bed. He leapt up and rested his hands on the sheet next to me, his eyes intent. From the dark smudges under them, *he* hadn't gotten much sleep. "How are you feeling?" he asked.

I shifted against the mattress, taking stock. A dull ache spread across my forehead. I touched the spot and found it bandaged. My arm was bandaged too—pads and swaths of gauze wrapped around my wrist and elbow where I'd sliced myself open with the shrouded dagger.

"I've been better, but I've also been worse," I said.

Tentatively, I pushed myself into a sitting position. My shoulder and my hip throbbed. The gold cuff no longer weighed on my thigh, but the muscle there felt tender. I lifted the sheet, eased up the skirt of my dress, and winced. Purple bruises mottled the skin from knee to hipbone.

But I'd take that over turning translucent any day.

I turned back to Bash. "Where are we? What happened after the eclipse?" I had a blurry memory of falling, flares of light and pain and voices shouting around me, but I couldn't piece together more than that.

"Your monsters took a good stab at getting you, but we were faster," Bash said. "You were banged up pretty bad, though. The good doctor did what he could for you, and I managed to arrange a private flight pretty quick. I figured the sooner we put distance between those things and the last place they found you, the better." He motioned to the window. "Rio de Janeiro. Not too far a hop but big and busy enough for us to go unnoticed."

"Good choice," I said. "It's only—that was all yesterday?"

He nodded. From the quality of the sunlight, I'd guess it was early afternoon now. I hadn't even been out for a whole twenty-four hours. Our Chilean adventure definitely could have gone a lot worse.

"John should probably take another look at you now that you're awake," Bash said. Apparently he'd gotten on a first name basis with at least one of the trio while I'd been unconscious. "Do you mind if I go get him?"

"If it'll make you feel better." I waved him off.

He went to the bedroom door and leaned out. "Hey, doc, your patient is awake."

John came striding in a few seconds later, and Sherlock and Garrett trailed behind him. It was kind of amusing seeing someone other than Sherlock taking the lead for once. The other two stood awkwardly near the end of the bed while John sat on the edge beside me.

"Hey," he said. "It's good to have you back with us."

"It's good to be back, considering I wasn't sure I was even going to make it through the eclipse alive." I raised my bandaged arm. "You do neat work."

He laughed, but concern still shone in his hazel eyes. "I haven't completely lost my touch. Can you move all right? Is your vision clear?"

"Everything feels pretty normal, just achy here and there. I think I'm through the worst. I wouldn't mind a painkiller if we've got any around. Not the heavy stuff, just to take the edge off."

Bash tossed over a bottle of over-the-counter pills and went to get me a glass of water. I gulped a couple down and turned my attention to the two men still standing vigil at the end of the bed.

"Can I assume that since we're in an apartment and not a prison hospital that you're not here to arrest me for something or other?"

Garrett shot Bash a wary look, maybe in recognition that even if they'd wanted to, they'd have had a tough time taking me into custody under my hitman's watch. Sherlock tucked his hands into the pockets of his trousers, studying me with his incisive gaze.

"I have no grounds on which to arrest you at the moment, Miss Moriarty," he said. "But I was rather hoping you could provide some illumination on the events during the eclipse. What exactly did you accomplish there, for example?"

"And what the hell were those things that were trying to stop you?" Garrett put in.

John hadn't told them the extra details I'd shared with him about the cult, then, even now that they'd seen plenty of evidence. I couldn't blame him for leaving that task to me—they'd have thought *he* was crazy.

An urge to lie coiled around my chest. My hands balled on top of the sheet. But what could I tell them that would sound any less crazy than the truth? What would it hurt for them to know?

These men had turned up and fought in my battle alongside me without any need to. They might very well have saved my life twice over now.

I wet my lips and looked at Sherlock. "Are you sure you're going to believe what I tell you? I think you know I'm not going to say it was an elaborate electronic light show. If you're only going to scoff, I'd rather skip that."

He shifted his weight, his mouth twisting into something between a smile and a grimace. "I was present for everything that happened. I can admit that the phenomena I observed cannot be explained by any scientific means I'm aware of. It may pain me to consider a less grounded explanation, but I can hardly call myself an objective observer of facts if I refuse the most fitting account simply because I find it difficult to accept."

Spoken like only Sherlock would. The fact that he was even willing to entertain the idea of something supernatural sent a flutter of affection through me for the proud, brilliant man in front of me. I had discovered many things I hadn't expected about myself in the last several weeks. Perhaps he hadn't come through that time unchanged either.

"I don't understand exactly what they are either." I leaned back on my hands as I chose my words. "There are beings with powers most people would call magic. They like our world—they like our sun. Left to their own devices, they can only create illusions, making themselves or other things visible but not really affecting anything. But if they can find people willing to worship them, to feed them with pain and blood, that gives them enough energy to have an impact on our world."

Garrett looked ill. "That's why the mutilated animals —the boy—all the things we found in the commune…"

I nodded. "Some of that might have been the fiends themselves, enjoying themselves after they'd been let loose. Their tastes tend toward the violent. But yes. Wherever they can find people who get off on being near creatures that much more powerful, they've fostered their cult of worship. We call them the shrouded folk. I grew up in one of their communes. I was still tied to them even after I escaped, but that ritual with the dagger means they have no more claim on me."

"Are you done with them?" John asked.

A laugh sputtered out of me. "Hardly. They—they killed my sister. They would have torn me apart and enjoyed it. And the people in the cult, like my parents, might as well be monsters too, considering the lengths they're willing to go to in service of those things. Now that I can take them on freely, I'm going to destroy every commune there is by whatever means necessary until there's no one left giving reverence. Until the fiends can't touch anyone here ever again."

The men around me were silent for a long moment. Garrett drew in a breath.

"These 'fiends'—they're what you meant," he said. "Before you took off on us in Split, you said there were worse things in the world than you."

The corner of my mouth quirked up. "Yes. So, I wouldn't ask you to stick your necks out again. I don't plan on setting up any schemes that would conflict with your work. I just hope you'll agree that letting me go to deal with these fiends is in everyone's best interests—not just ours, but every human being out there." I motioned to the world beyond the walls.

Garrett looked at the floor and then back at me. A fierceness had come over his expression. "What if we want to stick our necks out? I got into this line of work to make the world better. If those *things* are out there, killing and warping people to their wills… I don't know how I can manage it around the job once I have to go back—"

"I can handle that," Sherlock broke in. When Garrett's gaze snapped to him, he smiled thinly. "Your chief appreciates how many cases I manage to smooth along for Scotland Yard. I'm sure I could convince him that I had a great need of you being assigned to an undercover detail for an indeterminate length of time. No need to be on hand in the station." He turned his attention to me. "We might not even need to go very far to start, if this cult operates in Britain as well."

I stared at the two of them. A strangely bubbly sensation emerged from my gut.

"It operates pretty much everywhere," I said. "I'd be surprised if there isn't at least one settlement in the Highlands. It *would* be easier to tackle them with more minds and resources put toward the cause... Are you sure?"

"Take on the most challenging enemy I've ever faced or go back to the hum-drum grind of petty crimes." Sherlock arched his eyebrows. "The decision is hardly difficult."

John grinned. "If he's in, you know I am."

I felt I needed to clarify, just for the record: "You'd have to let me direct our moves—and not ask too many questions about how I acquire my own resources. I've been working toward this from the moment I understood what monsters the shrouded folk truly are. I'm not compromising this mission for anyone's morals."

John tipped his head to the other two. "I'm sure we can avoid prying when it serves the greater good, can't we?"

A sly glint sparked in Sherlock's eyes. "As long as your means never appear more of a concern than the enemy we intend to eliminate, I don't think that should be a problem."

Garrett cleared his throat. "Yeah. What he said."

I glanced at Bash in case he had an opinion about bringing the trio into the mix. I wasn't taking them on if it meant losing him.

He simply shrugged with a hint of a wry smile. "I can tolerate them if they're making themselves useful. It's up to you, Majesty."

I sat up straighter with a smile of my own, an energy flowing through me that was even more potent than what I'd felt in the grip of the dagger's power. "All right then. Let's take the bastards down."

ABOUT THE AUTHOR

Eva Chase lives in Canada with her family. She loves stories both swoony and supernatural, and strong women and the men who appreciate them. Along with the Moriarty's Men series, she is the author of the Looking Glass Curse trilogy, the Their Dark Valkyrie series, the Witch's Consorts series, the Dragon Shifter's Mates series, the Demons of Fame Romance series, the Legends Reborn trilogy, and the Alpha Project Psychic Romance series.

Connect with Eva online:
www.evachase.com
eva@evachase.com

www.ingramcontent.com/pod-product-compliance
Lightning Source LLC
Chambersburg PA
CBHW061318190726

48288CB00002B/563